T0288294

McKenzie Rising

McKenzie Rising

AN AMERICAN FROLIC

Miles Wilson

UNIVERSITY OF NEVADA PRESS | *Reno & Las Vegas*

University of Nevada Press | Reno, Nevada 89557 USA
www.unpress.nevada.edu

Cover design by Ter-AvanesyanZ / Ter33Design
Nuclear button © ylivdesign / Adobe Stock

LIBRARY OF CONGRESS CATALOGING-IN-PUBLICATION DATA
Names: Wilson, Miles, author.
Title: McKenzie rising : an American frolic / Miles Wilson.
Description: Reno ; Las Vegas : University of Nevada Press, [2022] |
Summary: "A lusty environmental picaresque, *McKenzie Rising* satirizes our shortfalls while celebrating our resilience and the triumph of community. As an instrument of social critique, satire operates on the premise that human folly is correctable. *McKenzie Rising* is intended as a spirited corrective to some of the amendable follies we lug with us as we careen on into the (post)-Trump, (post)-Corona years." —Provided by publisher.
Identifiers: LCCN 2022003414 | ISBN 9781647790639 (paperback) | ISBN 9781647790646 (ebook)
Classification: LCC PS3573.I4598 M35 2022 | DDC 813/.54—dc23/eng/20220415
LC record available at https://lccn.loc.gov/2022003414

The paper used in this book meets the requirements of American National Standard for Information Sciences—Permanence of Paper for Printed Library Materials, ANSI/NISO Z39.48-1992 (R2002).

First Printing

Manufactured in the United States of America

Christi

In Memory
Rob Cooley, Walter Spencer, Nat Spencer, Guy Lewis

McKenzie Rising

— 1 —

Here comes Buckthorn: his laces loose, his bowels clenched, the rain running into his eyes.

Because the starter on his pickup is uncertain, he leaves the truck chugging away as he pounds through the front door of Devaney's Mercantile. Devaney, who has heard the Chevy coming the last half mile of Hack Creek Road, is in the back skimming the index of the U.S. Postal Code. Besides Devaney, the only person in the store is Sarah Trip, who is opening her P.O. box. Her mail consists of returned manuscripts from the *New Yorker, Poetry,* and *Rural Womynhood.* Buckthorn, who once read one of Sarah's poems by mistake while hiding out in the stall of the women's john at the Pour House Tavern, emits an adenoidal rasp in Sarah's direction that is not unlike the ratcheting his starter makes when it goes out on him. Sarah has the red hair of an Albanian television set gone berserk, and Buckthorn growls again to mask his whimpering lust.

"You don't fool me," says Sarah, pivoting to face Buckthorn square in the chops. "Just because you pretend to be a jerk doesn't mean you aren't one."

Buckthorn's mind hums in neutral, and he begins to make nervous little sucking sounds as though he has false teeth. It's an old habit from high school German class, the mortal fear of being called upon and thereby magically rendered dumb. He tries to estimate whether his wheezling sucks could be construed as quirky and enticing or perhaps tragically stricken, heard in an amorous key. But Sarah is out the door, and Devaney is rounding the corned beef, cornbread, corn chips, corn dogs, cornflakes, cornpone, corn plaster, and cornstarch with Volume 27 of the Postal Code.

"You can't do it, Harley. It's right here in Section 139¶28.27[73] 609±π 4286-6b≥c{lx}1/8." Devaney knows what he's talking about because the man who delivers his contract rural route came in twenty minutes before and quit. He had been stuffing Buckthorn's box when Buckthorn rushed out of a clump of alder, picked up the rear end of the carrier's Subaru, and bounced it several times.

"You show up without it again," said Buckthorn, "and I will tear off your *Consumer Reports*-approved bumper and wrap it around your pre-goitrous neck. *Comprende?*" He bounced the Subaru once more for emphasis.

Devaney is patient as a stump, but Buckthorn has extended him. The last rural routeman was run off by the Gang of Four, and Devaney had high hopes for this one, a former franchisee for Sears siding. But rules were rules, and if Buckthorn shipped plastic explosive through the U.S. mail, appropriate authorities would have to be notified.

"What am I supposed to do?" says Buckthorn. "We're talking First Amendment here, freedom of expression. I'm a legitimate artist. I have an MFA; I have $90,000 in delinquent student loans; my NEA grant was singled out by Rand Paul on the floor of the Senate; my parents won't speak to me."

"The private sector might be the ticket."

"What?"

"Supply and demand. Adam Smith on the open road. Somebody, say, with a truck and ICC permits. And Harley..."

Buckthorn is gazing disconsolately out the window where a rinse of blue exhaust rises around his truck.

"...if you molest one of my carriers again, don't expect to find any more Puffy Cheddar Diesel Cheetos in stock."

Buckthorn bays in despair, but it is not, as Devaney supposes, over the Cheeto ultimatum. Hunkered down in the blue mist, a dog is gnawing at Buckthorn's right front tire.

By the time Buckthorn gets outside, the tire is leaking audibly and the Chevy is starting to list. The dog, a boxer named Chuck Wepner, is loping across the road heading for a blackberry thicket. Buckthorn grabs a tire iron from the bed of the truck and lofts it after Chuck, who scoots into the thicket and moments later emerges triumphant on the far side up an embankment jogging home to Juggernaut's.

On the off chance that his spare has air in it, Buckthorn roots debris to one side of the bed until he reaches the tire, which is flat.

Back inside Devaney has poured two cups of coffee. "I've never seen anything like it," he says.

"The hell you say. I paid $22.50 for it at Les Schwab. I even had the sucker balanced."

"To my knowledge, Chuck's never shown an interest in anything except BMWs and Saabs, maybe the occasional Volvo. Anything with Michelins. I've heard a few blow up on him lately; perhaps he's gone a bit punchy."

Buckthorn sticks his thumb in the coffee to see if it's cool enough to drink. "Juggernaut's got it in for me. She probably sicced him on me."

"Maybe you ran over a squirrel or something. Chuck fancies squirrel. Of course, there's no telling where Schwab gets his cappers. Could be you got into a batch where they mix in horses the pet food companies and Firestone won't take. There was something about that last year in *Entrepreneur*."

Buckthorn drains his coffee, buys a roll of Tums, goes out into the rain. Then he turns around, comes back in, and buys two more rolls. Then he goes across the road and begins to inch through the blackberries looking for his tire iron.

— II —

When Buckthorn arrives at Stanley's it's noon and there's no sign of life. Buckthorn pounds the steering wheel, but the horn isn't working today. Taking a chance, he shuts off the engine. Skirting the deepest gumbo and fingering a roll of Tums free in his pocket from a wedge between his right nut and corresponding thigh, Buckthorn walks around the side of the house where Stanley's truck sits up on blocks, gears scattered like whale vertebrae beneath. The truck is painted citron and lavender, the school colors of Emporia State where Stanley matriculated about three lifetimes ago. Crimson lettering on the side of the truck reads, "You Trash It—I Stash It." The rig, a custom Peterbilt garbage truck, has not stirred since Stanley's brother—mechanic and bookkeeper for the company—moved back to Kansas City in the middle of a tricky piece of mechanicing to sell derivatives for Merrill Lynch. No one else upriver can finish the job, and the cost of towing the truck to town is prohibitive, so there it stands, Stanley losing customers up and down the river as folks begin sneaking their garbage into the dumpsters at Forest Service campgrounds.

Buckthorn ambles up on the porch, knocks once, and when nobody answers walks in. "Hey, ace, you got anybody in the sack with you?" Buckthorn does not think this is likely, but it's polite to ask.

"Just leave me the fuck alone, Buckthorn."

Buckthorn goes into the kitchen, gets two Buds from the refrigerator, and walks on back to the bedroom. Stanley has pulled the sleeping bag over his head.

"Stan, my man," says Buckthorn, crushing a Tums and dropping it into his beer.

Stanley sits up. He looks like somebody's botched idea of Spike Lee as a young Rotarian. Stanley has taken his contacts out, and

Buckthorn, at 220 pounds, blurs around the edges like a watercolor. Stanley waves off the beer and pulls on his shades. "Man, you saw the truck, right? I can't do nothing till Jimmy comes back."

"That bro's long gone."

"I know; I've had it."

Buckthorn belches sympathetically. Stanley owes him $234,000 from a recent poker game where Stanley got drunk and Buckthorn, cheating only when necessary, won some big two-man pots. "I've got something that could put you back on your feet."

Stanley scrunches down into his bag. "No, no, no," he says. "No, no, no, no, no. Not Mexico. Not this nigger."

Within recent memory, Stanley has had some bad luck crossing from Juárez to El Paso in the very truck that now lies beached in his yard. In those days, he had a route in Aspen. Nailing a federal subsidy as an historically underutilized smuggler, he and some customers cooked up a little deal. Nobody figured that pre-9/11 Customs would be too scrupulous about rooting through a loaded garbage truck. Stanley stowed away the pot and then paid the owner of a private dump to fill him up. At the border, they found the pot and also a colony of Hammerhead Potato Borers, assorted body parts, and about thirty different toxic chemicals, with a little nuclear waste to sweeten the deal. Hunter Thompson's lawyer got him off on the drug charge, but the FDA, the EPA, the Departments of Agriculture, Energy, and Veterans Affairs (Stanley was on the VA's books for an Abrams main battle tank he checked out for the weekend and never brought back when he was mustered out of the National Guard), and the National Endowment for the Arts (a DNA match on the body parts indicated that Stanley was hauling the remains of B. Traven and Hilario Lopez Smith, progenitor of black velvet painting) busted him for the rest of the load. He spent eighteen months in jail, and although Thompson bought the truck at government auction and gave it back to Stanley, they later had a falling-out that required Stanley to leave Aspen precipitously. Buckthorn has seen the bullet holes in the driver's door.

"Not Mexico," says Buckthorn soothingly, "Quagmire, New Jersey."

Stanley shakes his head. "I don't think so."

"$234,000."

"Come on, Harley. We was playing for funsies."

"You also signed your truck over to me."

"Shit." Stanley hoists himself out of his bag and sits on the edge of the bed. Buckthorn hands him the beer and he drinks it. Like many houses upriver, Stanley's place is homemade and Buckthorn shifts his stance to match the pitch of the floor.

"If I do it we're even?"

"Right."

"And I get my truck back?"

"Right."

"What am I hauling?"

"You really want to know?"

"Yes. No."

Stanley looks bad, but he refuses Buckthorn's offer of a Tums.

"I know a mechanic from Weyerhaeuser who moonlights. I'll get him on out here." Buckthorn heads for the door, happier than when he discovered that Sarah Trip wrote poems with her clothes off and the curtains open.

Stanley's whine follows him out like a recessional. "Buckthorn, how am I going to do it?"

"This is America," says Buckthorn. "Blend in."

– III –

On the west slope of the Oregon Cascade Mountains, deep inside the Three Sisters Wilderness Area, Naughty Girl Creek rises on the flank of the South Sister and flows west and north some twenty miles into the McKenzie. It is an ordinary stream, bright as ice and dropping steeply once it leaves the high meadow country. It had been called Whorehouse Creek by miners with an eye for the obvious. The name was adjusted with the coming of the U.S. Forest Service and the federal tidying up of any monikers that might give offense to a crypto-sensitive proto-Palinesque Anabaptist under the age of consent. (In a later related development, Cripple Flat—renamed Differently Abled Flat in one of the Carter administration's notable domestic initiatives, prompting a lawsuit from the Frank Cripple family, after whose progenitor the site had been named—was rechristened No Entitlements Flat following the congressional elections of 2016, prompting Cripple's descendants to move to Australia.)

No trail follows Naughty Girl Creek, and its lower canyons are choked with rockslides, deadfall, and an impenetrable smorgasbord of rococo riparian extravagance. In a secret cave overlooking the creek, four men and something else sit around a little fire eating venison haunch, Spam, and rice. Blue smoke fills the cave. It is the legendary Gang of Four, scourge of the McKenzie drainage and coverboys on the latest ¡Earth Liberation Front! calendar.

The four are Hiro Ishimatsu, Imperial Japanese Air Force, escaped in 1945 from a POW camp in Milton-Freewater; D. B. Cooper, air pirate when air piracy was cool; Tony Ten-Toes Jr., last living claimant to the ancestral McKenzie lands of the Qnxtqkl tribe; and Carlos Castaneda, publicist.

The Gang of Four plus one is in deep debate over its collective *nom de guerre*. At various times, depending on the faction in power, it has excluded from the numeration Hiro (on grounds that he remains a sworn enemy of all we hold dear); Tony (on grounds that he is a savage); D. B. (on grounds of common criminality and refusal to recycle his bowel movements in Hiro's rice plot); and Carlos (on grounds of metaphysical hyperbole). Shifting alliances have produced a fragile coalition that now threatens to fly apart like a postwar Italian government over the matter of the fifth member of the group.

"I may be a savage," says Tony, "but he's an animal."

"And a legendary one," says Carlos. "If he's in the picture, I guarantee a spot on *Dr. Phil.*"

"Where does he stand on the Emperor's divinity?" Hiro wears a tattered Vanilla Fudge T-shirt, snatched off the back of the band's last living fan, who had fallen into an apparent stupor on the trail to Separation Lake, "You Keep Me Hanging On" cycling through his Walkman.

"The FBI eats cootie pie," says D. B., who is quite mad.

Sasquatch, who smells approximately like the sludge pond at a sugar beet factory, pops a roll of Tums into his mouth, breaks into a little soft shoe, and sings, sort of, "Ain't Misbehavin.'"

– IV –

The offices of the Estates at Rancho Rio, a project of MegaMax Corporation, are located in an aggressively restored two-story log lodge that once housed the stage stop for which McKenzie Station is named. Second-floor suites accommodate MegaMax executives who fly in from Bakersfield in their Gulfstream Aerocommander. The ground floor features a rustic lounge, the Buckaroo Room, which has a complimentary bar for prospective buyers who have come to preview Rancho Rio's three-thousand-acre planned community. Twelve-passenger buses decked out to resemble stagecoaches take interested parties on site tours. Although several inconvenient local holdings remain to be bought up, the project is 83 percent presold. The homes feature passive solar heating, graywater recycling, smoke scrubbers for fireplaces, water-permeable asphalt to reduce runoff, a Municipal Utility District with a sewage lagoon shaped to resemble Walden Pond, and a Municipal Eco Refuse Disposal Exemplum that will compost or recycle all garbage. Home plans range from the bold and rough-hewn Teddy Roosevelt to the delicately complex Annie Dillard. All models are named for heroes of the natural world: the John Muir, the Rachel Carson, the Gifford Pinchot, the Percy B. Shelley, and so on. Actual construction has not yet begun, but the last regulatory body at the table—a division of the Oregon State Department of Fish and Game responsible for preserving access to traditional sporting grounds for citizens who like to shoot things—is in the process of being kneaded by the same lobbyists who recently massaged the National Park Service into approving discrete Hopiesque condominiums served by cable car at a major rapids in the Grand Canyon.

The ground floor of the lodge also contains the office suite of the resident project manager, Marta Juggernaut. Marta, thirty-two, has an MBA from Wharton and is an adept of Maraca, an arcane Paraguayan martial art that makes spectacular use of her forty-four-inch bust. Known to her sparring partners as "Jugs" (if the right one don't get you, the left one will) and to everyone else as "the Juggernaut," Marta is a stunning six-foot, 160-pound blonde magnificently groomed in casual Eddie Bauer style. She plays golf and tennis with prospective buyers, crunches numbers on her Cray like a CIA analyst, and helps supply the muscle when some holdout balks at selling to MegaMax. Her only weakness is Chuck Wepner, whose appetite for tires is a source of growing dismay.

One of the holdouts, of course, is Buckthorn, whose grandfather left him five acres of cliff face overlooking what is now the Rancho Rio properties. Grandfather Buckthorn had won the parcel from Tony Ten-Toes Jr.'s great-grandfather, Tony Twelve-Toes, on a 1906 World Series bet. It is the only land on the upper McKenzie that Tony Jr. concedes was honestly lost by the Qnxtqkl.

Buckthorn and Juggernaut skirmished even before it became clear that not only wasn't Buckthorn going to sell, he was up to something fishy with his cliff. Juggernaut also suspects, correctly, that Buckthorn is the source of a recent bumper sticker: "Rancho Rio: Upriver, Upscale, and Up Yours."

Now they circle each other warily, awaiting the fatal advantage. To this mortal contest Juggernaut brings youth, cunning, patience, beauty, a 260-pound bench press, a 4 percent stake in Rancho Rio, an IQ of 153, and deep pockets. Buckthorn counters with luck.

In Marta's first week in McKenzie Station, Buckthorn tried to kiss her in the Pour House Tavern's parking lot to show that there were no hard feelings about her running the table on him twice in the pool tournament. That is, he was puckered up, smacking his lips while trying to smile like Prince Charming. Alarmed, Juggernaut grazed his ear with a left breast hook. Balance not being his long suit, Buckthorn wobbled, arms paddling air, wide open for the right mammary uppercut that whistled past his jaw as Juggernaut, distracted by the siren with which Reverend Endwell announces Friday night services at the Free Will Apostolic Church of the Doublewide (McKenzie Synod), missed by less than the length of a nipple, leaving Buckthorn with a Pendleton wool burn on his chin.

Except for Buckthorn, things are humming right along for the Estates at Rancho Rio. Juggernaut is confident that Buckthorn, too, will fall into place. The Cray is only a few hundred billion permutations away from cracking the IRS computer banks and retrieving Buckthorn's file. Juggernaut has lately arranged for Up against the Wall, MegaMax's beaux arts and personal security subsidiary, to buy several of Buckthorn's pieces for the Chamber of Horrors exhibit in the MegaMax Capitalism Theme Park just outside of Oklahoma City in Pud. She has seen to it that Buckthorn is paid in cash with appropriate receipts. The cash, she is sure, will never clutter up his 1040. No one else has ever bought one of Buckthorn's sculptures and he has no other apparent source of income, so an IRS judgment will cost him his property, which Rancho Rio will buy at auction. It's all so obvious that Juggernaut, bored by the inevitability of the scheme, has turned her not inconsiderable attention to finding some means of diverting Chuck Wepner from his diet of Michelins.

But all is not as it seems. Even as the Cray's screen is scrolling up *A Compendium of Canine Neuroses: The Warp of the Woof,* a technician from the Department of Fish and Game is floundering through a patch of distinctively-leafed foliage on the Rancho Rio holdings completing a survey that will reveal, his boss has assured him, neither beast nor fish nor fowl of remote interest to the Oregon sporting public. As he pauses to get his bearings in the late-afternoon drizzle, the technician is startled by the slow contraction of a tubular mass of glistening white mucus, transcendentally distinct from the ordinary Oregon slime, sludge, ooze, muck, mold, mire, quag, gumbo, rheum, sullage, and cable television providers. His heart lopes into his throat. It is, beyond all quibble, the legendary Albino Banana Slug. The last confirmed sighting was during Bob Packwood's run for the U.S. Senate in 1968, where it served as a folksy mascot. The slug thrived on the campaign trail, but was jettisoned after the election on the grounds that it did not represent the kind of image the senator wanted to project in Washington, though he did retain the slug-inspired slogan in subsequent campaigns: "Packwood: One of a Kind." The slug had been donated to the Portland Zoo, where it was promptly salted by vandals. Until this moment, the species had been presumed extinct.

A complex sob catches in the technician's chest. This will cost him his job. The department has made it clear nothing is to turn up that would interfere with granting Rancho Rio an unconditional use permit. The reappearance of a species thought to have taken the long ride will put most of Rancho Rio's holdings off limits to everybody except Exon Mobil and PBS (motto: "The Network with the Crash Dummy Logo") specials.

The technician lifts his boot, heel poised over the shimmering phlegm. At this decisive watershed in the epochal relationship of man and slug, the technician catches a cramp in his calf. Although not himself a religious man, the technician's wife, who watches Reverend Endwell on Springfield Cable Access Microchannel, has urged him to remain ever alert for signs of divine dicking around in human affairs. Supine and rubbing at his knotted calf, the technician is transfixed as a radiant shaft of light breaks through the drizzle, illuminating the slug and throwing the vegetation into sharp relief. The gathering sob bursts forth as he sees that the brush he has been wading through is poison oak.

– V –

Professor Freddy Waxwroth is watching Eyeclueless News when the technician—whom he recognizes as a former student who had repeatedly confused meiosis with mitosis in Biology 101—appears, rash-ridden, with the local anchorpersons and the Albino Banana Slug. The slug's whiteness reveals the anchorpersons' teeth to be liverish in comparison; its luminous sheen renders their eyes and hair as dull as Professor Waxwroth's professional prospects. Rod, trying to remember how to pronounce banana without slipping in an extra syllable, is oblivious, but Stephanie rushes off-camera during the first commercial to change contacts and renew the coat of Vaseline on her canines.

The technician, whose name the professor misses, rapturously describes his encounter with the slug. The slug, beginning to crinkle under the studio lights, oozes along a leaf of romaine lettuce looking for shade. Stephanie reads the newspaper often enough to know that although it does not fly or, yuck, poop in the woods, the Albino Banana Slug may be her very own Northern Spotted Owl and a ticket out of Springfield—to Medford, maybe, or even Spokane. She presses the technician with her best investigative technique, wriggling her nose, ratcheting her lashes, and bending towards him so that the technician—though not the camera—can catch a medium deep shot down her scalloped neckline. The technician, oak boils erupting in oily spasms, spills the beans about where the slug came from.

Twenty minutes later Freddy's phone rings.

"Is this Professor Waxwroth of MegaMax State University?"

Freddy is momentarily disoriented. It has been scarcely a month since MegaMax took over the college in a leveraged buyout of the North American Professional Wrestling Association, which had owned the college, then called Deltoid State, for less than a year, having purchased the school when Oregon decided to privatize higher education and sold off all but a 10 percent interest in most state institutions, including Central Oregon State University. Freddy fishes a new business card from his wallet and reads it.

"Yes."

"I understand that you're the inveterate biologist at MegaMax."

"Invertebrate?" asks Freddy.

"Whatever."

"It's sort of an important distinction," says Freddy pedagogically.

"I'm sure you're a busy man, Professor, so let me come right to the point."

"With whom am I speaking?"

"Mark Neighbors, Northwest Acquisitor, MegaMax Corporation."

Freddy, who has been rehearsing time management by trimming nose hairs while balancing his checkbook, drops the ConCo TurboShears and sits up straight.

"Here's the deal," says Mark. "You've heard about that slug?"

"Yes," says Freddy, batting a thousand so far.

"We want you to breed it or clone it or whatever it is you guys do. What we want are lots of slugs just like that one. We want the Oregon woods to look like slug Tokyo. We want a media feeding frenzy about children and family pets beslimed with them. We've already got Stephen King and Netflix in the loop on this one. Or we can work the lovable pet rock angle and bankroll slugfests all over the state. I can go either way, depending on our polling and how it plays in the House Environmental Affairs Subcommittee. All you need to do is turn out the slugs."

"I'm afraid that there are certain practical and ethical constraints."

Mark Neighbors lets the serrated silence whet its edge. Then he says, "I've got your résumé in front of me, Freddy. You couldn't get a job preparing lab specimens at the county morgue. Have you looked at the return address on your paycheck lately?"

"Slugs," says Freddy. "Lots of slugs."

"You got it, Professor," says Mark. "I've arranged with President York for you to be relieved of all teaching responsibilities.

You'll get a lab and an office of your own with a window, a phone, and a filing cabinet. If you come through on this, we'll double your salary."

"$40,000," says Freddy worshipfully.

"So get in there and slug away. And Professor," says Mark, his voice resonant with implication, "don't let us down on this one."

— VI —

President York sits disconsolately in his office overlooking the McKenzie River. The state had founded the school in the boom days of the early '60s as Oregon's arts and environment university. It had been ticketed for Astoria, but Astoria lobbied successfully for a division of the state hospital that contracts with mental health agencies throughout the nation for treatment of hydrophobics. Central Oregon State University—as it then was—was built on pristine riverfront twenty miles downstream from McKenzie Station. State and county zoning ensured its monastic isolation. The early buildings resembled tepees, yurts, hogans, and dodecahedral domes. As the money ran out, the dominant architectural style could best be described as post-coital.

President York is himself a veritable institution, having been at MegaMax—as it now is—since 1969, when the founding president got into a bad batch of LSD and drove his VW Beetle up two flights of stairs in the women's residence hall.

President York is greatly downcast because Mark Neighbors has just pulled another faculty member out of the classroom. This drops the actual teaching faculty into single digits, not counting the faculty spouses (formerly the faculty wives) who teach introductory courses for $750 a semester. Everyone else has hustled some kind of grant, has assigned time for multigender polycultural monounsaturated curriculum development, is on loan to MegaMax, has moved into administration, or is a full professor.

To cheer himself, President York has his secretary fetch the entries in the recently concluded competition to replace the university's motto: "Deltoid State: Steroid Built and Proud of It." The first submission reads, "MegaMax State: The Progressive University with a Proud Past." A tear starts in President York's eye. This is the very slogan that once had appeared emblazoned in Latin on the school seal, a sleek creature who gamboled mascot-like on the quad in the 1970s during the annual intercollegiate hacky sack Slacker's Cup competition with Reed College.

There are three other entries: "MegaMax State: Why Not the Minimum?"; "MegaMax State: Where the Inconceivable Is Not Necessarily the Unlikely"; and "MegaMax State: Just as Bad as You Thought."

President York tries to recall happier days when he harbored a not unrealistic hope of being tapped for the Board of Governors of the American Association of University Presidents. Since then, his school has been censured by that group as well as by the American Association of University Professors, ¡Earth Liberation Front!, the International Federation of Professional Wrestlers, the American Dairy Council and, most recently, the Rumanian Union of Machinists and Pipefitters (apparently MegaMax Corporation had a cozy deal with the former Rumanian regime to train and smuggle into the country Turkish workers who labored in secret factories to assemble for wages less than President York pays his part-time faculty Rumania's answer to the Yugo—the Rumatic ((motto: "*Sic Transit Amalgam,*" which roughly translates as "It Will Make the Fillings Fall out of Your Teeth"))).

President York takes a Tums and consults his appointment book. An assistant professor of art, Mable Goodchuck, wants to talk to him about the conversion of her studio into what a fresh sign on the door identifies as a slug lab. President York hired Mable when the neo-realism of the '90s filtered out to Oregon in the nick of time via South Carolina, Nebraska, and the Northwest Territories, dictating that paintings ought to look like something. He had checked out the art faculty on the off chance that somebody might be able to paint something that looked like what it was supposed to be. Nobody could. Mable not only painted things that looked like things, she specialized in hills and trees and brooks and clouds. You could step right outside and it would look just like one of Mable's paintings. President York blocks out two minutes for Mable.

His other appointment is Lunelle Johnson-Bender, provost of the university. President York pops another Tums and wonders whether he could score some LSD from any of the current students.

— VII —

If Amanda Pennypacker were any cuter, she could have brought the 1950s back single-handed. Pert and scrubbed, blond and buxomesque, she is spending a year in McKenzie Station coordinating a Ford Foundation community development pilot project. The foundation has singled out McKenzie Station because it clings relentlessly to the bottom of the last quintile of all relevant demographic, economic, and cultural indices, fractionally beating out Bent Organ, Mississippi; Gristle, Wyoming; and Sludge, West Virginia. Amanda is also here because her two beaus—Princeton and Columbia Law—are working off the curse of family wealth and burnishing their political résumés in Arkansas (motto: "Thank God for Mississippi") and West Virginia (motto: "Thank God for Mississippi"). Amanda believes in the inherent goodness of the common man, the virtues of prayer and Belgian hair conditioner, waiting until you're married, and the likelihood that one of her beaus will some day be president of the United States. Preening only the teeniest bit, she assumes it will be the beau of her choice.

There is, of course, a darker side, which emerges nightly as Amanda, in a Céline Dion flannel nightgown, kneels at her bed. As she makes her mind blank for God, in rushes Daddy, Florsheims tracking the past all over her *tabula rasa*. The dialogue is unvarying, has not changed since Amanda was twelve:

"Cute," her father intones, "has a shelf life. Character is what goes the distance. Your mother's shelf life, for example, expired at thirty-four."

"You mean," says Amanda winsomely, "you can't eat Mommy anymore?"

Mr. Pennypacker has risen to CEO of Haverford Coil and Capacitor by dint of an operatic baritone, his six-foot, four-inch frame, and an IQ that occasionally exceeds his golf score. Amanda, of course, yearns for her father's approval and dares to hope that doing CPR on the McKenzie Station civic corpse might yet turn the trick.

So far, Amanda has managed to establish a bi-monthly video club and sing along at Loretta's Curl Up and Dye Shoppe of Beauty and persuaded Devaney to stock male birth control devices. Since Devaney's inventory is arranged alphabetically, Amanda reluctantly agrees that the devices will be considered rubbers instead of prophylactics so that they can be shelved within easy reach of one of Devaney's big sellers, Root Wad Chewing Tobacco. She has also tapped MegaMax for a donation to fund a community fair. It will be the biggest thing upriver since Buckthorn, having lost a bet, drank a pint of Old Mortuary while walking naked up the center stripe of Highway 123 from the Pour House Tavern to the turnoff for Foley Ridge playing Mozart's Piano Concerto #7 on a borrowed accordion. Amanda has captured that episode in *Magic Moments on the McKenzie,* the monthly newsletter she produces to help residents take pride in the accomplishments of their fellow citizens. Buckthorn, who she thinks is a little sweet on her, has promised to symbolically reenact his heroic trek at the community fair.

Amanda's horizons, straight and narrow as George Will's scoutmaster, are about to be widened and warped.

– VIII –

Like many revolutionaries, the Gang of Five (Sasquatch having been admitted as a provisional member) has a hard time agreeing on the shape of the world once the revolution is won. Tony Ten-Toes Jr. wants to remove all non-Indians save Buckthorn from the upper McKenzie valley to Lake Oswego, Oregon, where they will support themselves by learning to fabricate characteristic ethnic artifacts such as pull tabs, pocket protectors, black sandal-length socks, Miracle Whip, and polyester golf shirts in schools run by the Bureau of Chuck Affairs. He then plans to open a floating bingo parlor anchored just upstream from the Pour House. Hiro Ishimatsu, having never tuned in Eyeclueless News with Rod and Stephanie, lags even American teenagers in his knowledge of current affairs. He believes he will yet live to see Roosevelt eat sushi. The others have not broken the news that Japan is now winning without him, since they do not wish to lose Hiro's mechanical dexterity and **** Spam Stir-Fry. D. B. apparently hopes to go into politics, often rehearsing his campaign slogan: "Get off your pooper and vote for Cooper." Carlos thinks both major parties might be interested (like Dolly Parton's, D. B.'s political affiliation has been a matter of keen speculation) since D. B. could run on an irresistible campaign pledge: "The only candidate for whom the statute of limitations has run out." D. B. also seems to have deep pockets, vanishing from time to time farther into the wilderness to return with a wad of bills. As for Carlos, he wants only to bring to the world the heartwarming story of the gang, hoping thereby to refurbish his literary stock, which plummeted still further when Don Juan signed with Scott Meredith, who auctioned in the high six-figure range *The Road to Cancun: Ixtlan in My Rear-view Mirror* and *Follow Your Bliss*, co-authored with Bill Moyers, Deepak Chopra, Nicholas Sparks, and Khloe Kardashian.

Sasquatch, though he continues to smell like a bad day downwind from the pulp mill, is on his best behavior during the trial membership and agrees with everyone. As it happens, he learned to communicate by memorizing sheet music he filched during the ransack of a summer home. He now entertains the group evenings around the campfire with a medley of old standards including everybody's favorite, "Beauty and the Beast."

What has been agreed is that the boys have grown out of touch and perhaps a tad rusty since their last raid, when they hijacked a rural mail carrier, stripping his car of distributor, gearbox, and clutch housing, which Sasquatch carried back for use in the ultralight Hiro is assembling.

Periodically, Carlos steals into the lower reaches of the wilderness, where he picks up cases of Spam and cartons of Tums brought to a secret clearing by C. C. (Cash Crop) Fellows, who uses the site to grow a stand of McKenzie Mauve, judged eight years running at the Lane County Fair the finest sinsemilla north of Mendocino.

Carlos first met C. C. while dangling from one of his snares when Carlos happened upon the patch trying to follow D. B. to his cash cache. After some awkward moments, Carlos managed to introduce himself, and since Carlos was suspended upside down ten feet in the air, C. C. set aside his twelve-gauge Browning over-and-under and allowed as how the name was familiar. When Carlos said that he had written the Don Juan books, C. C. cut him down at once and they blew a little smoke. C. C. asked if Carlos would autograph his copies, not yet having come across Don Juan's recent endorsement of MD 20-20 in *Cirrhosis Quarterly*.

They blew a little more smoke, and C. C. asked Carlos what he was doing in these parts. When Carlos explained, C. C. thought about it and then said he'd like to sponsor the gang: T-shirts, Christmas party, entry fee in the Springfield slow-pitch softball league—the whole caboodle. A California company, he said, wanted to build a big development in the upper valley. That meant more people and more attention, maybe even a resident deputy sheriff. It would be harder to do business, and besides all that California money meant cocaine, which would erode his local market share. Not to mention that the McKenzie would be forever Californicated. C. C. had undertaken civic endeavors before, having endowed a cannabis chair in the biology department at Deltoid State to develop uses for marijuana modeled on how Booker T. Washington had diversified the peanut. As it turned out, by the time the money reached Freddy Waxwroth it had been folded into a grant from the North American Professional Wrestling Association to derive human-compatible growth hormone from musk oxen. Since the endowment had been paid entirely in small bills, C. C. didn't have any leverage. Now that the college had changed hands, C. C. had heard that the professor who held the chair had moved on to slug research.

The deal, then, was this: C. C. would provision the gang if they would do what they could to thwart the Estates at Rancho Rio. The alliance was ratified over another soupçon of McKenzie Mauve as C. C. and Carlos shared some munchies, a tin of Spam Crispies C. C. had brought along.

On his most recent visit to the patch, Carlos has learned from C. C. of Amanda Pennypacker's forthcoming community fair. Thinking it a perfect opportunity to get the lay of the land, the drift of the wind, and perhaps to beguile the hearts and minds of the natives, Carlos resolves to come in. Long into the night, the Gang of Five lays their plans as Naughty Girl Creek babbles like an idiot child and a shadow passes across the moon.

— IX —

The shadow across the moon is both literal—a Gulfstream Aerocommander—and figurative—the MegaMax Rancho Rio executive group, all of whom are named Herbert Walker to confuse competitors and engender team spirit. Due to construction constraints pending final state waivers for Rancho Rio, the Gulfstream must land at a U.S. Forest Service airstrip. The airstrip, a grass field with a windsock, has a 183-foot elevation differential east to west, a 15 percent tilt north to south, and is approximately the length and width of a bowling alley lane. It can accommodate deer, bear, resident and migratory birds, pickup drag races, teenage front-seat gropers, and the DC-3s of Air Error, which are the cheapest plane the Forest Service can lease to fly their fire crews around in. On FAA civil aviation maps, the field is designated as KYAG-87-532 and is widely known among aviators as Kiss Your Ass Goodbye Many Times.

The MegaMax pilots—Tice, an F-4 jockey with forty-three missions over Hanoi, and Wally, a thirty-year veteran of the ivory trade in Africa—flutter the Gulfstream in, reversing thrust in the air and dropping like a Lloyd's of London nightmare. Wally and Tice play rock-scissors-paper to see who has to land at McKenzie. Win or lose, Wally shuts his eyes after they clear the last stand of old-growth Doug fir and, if he's flying it, sets the Gulfstream down by feel and terror.

In the back, the Herbert Walkers discuss rollover stock options and sip MegaMax Glenaerie Corporate Reserve Brandy. They are met at the strip by Juggernaut in a stretch Jaguar Land Bruiser with smoked windows, satellite uplink, Soloflex, and hot tub. They come and go only at night, wearing infrared goggles to tour the project, occasionally stepping out to piss so as to get the on-site feel. On the infrequent occasions when the Herbert Walkers stay over, they remain upstairs in their rooms.

The only man on the team not named Herbert Walker is Mark Neighbors, and that is because he is the boss. Sometimes he tries to disguise himself as one of them and slip unnoticed onto the Gulfstream to gauge morale in the ranks of middle management. But like an alien in an old TV series, he misses some detail of dress or decorum—too subtle a pair of cuff links, too quick to laugh at corporate jokes—so that the Herbert Walkers spend the flight winking and nudging each other until Mark Neighbors has to admit that he's been found out again.

The Herbert Walkers think he's a good sport about this, but in fact their composition turns over as rapidly and subtly as the body's cells. Since each new Herbert Walker is indistinguishable from his predecessor, nobody can tell the difference. Whenever Mark is found out, he transfers the Herbert Walker he thinks first fingered him to one of the MegaMax convenience stores in the Texas Panhandle District. Herbert Walkers currently manage MegaMaxMarts in Mobeetie, Goodnight, Muleshoe, Farfetched, Migraine, John Wayne, Testosterone, and West Jesus.

On the night the Gulfstream eclipses the moon over the Three Sisters Wilderness, Mark Neighbors flies in with the Herbert Walkers and they tour the *déclassé* section of Rancho Rio set aside for those who have to ask the price (which, as it happens, is $100,000 for a starter lot). Up Buckskin Boulevard, along Appaloosa Avenue, down Drover Drive, across Conestoga Court, past Polecat Place, around Lariat Loop, over Wrangler Way, into Chuck Wagon Circle, and finally debouching onto Stetson Street they drive.

Since Mark is cognito by this time of the evening, he rides up front with Juggernaut. At each newly pre-sold lot, Mark and the Herbert Walkers climb down, join hands, and do a little corporate jig around the sign while Juggernaut, flexing her breasts, scans the looming woods with her nightscope. Later, as the Herbert Walkers are snacking off the catered tailgate of the Land Bruiser, Mark walks Juggernaut down to the river and makes his move.

"Marta," he says, keeping well clear of her 44s, "I must declare myself." Mark's Belgian body talc clots between his cold sweat and the mist swirling up off the river. “I am not who I seem. I was once an English major at Cal State Merlot. Come away with me. I am provisioned with zero-coupon municipal bonds. We could restore an authentically neglected Victorian on the coast, convert it to a bookstore, bed and breakfast, and studio for Maraca. Say the word,” says Mark, rising to the occasion, “and they are mine.”

Juggernaut surmounts an insurmountable giggle that she last giggled in eighth grade when Gary Farragut bet her they weren’t real and had to eat Jell-O salad in the cafeteria all semester for losing the wager.

“That is, they are yours. No, yours are mine, they are it—I mean, those are some hooters.” Sparks fly as the head-up display on Mark’s Blackhawk nightscope goggles shorts out in the McKenzie drool and his text vanishes in a puff of blue smoke.

Juggernaut gazes demurely down. “I’ll think about it after I bank my second million.”

Back at the airstrip, Mark is a smorgasbord of emotion. He is anxious to return to Bakersfield where he will drain Marta’s Cray into his Fujitsu and ransack it for a clue to her heart. Eager to be off and vexed at the delay, he reaches up reflexively to twirl the ends of his moustache, momentarily forgetting that as a contemporary villain not only is he psychologically multitextured but he has no moustache. At the last moment he recovers, reaching instead over the chrome-tanned leather to twirl the ears of the Herbert Walker seated in front of him. Just then, Wally enters the cabin, followed marginally by Tice. Mark turns loose Herbert Walker’s ears, which unwind like a tire swing.

“Mr. Neighbors,” says Wally, scuffing his Justin Roper at the Karastan, “some wild animal has et our tires plumb off the rims.”

– X –

Buckthorn parks his truck at the laundromat, where no one will think to look for him, cuts across the Forest Service compound past the Oregon historical plaque commemorating the site where Further, the Pranksters' bus, blew its first water pump on that legendary journey, and loops up behind the Church of the Doublewide. Beyond, the dark wilderness closes.

Buckthorn is bound for a small gingerbread cabin tucked into a notch of private land in the Cut-and-Run National Forest. Sarah Trip lives in the cabin, and it is, by Buckthorn's reckoning, the night of her menstrual full moon when Sarah sits in the buff, lantern-lit, writing poems like the ones that have led to reviews of her first book, ⚦, in *Playboy*: "Take a trip with Sarah—she has met the enemy and he is us. These poems will grab you by the short-and-curlies and yank"; *You Go Grrrl*: "Makes Anne Sexton read like a whiny New England housewife and Sylvia Plath like a jingle writer for Magic Chef. Sisters, this is the real stuff"; and *Library Journal*: "Not for the faint-hearted... recommended for mature collections only."

Reaching the cabin, Buckthorn shinnies up to his perch in a yew tree and gazes in reverent lust through the uncurtained window. Facing him, cross-legged on a small rug and bending to her task, is Sarah, neon-red on top, a deeper burgundy below, breasts flushed and freckled like a rainbow trout, lantern light streaming into her lap. Sarah shifts on the rug, and her hair flares as she shakes it back.

Buckthorn's groin twitches, and he drifts in reverie back to his years at the Rhode Island School of Design and his old roommate, John Shine, who regaled Buckthorn with tales of his amorous escapades featuring Captain Howdy, as Shine had familiarly dubbed his member. Buckthorn—who had seized onto the term "Johnson" when he first heard it used by a Standing Rock Sioux attending high school in Gruel, South Dakota, as an exchange student (they referred to all white pricks as "Custers")—was awestruck by how Shine dazzled his dates. Scar tissue from an old injury to Captain Howdy enabled Shine to raise erections in the approximate shape of a question mark. What woman could say no to such a charmingly posed physiological query? Few of Shine's dates, in fact, could. Often, after a luckless night in the pubs of Providence, Buckthorn would return home only to hear "Shine on" from his roommate as he rattled the doorknob. This meant that Buckthorn would have to spend the night on the couch again since the apartment had but one bedroom.

In their last year, Shine had a regular girlfriend, also a student at the Rhode Island School of Design, who did installations featuring polystyrene, bronze, sourdough (baked and garnished with ConCo TurboRoach Powder), and wilted lettuce casts of the penises of her lovers that she arranged in vases like still lifes. Once when she was trying to finish a piece in time for her MFA show, Phyllis tried to entice Buckthorn into the sack so she could round out her thesis with an even dozen. She also said she wanted an honest, Lutheran, corn-fed midwestern cock in the show—the kind that kept *Reader's Digest* in the bathroom instead of *Penthouse* and didn't shake drops all over the floor when it peed. Buckthorn, stricken with ordinary male size anxiety, resorted to a phallic trick Shine had taught him and played dead, embarrassing himself privately but avoiding potentially catastrophic public display. Phyllis coaxed and prodded, but she couldn't get a rise out of him.

Later, Shine moved into performance art, and Buckthorn had once seen a video, *Further Adventures with Captain Howdy*, rented apparently for bachelorette parties and featuring the indefatigable Shine (the scar tissue was distinctive) doing charades and shadow art on walls.

Sarah arches a kink out of her back, and Buckthorn struggles against a faint stirring in his loins. Nothing, he knows, will come of it. "Never up, never in," Shine used to say, walking around with an interrogatory lump in his pants. Buckthorn imagines he is saving himself for his art, that he must husband his precious bodily fluids for the work ahead. In fact, he has not had an erection in months. Chaste as the '90s but randy as the '60s, Buckthorn groans, works his way down the yew, and returns, whimpering, through the drizzling woods.

– XI –

On Friday nights, the Reverend Endwell makes ready the Church of the Doublewide for his flock. The reverend has a lopsided grin, a shock of creamy black hair, and the energy of an amphetamine-fueled slot machine. He also has a portable signboard down by the highway advertising services and passing along a thought for the day. He tries to perk people up spiritually with the messages. Although Catholics now use kazoos at Mass and have beatified Crescencio Domino, purveyor of pizza and young boys to the College of Cardinals, and the Presbyterians have ordained imams, fakirs, dervishes, and mongeese in the spirit of ecumenicalism, organized religion, like organized crime, has ossified, he believes. It is an indigestible dumpling in God's gut. The Reverend Endwell thinks of the Church of the Doublewide as ConCo TurboFleet for God.

For several months, the messages have consisted of the reverend's own translations of the Ten Commandments, whose linguistic subtlety seems to elude much of his congregation in any currently available rendition. This week's commandment is #7: "GuYs—Keep it in Your Pants. GalS: See to it that He DoeS." Due to space limitations, the reverend worries a moment that the passage might be taken to prohibit lawful conjugal relations, but he supposes that any conjugality that has survived ESPN will not easily be daunted by the misconstrued word of God.

The reverend struggles mightily to tamp down the pride he takes in his work, pride being one of the seven deadly snakes indigenous to the spiritual brambles. In fact, Reverend Endwell had nailed a cool "A" at Bible college in Antepenultimate, Nevada (a western branch of the mother seminary in Mumble, Maine) in the seminar "Signified and Signifier: Signage along the Road to Salvation," a course taught by a former member of the faculty at the Yale School of Divinity whose tenure had been revoked when it was discovered that he actually believed in God.

Although Amanda Pennypacker has been raised Episcopalian, in McKenzie Station she chooses to attend the Church of the Doublewide. Amanda had never been in a mobile home before (in fact, she could not recall ever having seen one), but the services have the folk charm of a native quilt—though, to Amanda's dismay, not only does no one upriver quilt but hardly anyone sews or whittles or puts up preserves, dashing her hopes for a cooperative indigenous craft shop since the crafts passed down river families for generations consist largely of fabricating gill nets and shocking devices for salmon, making salt licks disguised as mushrooms to set out for deer and elk, carving bongs from madrone, and ransacking cars parked at wilderness trailheads—especially the occasional glossolalia, which gives her something to write Handler, who early on had told her about the dirt eaters and snake fondlers far back in the Ozarks, concluding, in a rare moment of despair, that Arkansas was God's best argument against incest.

The Crease family—Orville and Everline and their children Willa, Waylon, Wick, and Iphigenia—also belongs to Reverend Endwell's congregation. Amanda thinks they might have come from Arkansas. In season, the Creases collect fern, fronds, forbs, and sphagnum moss to sell to local florists; returnable cans and bottles from Forest Service campground dumpsters; yew bark for local distillers; and anything that doesn't seem especially attached to its owner for Easy Ed's Pawn and Appliance in Springfield. Mr. and Mrs. Crease pray lustily, and Amanda had let Willa play with her radiant tresses until she began to miss small patches of hair that Willa was assembling into a fall to sell to Loretta, who carries wigs at the Curl Up and Dye for customers who had not gotten out of California soon enough. In fact, Reverend Endwell has been constrained to see to it that the collection plate always begins at the row where the Creases sit, so that as the offertory, "(Money) Can't Buy Me Love," is sung, the plate does not emerge from the row appreciably lighter than when it entered.

Although a man of the cloth—more precisely, the polyester double knit—Reverend Endwell cannot help but notice the cherubic Amanda, her pert nose and fawn-brown eyes enough to bring a saint shinnying down from his pillar of salt in the desert. As the camcorder hums away for Springfield Cable Access Microchannel and Orville Crease eyes the equipment, Reverend Endwell reminds himself of his responsibility to his extended flock: if he is not soon implicated in a sexual peccadillo (a full-sized cigar being out of the question), people will lose interest.

– XII –

Devaney's Mercantile is one of the twin pillars of commerce in McKenzie Station, the other being the Pour House Tavern. Provisioned by his contract with the Postal Service and his pension from the Federal Bureau of Weights and Measures, Devaney can turn a modest profit by selling goods at no more than three times the price you could buy anything for in Springfield. Like the Pour House, he will also run a tab. When the tab exceeds the limit worked out on a sliding scale Devaney guards as if it were the all-purpose formula for Brylcreem and Twinkie filling, he insists on payment. Firewood (no cedar, alder, or chinquapin; bonus for madrone), trout, venison (backstrap only), elk, elderberry brandy, dressed quail, blackcap raspberries, morel mushrooms, and information pertaining to the whereabouts of the Gang of Four can be used to reduce the balance.

Devaney has shelved his goods alphabetically after early ill-fated experiments with displaying them according to the Dewey Decimal System and the Periodic Table. He intractably refuses to use the standard categorical arrangement originally worked out by Benjamin Franklin at the A & P in Otiose Heights, Pennsylvania. He believes that his current shelving system is a civic responsibility, prodding the locals to refresh their familiarity with the alphabet, which they often leave behind when they drop out of school in the tenth grade. The crafty locals, of course, soon memorize the location of typical purchases, so Devaney, like a greenkeeper resetting the cup, will sometimes stay up all night revising the shelving so that the "A's" start, say, by the beer cooler instead of the door.

Sheila Wallop, manager of the Pour House for a group of silent partners, swings by the Mercantile from time to time to see if Devaney is ready to marry her yet. Both have lost spouses—Devaney to boredom; Sheila one each to the State of Georgia, a 780 triglyceride level, and bad luck in Bolivia. Devaney is smitten with Sheila: her tidy ankles, her Tequila Sunrises, her ownership of one of the last pieces of property other than Buckthorn's that Rancho Rio needs to complete its holdings. Still, Devaney—whose idea of pushing the envelope is flushing the toilet again before the tank has filled—demurs.

On this day in July when no one will answer the phone at the Oregon State Tourist Commission because staff is working on a new promotion: "Oregon: 70 Percent Less Skin Cancer Than Alabama," Sheila and Devaney sit on stools fore and aft of the cash register watching Devaney's gas pumps rust in the summer rain.

"What the hell, Billy, you could save a bundle at the laundromat and maybe I could put a little fire back in the old furnace." Sheila pinches Devaney affectionately on the thigh through his tweed trousers.

"I'm worried about Buckthorn," says Devaney.

"I'm worried about *us*," says Sheila. "There are those that would jump at the chance. I could be snatched off the market just like that."

"He just hasn't been the same ever since I told him he couldn't ship plastic explosives through the U.S. mails."

Sheila lights up a Kool and Devaney waves his hand at the smoke.

"He's in love, that's all."

"With who?"

"Sarah Trip and what's her name—you know, Miss Goody Two-Shoes from back east—and also Marta Juggernaut."

Devaney whistles in sympathy. "No wonder he looks so bad."

"If he'd just settle in with a nice girl, he'd perk up in no time. It's a proven fact that married men are happier. Live longer, too." Sheila shoots Devaney a meaningful look.

"Apparently, the statisticians missed your husbands."

"That's not fair and you know it, Billy Devaney. Why, there's not a one of them wouldn't have died years sooner if I hadn't taken an interest."

Around the corner from the gas pumps comes a customer. It is Carlos Castaneda, sporting a false moustache, false glasses, a false limp, a real hairpiece, and a Nebraska accent. Devaney punches open the register, grabs the big bills, and stuffs them down his socks as the bell over the door jangles behind Carlos.

"Mister," says Devaney, "all those disguises don't fool me one iota."

"What?" says Carlos.

"And neither does that phony Nebraska accent. If you aim to rob this store, I'd thank you to let me get one of my sweaters for the Widow Wallop here so she won't be too discomforted when you lock us in the cooler."

"Tums," says Carlos. "I need to buy some Tums."

"Big seller these days," says Devaney, and points him down aisle 2.

After Carlos leaves, Sheila plants a large kiss on Devaney, who reels from the waft of menthol. "Why, Billy, you old romantic. To think you wanted to snuggle up with me in the cooler."

"What I wanted to snuggle up to in the cooler," says Devaney, "was my socks."

– XIII –

Amanda Pennypacker has gone over the vital statistics three times. There can be no mistake. No baby has been born upriver in fourteen months. Moreover, guarded inquiries at Loretta's Curl Up and Dye have revealed no present pregnancies, not even among the Creases. At first, Amanda fears her family planning venture has succeeded only too well, but on checking with Devaney she learns he has sold only three boxes of Trojans: one to a trucker, one to the co-anchor of Eyeclueless News, up for an afternoon to float the river with the winner of a Campfire Girls group leaders' membership contest, and one to Sheila Wallop.

Amanda does not include, of course, U.S. Forest Service personnel, who breed like beavers. Scarcely any Forest Service pregnancy runs its course upriver, though, since the government, like a colonial power, rotates its rangers out every six months to keep them from being corrupted by long association with native custom. The Forest Service overhead lives mostly in Springfield anyway, drawn by the cultural seductions of Oregon's seventh largest city. Locals who work seasonally for the Forest Service have spawned no more than their civilian counterparts.

Amanda, deeply troubled, makes an appointment to speak with her pastor.

– XIV –

Buckthorn sits on a stool at the Pour House near the telephone. Stanley has made a long-distance call, word was passed, and now Buckthorn waits morosely for the return call. Stanley would not be phoning with good news; given Stanley, the bad news could be spectacular.

Above the bar, Sheila's thought for the week is written in red chalk on the blackboard that also announces drink specials and the names of those who have exceeded their tabs and get no more credit even if they are screwing one of the barmaids. The thought for the week is this: "BOSSES ARE LIKE DIAPERS—FULL OF SHIT AND ALL OVER YOUR ASS." The week's thought usually recycles out front where Sheila has put up a portable signboard directly across the road, as it happens, from Reverend Endwell's. She and the reverend had gotten crossways some years back when the Pour House featured topless barmaids, and there are still hard feelings on both sides. This week's public message reads: "OLD PREACHERS NEVER DIE—THEY JUST SMELL THAT WAY."

Sheila and Buckthorn are alone in the bar. They go back a long way, to the time when Buckthorn stepped in as a speed bump for three fraternity boys, decathletes of debauch on their way home from a weekend skiing Mt. Bachelor, who had stopped by the Pour House to prove that when they're on, nobody can touch a Kappa Sig for all-around assholery. As it happened, there were no loggers in the Pour House that night, so Buckthorn himself had to stuff them individually through the sunroof of their BMW, picking up the back end and bouncing it once for emphasis as he sent them on their way.

Buckthorn remembers that incident now and remembers, too, what he had always meant to ask. "Sheila, you've lived in New York. What percentage of the world would you say are assholes?"

"About 5 percent, Bucky," Sheila says, pouring some Scoresby into a Glenlivet bottle. "But they get around a lot." She finishes with the Scoresby and starts adding MD 20-20 to the MegaMax Glenaerie Corporate Reserve Brandy.

At the Pour House, Buckthorn drinks only from bottles he can watch the seal broken on or the cap popped off of.

Sheila interrupts her chores to buy Buckthorn a Bud on the house. "Buckaroo," she says fondly, "why don't you just get the fuck married and let the gal make something of yourself. You're likely to go sooner or later, and later your options are going to thin out and fatten up, if you get my drift. Any one of them would do—even that Miss Priss from back east."

This last is fairly heretical. Oregonians learn at their mother's breast that except for a major California tributary, all rapaciousness, gooey-brained middle management, good tans, and bad manners arrive in the state from back east. Buckthorn, who had not thought his hypothetical love life a subject of local speculation, blushes. "Why don't you?"

"Can't get Devaney's nose out of his business long enough to sniff my assets."

"What he sniffs," says Buckthorn, "are your Kools."

Sheila makes a rude noise she learned living back east.

The phone jangles, and Buckthorn accepts a collect call from Stanley, who is in East Quagmire, New Jersey. At first, Buckthorn listens. Then he yells. Then he listens some more, slumping over the receiver as though the beams and joists of his body have turned out to be a house of cards, as it were. The deal is this: for reasons inexplicable by any calculus of the combinations and permutations of stupidity, beyond even the random lunacy theory of cosmologists, Stanley is in the back room of Mom's Cafe and Bar, a woman named Doll on his arm, playing poker with a man called Doc.

So far, Stanley has lost two-fifths of the garbage truck; the rest is riding on the hand before him on the table. He has called Buckthorn for advice, Doc loaning him a quarter for the pay phone in the men's room. They are playing five-card stud with the last card down and dirty. Doc has two sevens and a king showing. Stanley has a nine, a five, and a six. He tries to explain to Buckthorn that he'd be doing a lot better if Doc would just agree to play with jokers and one-eyed jacks wild, but Buckthorn starts yelling again, hurting Stanley's feelings. Stanley is about to hang up when he remembers that win or lose, Buckthorn is going to have to wire him some money if he's going to get home, Doc having lifted his bankroll before he started in on the truck.

Buckthorn waves frantically to Sheila, jabbing his finger in the direction of the Stupefaction Tequila until she gets the right bottle and pours him a shot. Buckthorn has to decide whether to wire Stanley money to finish the hand or let him bet the rest of the truck. If he folds, Doc gets another fifth and with it majority ownership. Buckthorn tosses off the shot and waves for the bottle. He has seen Stanley lose on hands that other men would kill for. Stanley's hole card is an eight, he whispers into the phone. Buckthorn drinks, gags, shudders, and tells Stanley to go the whole truck drawing to an inside straight. Luck—blind, deaf, and dumb—is their only hope. Doc deals the last round and bumps the stakes until the entire Peterbilt is in the pot, stem to stern. Then Doc flips over his hole cards: an ace and a seven.

Buckthorn bays in despair. Passing on the highway, a vacationing mother from Prozac, Connecticut lunges instinctively across the back seat of the family Volvo where she has been reading gender-neutral, pancultural, gluten-free fairy tales printed alternately on acid-free and biodegradable paper and tries to shield her child's ears from the sound. Down the road, Devaney wonders if Buckthorn has lost another tire.

On the phone, Stanley is giggling. In a remote crevice of his brain where Buckthorn imagines such creamy pleasures as the complete *oeuvre* of Yanni piped in to a reunion of MTV programmers, he begins to formulate what he will do to Stanley.

Stanley's last card is a seven.

Buckthorn accelerates off the barstool, whooping around the dance floor slapping himself upside the head. When he returns to the phone, Doc is on the line.

"Your friend," he says, "is short the table rent."

"Table rent?"

"We don't play for free here, bub. Either I see $250 or Stanley ends up in the Hudson and the truck gets buried with Jimmy Hoffa in the end zone of Giants Stadium."

Buckthorn wonders if Doc doesn't have it backwards, but this is no time to quibble. He catches Sheila's attention, puckers up, and blows her a round of kisses.

"How much?" she asks.

"$300?"

Sheila scrunches her brows together. "You swear to get married inside a year and $300 it is."

Buckthorn gags and shudders. "You got it."

As he makes the necessary arrangements with Doc, he watches Sheila pour paint stripper into the diminished bottle of Stupefaction.

– XV –

Lunelle Johnson-Bender is in President York's outer office, held momentarily at bay by his secretary, who is under orders to grab her by the hyphen if she tries to barge in before his Tums have taken hold. Lunelle, a sociologist, has been provost of the university since President York found he could limit the harm she caused as a faculty member by putting her in charge of assigning keys and classrooms, selecting the menu for receptions following commencement, and counseling students in jeopardy of academic probation—that is, those whose GPAs were so microscopic that they had fallen beneath the benchmark Quayle-Palin-Lindell Line (a not inconsiderable achievement given MegaMax's new mastery-based academic scale which awards only two grades: passing and not yet passing), suggesting that it would be nip and tuck in the College Bowl if they came up against a loaf of Velveeta cheese.

Since MegaMax bought out the university, Lunelle has become increasingly emboldened, sometimes brushing past President's York's secretary into his inner office and recently calling a faculty convocation where she delivered a paper she had written in 1983 but had yet to place at a conference: "Field Validation of Statistical Norms of Cross-Gender Public Restroom Entry as a Function of Signage." She guesses, correctly, that MegaMax understands that President York is essentially harmless and has left him in place to keep the tax-free status the university retains so long as its president has been named by the State of Oregon. Their only administrative restructuring thus far has involved sacking the vice president for financial affairs so all the money can be handled in Bakersfield. President York fears that Lunelle wants to bend his Johnson. In fact, she hopes to catapult past him into the position of chancellor.

While he waits for the Tums to absolve him of lunch at the

University Club and buffer him from what is to come, President York gazes from his window, sees some flotsam or jetsam bob past (the McKenzie, high and sludgy from rain, blurs the distinction), and thinks fondly of Thurge, his former vice president for financial affairs. Thurge was of the old school, handling university finances like a man burying tin cans full of money in his backyard and then forgetting where he had put them. President York could find the cans (even the Merrill Lynch derivatives purchased through the Silage, Iowa branch of their Kansas City office) often enough to keep the university afloat in a sea of fiscal woe. No more—neither cans nor woe. MegaMax had doubled tuition, halved faculty salaries, and tripled enrollment by an aggressive marketing campaign—"MegaMax U: Cowabunga, Dude—Like, Is This a Great Place or What?!"—and by requiring all domestic MegaMax employees to send their children here.

What may or may not have been a Porta Potty sails past, and President York's thoughts turn to his next appointment. Scorned by scientists and humanists alike, sociologists were now thriving at the university, having lost their one saving grace, embarrassment at their field. MegaMax had most of them on consulting contracts to match individualized fleecing techniques with site-discrete crowd behavior at various MegaMax theme parks (example: at the State of North Dakota Theme Park, the consultants had recommended replacing the Lawrence Welk talking doll—"Cowabunga, Dude: Like, Is This a Great State or What?!"—with Windham Hill recordings of wheat growing). It is President York's fervent hope that MegaMax will find a consultancy for Lunelle, perhaps at their theme park in Hallelujah, Tennessee, where the seven days of Creation are reenacted with God turning the whole deal over to the Baptists on day 8.

President York can put off no longer his post-prandial comeuppance, and he buzzes Marsha to send Lunelle in. She marches resolutely through the door straight to President York's desk, where she stops. President York rises, gestures in courtly fashion to the chair directly beside her, and remains standing until she reluctantly but substantially fills the *faux* vinyl. Seated, Lunelle does a quick little twitch, smoothing some of the scrunch out of her girdle. She is, President York supposes, the last person besides Donald Trump who wears one. Perhaps if someone had snapped it once in her life...

"Walden," she says, hoisting one thigh up and over the other as nylon whisks and latex groans, "you really must do something about the faculty."

"What I hear you saying," says President York, who has recently read a book on management, "is that I really must do something about the faculty."

"This time they've gone too far."

"Have they?" says President York, hoping the tale will take a prurient turn but, given the collective faculty libido, doubting it.

"They're never in their offices."

President York nearly suggests that they may be in their classrooms, but catches himself in time. Nobody, of course, is in the classroom anymore. Having just avoided stepping in the cow patty, he plunges thigh-deep into rhinoceros shit. "Have you checked the library?" His bowels quake at the blunder, but by the time he thinks to laugh it is too late: Lunelle has seen that he meant it.

"Why, Walden, you're such a sentimentalist. I hope MegaMax appreciates what an important link you are to everything dead and gone."

"Dead and gone," thinks President York wistfully, catching a fleeting reflection of himself in Lunelle's tinted contacts. The Learning Resources Arcade (formerly the library) has been converted into a vast video mall, its books having been given to foreign relief agencies, the state hospital, or local museums. In the Learning Resources Arcade, students access their self-paced, non-prescriptive personal enhancement portfolios on computers manufactured by MegaByte SA, a Peruvian subsidiary of MegaMax. The MegaByte logo consists of a worm, wearing what may or may not be an Inca death mask, emerging from an apple as a Blakean Adam and Eve plunge headlong from Paradise. The computer features technology pilfered from the microprocessors General Mills gives away in boxes of Chocolate Sugar-Frosted Marshmallow Bran upgraded with MegaByte's revolutionary drool gutters and splash guards for the slack-jawed, who seem to arrive in greater numbers each semester.

President York remembers watching a Learning Resources Arcade waitperson (formerly a librarian) access a specimen student portfolio. He remembers the screen blazing to life: "Cowabunga, Dude: Can you divide the little number by the big number?" Then he remembers nothing.

The faculty is not in the Learning Resources Arcade, of course, because the scientists have real computers and lab equipment they have bought with grant money and stashed in their basements, garages, and attics or in space donated by industry. The humanities faculty is not in the library because they keep getting their fingers stuck between the MegaBytes' keys, leaving them hapless targets for student pranks.

"I'm going to insist, Walden—with your permission, of course—that faculty remain in their offices from 8 to 5."

President York scoops a handful of Tums from his candy jar and pops them into his mouth. "Breath mints," he says, grinding away.

Lunelle uncrosses her thighs, plants her feet squarely, and heaves herself up. "Well?"

"Run it by the faculty senate."

"The usual?" asks Lunelle.

"I suppose so," says President York.

"Then it's settled: I'll draw up a draft operating letter that prohibits faculty from using their offices between 8 and 5 and ask for senate input."

"That should do it."

Lunelle turns to leave.

"Dr. Johnson-Bender," says President York. "Are you by any chance a Baptist?"

"I beg your pardon?"

"Never mind," says President York, waving off the question. If not Hallelujah, Tennessee, then perhaps a consultancy at the Cabbage and Tuber Theme Park in Dniepropetrovsk operated by the Russian franchisee, MegaBorscht (formerly MegaMarx).

After Lunelle leaves, President York returns to the memo he was working on before lunch.

To: Mom
From: Walden York, PhD
Subject: My shorts
More starch.

He initials it familiarly "WY" and drops it in the outgoing mail.

– XVI –

On the seventh day of the seventh month, as pockets of evening mist rise from the virginal forest, a stranger crosses over McKenzie Pass from the east, curls down the switchbacks of Highway 242 and on into McKenzie Station. He drives alone in a bronze Jimmy six pack, his falling gear in the back. In the silvering dusk, his ConCo TurboSaw gleams in the truck's bed, the naked chrome of its two-liter eight thousand rpm engine giving back shards of light as it sways in a leather sling, its sixty-inch bar with a skip-tooth chisel bit chain protruding like the Johnson of fate.

Pulling into the Pour House's parking lot, the stranger climbs down and passes into the bar. In all details save one he resembles a logger: hickory shirt, stagged Frisco jeans, suspenders, tin of Root Wad chewing tobacco. His shirt, however, is accessorized with a lavender Giorgio Armani scarf knotted around his left biceps. At a far table, a runty green chain puller nudges his partner and slips out the side door.

Sheila, having sized the stranger up as no matrimonial prospect, nevertheless gets an edgy little triboluminescence in her diaphragm that she recognizes from its association with one of her former husbands who had been engaged in an agricultural export venture in the Cochabamba Valley of Bolivia when he made her the Widow Wallop. The stranger orders a shot to go with his beer, and Sheila forgoes the house whiskey—Old Undertaker cut with diet Dr. Pepper—and serves him a straight jolt of black Jack Daniels.

As night falls, one by one loggers filter into the bar until it is packed, but uneasily hushed. No one claims the stools on either side of the stranger. At last a pop-eyed choker setter approaches him. The lad, a suitor of the younger Crease daughter who had been rejected by the family on aesthetic grounds, blurts it out all at once. "Are you the Fall Feller?"

A hush descends upon the hush of the bar.

Finally, a cat skinner clears his throat. "What he meant to ask, mister, was, is you the Fell Faller?"

The stranger swivels around on his bar stool. "You got that right, boys," he says in his legendary squeak.

At once, a dozen men clamor to buy him drinks, and the bar surges forward into a respectful semicircle around him.

"Is it true you cut ten thousand acres of New Guinea on one chain and never busted up a tree?"

"It is."

"They say it was you got the Treaty Eucalyptus where they signed the shit about no more logging at that confab in Rio."

"Don't ask, don't tell."

"And the redwood that was Ms. July on last year's Sierra Club calendar?"

"Let's just say I believe in tough love: fondle them and fall them."

Hearty huzzahs erupt and the runty green chain puller breaks into a little jig.

"What you been up to lately?"

"Most recently, I dropped the last tree in Kansas. Before that, the Tree of Life in Bhutan."

"Sure, that had to be you."

"How about now? You hiring out to somebody hereabouts?"

"You peckerbrain, Carlin, the Fell Faller don't work for no man."

"That's right, friend, but I work for money and there's some of that money for the man who can show me to my next job: a long-standing photosynthesis junkie out there somewhere contributing to the shortage of affordable housing for all Americans."

"How do you mean?"

A rehush falls across the bar.

"I'm looking for Moby Fir."

"You mean *Pseudotsuga menzeisii humongous*?"

"One and the same."

No one in the bar has laid eyes on the legendary Douglas fir, though all know of those who have come to a poor end in seeking it. Qnxtqkl legend foretold the withering of appendages on any man who sought the tree with ill intent. Should the tree ever fall, another Qnxtqkl legend goes, a mighty plague of California turbospeak would pass across the land, bringing with it the end of civil discourse between man and nature.

Everyone knows that Georgia-Pacific has a standing offer of $27,237.47 for a round from the butt cut of Moby Fir for their tree museum. Rumor abounds that Weyerhaeuser would do even better for the whole log, which they want to photograph running through the gang saw in their Springfield mill for the cover photo on their annual report.

"You looking to peddle it to G-P or Weyerhaeuser?"

The Fell Faller's face clouds, and everyone takes a reflexive step back.

"They had their chances. I'm an America-first man myself—I tell you I wept when I heard that the Sultan of Brunei bought Yellowstone and had an option on the Green Bay Packers—but I'm not giving you boys any news when I say it all comes down to money. On this one, I'm dealing with Japanese interests, so there's plenty to go around, never mind what you may have heard about the fall of the yen relative to the dollar and Asō's resignation as minister of finance. Now, who's the man here who can show me this tree?"

"I am," says Chip, the plucky young choker setter who had broken the silence earlier that night.

"You couldn't find your ass with both hands and a searchlight."

The Fell Faller gestures and all fall silent.

"Well?"

"I mean, I think I know somebody who knows somebody."

"Yes?" On single syllables, the Fell Faller is especially squeaky, but the loggers betray no hint of smirkishness.

"I mean, I know somebody who thinks they know somebody."

"Can we do any better than that?"

No one can.

"Well, then, get on after it." The Fell Faller tosses off the last of his whiskey and rises from the stool.

“Where you gonna be so I can tell you if I find out what you want me to find out and tell you?”

“Around.”

The Fell Faller moves down the line of men toward the door. He walks on past the choker setters and whistle punks, the yarder operators and cat skinners, but at every faller he pauses, claps the man on the shoulder, and then dips his own shoulder in return. Each faller gives him a solid thwack there on the hump of gristle and bone spur that rises across the broad expanse from years of packing his ConCo TurboSaw. Though they seldom wash except for new girlfriends and court appearances, the fallers would sooner cut off their fist than tidy the hand that touched the Fell Faller’s hump.

– XVII –

Amanda Pennypacker schedules the first annual Upper McKenzie Community Fair for Saturday of the full moon in July. The Forest Service has made their landing strip available and sets up great open-sided tents used in fire camps. The Forest Service has also supplied one of their seasonal workers, outfitted in a Smokey the Bear suit, to pass out balloons and safe camping tips. Food and drink is provided in prodigious quantity by MegaMax, and a band, Loraine and the Lumberjills, has been engaged.

The day of the fair dawns drably, but by midmorning the clouds have lightened to a more hospitable gray. As afternoon sluggishly succeeds morning, citizens of the McKenzie Valley stream onto the grounds. Many are festively arrayed at Amanda's urging; some are costumed. Sheila Wallop, scalloped into a T-shirt reading "Ask Me about My Former Lives," is impersonating Shirley MacLaine. President York, threadbare in his academic robes, resembles a mendicant. Descending from their DeSoto station wagon, the Crease family seems, at a distance, Snopesesque, but on closer examination is merely Dickensian.

No one can guess the identity of five men who arrive together, so cleverly are they fabricated. One (Hiro Ishimatsu) is dressed as Uncle Sam, that being the only costume left at Easy Ed's Pawn and Appliance; another (Tony Ten-Toes Jr.) comes as Roy Rogers; a third (D. B. Cooper) appears as a wanted poster of himself; while a fourth (Carlos Castaneda) is disguised as Thomas Chatterton. The fifth appears to be a bear with sloppy detail work, although even the loggers agree that he's got the smell down to the last gagging pheromone and make a point of staying well upwind of him. Amanda herself is festooned as Julie Andrews in *The Sound of Music.*

The day's schedule of special events looks like this:

12:00	Invocation: Reverend Endwell
12:30	Welcome: Amanda Pennypacker
12:32	Log truck drive-by and jake brake decibel competition
1:15	Latest hairstyles demonstrated (cornrows or corncobs—what's phat for you?): Loretta's Curl Up and Dye
1:30	Recitation from memory of the U.S. Postal Code: William Devaney
2:00	Skidder race
2:30	Poetry reading: Sarah Trip
2:35	Naptime (sponsored by USFS Civil Service employees)
3:00	Selected airs from the *Der Ring des Nibelungen*: McKenzie High School Pops Choir, Professor Wolfgang Glockenspiel, MegaMax University, conducting
3:30	Best biceps (men)
3:45	Best biceps (women)
4:00	Drawing for an opportunity to appear in a MegaMax brochure showcasing friendly and colorful natives available for yard and domestic work at Rancho Rio
4:15	Blessing of the chain saws: Reverend Endwell
4:45	Log-bucking competition
5:00	Charcoal portraits of your pickup, pets, deer rifle, unemployment check, Rottweiler, probation officer, etc.: Mable Goodchuck, MegaMax University (donations accepted)
5:30	Presentation of Miss Timber Topper and her court: Noxene (Mrs. Bud) Nickers, Mrs. February centerfold in the Lane County Extension Service *Homemaking Hints*
6:00	Special announcement: Mark Neighbors, MegaMax Corporation
7:00-?	Loraine and the Lumberjills

In all, a heady mix, even for those who have bypassed C. C. Fellows's complimentary samples of McKenzie Mauve custom rolled in special papers embossed with a mellow bear and the words "Smokey Likes It."

But more is afoot than meets the eye. One by one the Gang of Five slips away into the woods, leaving behind only Carlos who, in helping C. C. prepare his complimentary tokes, has succumbed to the classic cook's temptation and sampled the pot overmuch. The remainder of the Gang have made their way to a little-used rest stop on the McKenzie highway. With Carlos out of commission, Tony Ten-Toes assumes leadership of the group. Careful intelligence has established that twice a week an eighteen-wheeler filled with nitrous oxide passes through on a run to the offices of Dr. Dementia, the hippie dentist of West Springfield. Field observations have confirmed that the driver unfailingly offloads his bladder here before taking on the kidney-punching chuckholes of the lower McKenzie highway. Drawing on D. B's expertise, the Gang has laid plans to hijack the truck.

At the customary hour, the Red Ball Express rig pulls into the rest stop and the driver, imitating drivers who imitate cowboys, steps down in his boots, hat, and belt with a rodeo buckle. He leaves the truck running as he ambles to the john. The moment he's inside, Hiro slaps a padlock on the door and Tony climbs behind the wheel. The truck has a sleeper cab, so the Gang fits comfortably, though comfort is always a problematic concept within olfactory range of Sasquatch. After several false starts, Tony's National Guard truck-driving training pays off and they lurch onto the highway.

The plan is simple but stupid. Back at the airstrip, they will park the truck on a spur road uphill and upwind from the platform where Mark Neighbors is scheduled to speak. Heavier than air and nudged by a down-canyon wind, the nitrous oxide will roll into the assemblage, turning Mark Neighbors into a laughingstock. Not much as plans go, Carlos admits over Spam Surprise the night before the fair, but fractionally less of a Topeka than Hiro's suggestion of an ultralight bombing run on one of the MegaMax tour buses or Tony's Blockbuster of a scheme to render Rancho Rio uninhabitable by transplanting tubfuls of giant white slugs that have begun to turn up in alarming numbers in Hiro's rice paddy.

As they whine down the highway at seventeen miles an hour in compound low after Tony blows out the clutch trying to find a higher gear, Hiro comes across invoices and bills of lading. Rifling them for industrial secrets to pass along to Japanese intelligence, he stumbles upon the provenance of the laughing gas. The shipment originated at the Umatilla Army Depot where the government has been dismantling its chemical warfare weaponry. The munitions, from ten-ton bombs to grenades, have apparently been filled these many years with nitrous oxide. A blunder? Umatillagate? A dark, Strangelovian scheme whose outlines are lost in the mists of the Cold War? A perfectly reasonable approach to chemical warfare predicated on the unlikelihood that a laughing man will shoot you? These possibilities and more are carefully weighed by the Gang along with Tony's recollection of a rumor from his National Guard days of a four-day food fight in the Klamath Falls High School cafeteria that was finally broken up by guardsmen who induced paralytic laughter in the participants. Tony has always assumed that this was because everybody knows the Guard is a big joke (Q: What's the difference between the Boy Scouts and the National Guard? A: Adult supervision), but perhaps there was more to it after all.

Not long before the turnoff to the airstrip, D. B. slick as a whistle opens the window of the sleeper compartment, slips through, and straddles the trailer coupling while strapping on a parachute he has unwadded from his pants.

"No plane, no gain," howls D. B., preparing to jump.

In the nick of time, Sasquatch reaches out of the cab and yards D. B. back in, sedating him with his last roll of Tums. In this fashion, the Gang lumbers up the spur road into position and Tony kills the engine.

They have timed their arrival impeccably. Mark Neighbors has just mounted the platform and the MegaMax PR cameras have started to roll. Marta and the Herbert Walkers let it be known that MegaMax-donated kegs will be tapped after the announcement, so an attentive crowd has formed. Mark surveys the eager, upturned faces with the easy assurance of a hedge fund manager lounging atop the food chain. Back in the woods, the Gang pops the valve on the tank.

"Friends, I think most of you know who I am, but let me introduce myself to the rest: Mark Neighbors of the MegaMax Corporation. Now, you didn't come out here to listen to speeches, and I'm not going to give one; I'm just as anxious to get back to the fun as you are. In fact, I can hardly wait to dance my Weejuns off to Lulu and the Lumberlungs. But first I have an announcement that I think will interest you. As you may know, someone recently discovered a rare and endangered species on Rancho Rio property, the Albino Banana Slug."

Cries of "Salt 'em! squash 'em! feed 'em to the owls!" break out semi-spontaneously, and Mark Neighbors raises his hand.

"I know, I know, I feel exactly the same way, but the fact is the bureaucrats back in Washington care more about an uncommon slug than they do about the common man." Mark pauses and the Herbert Walkers cheer lustily, knowing that Mark has spent weeks crafting the last phrase himself. "So we just need to be a little smarter than they are, which means we've got to get our boots on the right feet two out of three tries."

"Mama, is that man making fun of Wick?" Willa Crease asks her mother.

President York is reminded simultaneously of his senior faculty and student body.

Buckthorn, pretending to scuff some dirt, looks down surreptitiously at his boots.

"Ha, ha, ha," go the Herbert Walkers.

"So here's the deal. MegaMax will pay $25 for each and every authenticated Albino Banana Slug delivered live to our Rancho Rio office. If we can turn up 5,001 of the little critters, the Environmental Protection Agency has to classify them as threatened instead of endangered, which would let us go forward with our vision of making the McKenzie Valley a better place for all of us. So what do you say to that?"

The loggers, who have trouble counting to twenty-one without shucking their boots and dropping their jeans, are silently trying to estimate what size take they might be in for. Orville Crease is silently speculating on whether a little bleach or white paint might turn the trick with the common banana slug, a species so numerous that it is capitalized neither in Latin nor English. Mable Goodchuck is silently assessing her chances of getting a little something going with Freddy Waxwroth, a dalliance that might lead to a grant for slug portraiture. Reverend Endwell is silently praying that Amanda will linger after the dance for cleanup vespers. Sarah Trip is silently penning a furious screed assailing the phalloform of bananas.

The offer would have been of great interest, of course, to the Gang of Five, but Carlos is nodded out behind Loretta's demonstration booth and the rest of the Gang is upwind and out of earshot.

Near the back of the crowd, Sheila turns to Devaney. "You know, Billy, it's the damnedest thing; I feel just like having some root canal work done."

Mark Neighbors shifts uneasily behind the podium and the Herbert Walkers buzz uncertainly, ready to loft three cheers but only in swelling chorus with the adoration of the locals so that they will not be thought provocateurs. Just then, a titter breaks the hanging silence, giving way directly to a snigger, a giggle, a chortle, a guffaw, gelasmus, and finally to wholehearted cachinnation.

Sheila Wallop has thrown her arms around Devaney, blurting out between shrieks of laughter, "A root canal, yes, yes, I will, a root canal, yes." Devaney snuffles a tweedy laugh in return, but the sound is washed away in the braying of the Crease family as the nitrous oxide eddies on. Beyond the Creases, Miss Timber Topper and her court have swooned like pansies except for the third runner-up whose legs are pumping energetically as she whinnies with laughter flat on her back. The Herbert Walkers mill about bumping into each other like faculty trying to line up for commencement. Several at the back of the crowd boom out with a hearty corporate laugh.

Red shading towards puce, Mark Neighbors appears to be either inhaling or holding his breath. Juggernaut springs to his side and hustles him off stage and into the Land Bruiser as Buckthorn whoops like a siren. Out of range of the gas, C. C. Fellows grudgingly extends his admiration to the competition, whose free samples are blowing his McKenzie Mauve right out of the water.

Thinning as it spreads, the gas wafts on like KINK, Springfield's lite-and-easy classic rock station, leaving in its wake mellow citizens who would happily ride the elevator all day. Inside his Smokey the Bear suit, the Forest Service employee shuffles dreamily through the crowd. Reverend Endwell has a beatific vision of celestial laughter, and Sarah Trip's anti-banana poem shifts mid-stanza into a rhymed anapestic ode.

As the tank empties, the Gang slips away, skirting the edge of the woods out of reach of the gas.

> *"And if the Babe is born a Boy*
> *He's given to a Woman Old*
> *Who nails him down upon a rock*
> *Catches his shrieks in cups of gold"*

says D. B., who has wandered in front of the spigot and caught a whiff.

The Gang keeps watch as the amiable pandemonium ebbs and flows. Loraine and the Lumberjills have taken the stage and are belting out a medley as Loraine and the drummer do "Something Tells Me I'm into Something Good" while the steel guitar and accordion are working out on "The Beer Barrel Polka."

In the general hubbub, Sasquatch tucks Smokey under his arm and makes off for the deep woods, humming "Getting to Know You" in an amorous key.

– XVIII –

Downcast in a winsome funk at the unseemliness prompted by the nitrous oxide though grateful that the Ford Foundation field representative had canceled at the last minute, ponytail bound in a funereal black bow and ruffled collar of her starched white blouse buttoned above the hickey that someone who may have been Buckthorn gave her when the Lumberjills' amps blew the lights during "Mamas, Don't Raise Your Boys to Be Loggers," Amanda raps pertly at the aluminum door of the Church of the Doublewide.

In his parsonage to the rear of the sanctuary, Reverend Endwell startles from the bathroom mirror at the knock. His white turtleneck springs back into place, covering the hickey given him during lights-out by the powerful stranger who had won the chain saw competition. Since the rear of the doublewide is warped somewhat off rectangular, Reverend Endwell can cop a look out his window to ensure that he's not answering the knock of the Sears siding man who had sold him (in a flusher and weaker moment, to be sure) a makeover of the doublewide and has been relentlessly trying to collect the disputed balance for some time. Seeing Amanda, Reverend Endwell bolts to let her in, grabbing his powder-blue leisure jacket from the vestry on the way through. He flings the door wide, nearly knocking Amanda back down the steps.

"Reverend Endwell, I was wondering if I might—"

"Yes, please do, by all means, absolutely!" The polyester fibers in the cobalt piping on the lapels and pocket flaps of his jacket give off an iridescent blue glow like moldy cheese or the instrument panel of a 1958 Lincoln. Reverend Endwell ushers her in, composes himself. He is reminded that nowhere is it written that the sins of the flesh require buffoonmanship.

“My child,” he says, starting over with a line from a Spencer Tracy movie he saw in his youth, “I can see that you’re troubled.”

Amanda’s visage puckers and she bursts into tears. “Oh, that awful Gang of Five.” She stamps her tiny foot. “I do try, really I do, but I can’t find forgiveness in my bosom.”

At the magic word, Reverend Endwell’s eyes fix on the anatomy in question, now heaving beneath a swirl of starched ruffles. Centuries pass. With a mighty effort he tears away first his obedient right eye and finally his roguish left and locks his gaze on Amanda’s niblet ears, one eye per ear. “I can imagine just how you feel. I myself have harbored such resentments.”

“You have?”

“Only last Holy Week I fell victim to similar spiritual shortfall. You may remember my Easter message on the signboard?”

“Daddy flew me to Vail for the weekend,” says Amanda sheepishly.

“Yes, well, the message read, ‘Here Comes the Son.’”

Amanda claps her hands. “How cute.”

“And theologically *a*cute.” Reverend Endwell chuckles at this nifty turn of phrase. Amanda looks at him blankly, and Reverend Endwell recalls that his professor of homiletics at Antepenultimate Bible College had proscribed the pastoral chuckle on the grounds that nowhere in either Testament does God or any of his stand-ins, hangers-on, or special effects people laugh.

“Yes, well,” the reverend goes on, “in any event someone—most certainly either the Widow Wallop or Brother Buckthorn, neither one a pal of God’s, I must say—doctored the sign to read ‘Never Up, Never In.’”

Amanda frowns and nibbles her lip; then her mouth makes a little round “O” and a blush spreads across her cheeks.

“In this matter, I too have fallen short of perfect forgiveness. But sin I must, according to divine writ; sin we all must,” the reverend pronounces, warming to the message as his left eye, rolling bosomward, throbs and burns in its socket.

“You might say,” says the reverend, taking the King James into untracked regions of exegesis, “that sin is the father, forgiveness the child.”

"That reminds me," says Amanda, an uneasy, half-formed scene from "Little Red Riding Hood" drifting in and out of focus, "that I really came about children. That is, there aren't any. I mean, not one baby has been born in months and months, and nobody is in a family way."

Under the heading of coming attractions, a crisp, fully formed scene from *Swaggart and Bakker: Two Jimmies Abed in the House of the Lord* pops up as Reverend Endwell's libido unspools like a wriggling snake. "I believe," he says, "that anthropological data suggest that in moments of cultural and economic stress, the progenitorial instinct is eclipsed."

"Just as I thought," says Amanda. "But we must do something. The Ford Foundation directive on community development is exact: a fertility rate of 1.78 per couple, give or take a decimal point or whatever. Why, a community without children is like a fish without a bicycle—no, wait, that's not exactly it." Amanda tosses her ponytail in frustration.

"Be fruitful and multiply?" offers the reverend helpfully.

"That's it," says Amanda, "that's it exactly. But what can we do?"

Drawing on dwindling reserves of reticence, Reverend Endwell forbears the possibility that immediately erects itself, settling instead on a more circumspect alternative. "There is," he says thoughtfully, "something from Qnxtqkl lore that might be worth a try. I do like to incorporate indigenous ritual into Christian service as I can. You understand, doctrinally this is cutting-edge stuff, but I believe it may be our best shot."

Amanda claps her hands again. "How does it work?"

"Well," says the reverend, stitching it together, "it's a ceremony loosely translated as the blessing of the womb. It requires, I believe, a virgin—"

Amanda looks stricken.

"—or near approximation," the reverend quickly adds, waggling his hands in dispensation.

Raised not to be one who thrusts herself forward, Amanda quickly reviews the skimpy possibilities up and down the McKenzie. When the inventory reaches Miss Timber Topper and her court, Amanda recalls mention of some similar gynecological requirement for the contest. Amanda cannot know, of course, that at this very moment a swim-suited Miss Timber Topper is about to bolt from the stage, where the preliminary round of the Ms. Lane County competition is underway, the aforementioned bolt prompted by the unseasonably hot seventy-eight-degree July afternoon melting her pancake body makeup to expose a hickey matching Amanda's in size, location, configuration, texture, and color. Miss Timber Topper is, in fact, the last near-virgin, save Amanda, on the McKenzie. The telltale hickey, however, will drive her in humiliation from the county to the squalid life of a test dummy for press releases from We Two, a public relations firm for consensual assaults, and finally into the moral cesspool of the division of Disney responsible for inserting liminal and subliminal nasties into children's movies.

"What if," Amanda asks timorously, "such a person were found, either real or *trompe l'Johnson*?" (Mother had insisted on etiquette lessons in French).

"I'd have to consult my local sources," says Reverend Endwell, "but I believe it would involve ritual deflowering by a community shaman."

"Why, Reverend Endwell," says Amanda, "I believe you have just described an act that might best be described as an act of cultural relativism." Amanda teeters on the carnal brink. Before being sent in-country, she had been warned in orientation against the seductive nuzzle of native custom. Yet the higher good of the community would seem to call for extreme measures. If Miss Timber Topper turned out not to be a Cinderellic fit for the Glass Johnson, Amanda herself would have to come forward.

A troublesome detail, though, nags at Amanda. "How can you tell, reverend, if we really have a virgin? You know, girls still fib about that sort of thing."

The reverend claps his hand over his left eye as it begins to wheel wildly in its socket. "Trust me on this one."

Amanda rushes forward. "You poor man; my father has migraines just like that."

Amanda begins to massage Reverend Endwell's temple while at a window Orville Crease hums a favorite hymn—

I was just another wobbly wheel on the grocery cart of life
Till Jesus oiled my casters and set my basket right

—as his camcorder rolls and he wonders if he could get Easy Ed, a notary public, or someone from the Columbia Log Scaling Bureau to certify Iphigenia a virgin.

– XIX –

Not long after the McKenzie Fair, a structure appears beside the Forest Service airstrip. A small tower with a radar installation on its roof, the building has been donated by MegaMax in a deal with the government. For its part, the Forest Service pulls some inter-agency strings with the Federal Aviation Administration and gets a class 3 air traffic controller assigned to the field. These improvements are necessary due to a logistical oversight that required the MegaMax Gulfstream to land once at the strip in daylight. The sight of what actually transpired aeronautically between an altitude of one thousand feet and touchdown moved the Herbert Walkers' bowels to such extremities that they were all but useless for days after the flight.

A class 3 controller is licensed to work airfields where you can't kill more than fifteen people at a pop. The controller assigned to KYAG-87-532 is one E. E. (Earlier and Earlier) Everclear, a devotee of that eponymous beverage distilled by a collateral branch of Everclears. E. E. takes full advantage of the family discount, drinking on and off the job on the grounds that (1) It is emotionally risky to separate one's life from one's work; (2) As lots of pilots drink too, he can better tune in, as it were, to their frequency and is therefore not so likely to get cranky when they pull some of their stunts and turn off the radar, directional beacon, and runway lights as his untuned colleagues are wont to do; and (3) Ever since Reagan fired the real controllers, the only actual job requirement is being able to recite during a surprise inspection by the FAA the Controllers' Creed: "What goes up must come down."

E. E. was most recently stationed at Mucus, Louisiana. Refusing to fly, he drives across the country to his new assignment. Passing down a deserted stretch of highway from Texas into New Mexico, dragging his past behind him like old, rusted cans, E. E. has an epiphany induced by the flotsam and jetsam of clouds racing through the western sky in advance of a giant thunderhead. It looks to E. E. as though God had laid a big hickey on the horizon, and it makes him think his life has not come to much, weighed in the cosmic balance. It is a small thing, after all, shearing the landing gear off planes by bringing them down here and there rather than where they had expected to land. The novelty of it has, frankly, worn thin. E. E. sees his life stretch out ahead: a tag team match of incident and reprimand until he is finally promoted to a class I field where he can knock off several hundred citizens at a whack in a major media market and will have to be pensioned off or transferred to the IRS.

The predictability of it all brings him to the brink of despair, and he searches the hickey-laden, oracular landscape for a sign. Will it be life or death? The next vehicle shall determine his course. He will wave in comradeship at the driver. If the wave is returned, he goes on to McKenzie Station. If not, he will slip the surly bonds of earth, launching his Ford into the nearest western abyss.

On the horizon a vehicle appears, bearing down. It looms larger but less credible as it comes, a truck of some sort, the color of the DTs, driven, as it waggles down the highway and into apparent focus, by a black man boogying in the cab to his iPod, no hands on the wheel. E. E. raises his palm in astonished salute. In return, the driver of the truck does a little two-handed jive out the window and the apparition blows past, veering extravagantly into E. E.'s lane and searing into his potholed retina the words "You Trash It—I Stash It."

– XX –

Buckthorn's introduction to environmental sculpture came during his first year at the Rhode Island School of Design when Terrell Crisco was in residence for a week. Crisco had arranged Buckthorn and forty other underclassmen in the shape of a double helix in a local park, encasing them in strapped-on solar panels topped off by a massive fiberglass beanie with a miniature wind turbine supported by a neck brace. Each member of the installation was harnessed into a grid: the energy produced by the collective electrical emissions powered a computer. The computer was programmed to assemble an image randomly generated by the erratic voltage that flowed and ebbed through the system. The resultant image was to be converted into a hologram that would be projected over a fossilized Paleo-American compost pit outside of Nattering Falls, New Hampshire, a site already in the hands of the Nature Conservancy. The hologram would be triggered each year at planting time and harvest by the precise azimuthal configuration of the constellations *Madona Giganticus* and *Homo Patheticus.* Starlight from the constellations, concentrated through a system of mirrors, would activate the hologram.

The initial image, the singular universal finger, stubbornly persisted even as Crisco rearranged the students into symbols for infinity, a monocarpous perennial fescue, and Remains to Be Seen, a drive-through funeral parlor and facial boutique in Novelty, California, owned by Beau Tox, specializing in the John Kerry look and featuring proprietary facial recognition software, The Right Stiff. Crisco was reprogramming the MegaByte 086 when a reverse burst of power surged back into the grid, toppling seven of the participants before the system shorted out. Of the seven, only Buckthorn emerged unscathed. Four of the others—whose electroencephalograms now resembled a John Cage score inscribed on a Twinkie—went on to careers in various branches of psychotherapy. Two of the most profoundly affected ended up in dental school. To be sure, Buckthorn sustained a droning in his skull, but it differed only in pitch from the residual hum from twelve years of American public education. Also, before major electrical storms his Johnson would emit a palpable spectral glow and draw to itself any spare change and keys in Buckthorn's front pockets.

None of this, however, dampened his enthusiasm for environmental art, and the summer after graduation he jumped at the chance to sign on as a roadie with the ¡Earth Liberation Front! Artcommandos' Western Tour. Working principally from a camouflaged hot air balloon, the group's mission was to raise the environmental consciousness of the American public by trashing various natural wonders. They had festooned the General Grant Sequoia with toilet paper, hooded Devil's Tower with a condom, and inscribed syphilitic lesions across Jefferson's face on Mount Rushmore. So that the American public wouldn't get the wrong idea, manifestoes were left at the scene and released to the media.

Roused from its environmental stupor, the American public seized the day and balloonists when they made a forced landing on the rim of Crater Lake after dropping black dye in the water, brought down by a hand-held, heat-seeking missile that a retired lieutenant colonel from Hominy Junction, South Carolina, providentially carried in his recreational vehicle. By the time Park Service rangers arrived, Buckthorn's chums had been stripped, trussed, coated with what remained of the dye, and forced to sing the Union Carbide company song (to the tune of "Smoke Gets in Your Eyes"):

They asked me how I knew
that Bhopal had blew.
I of course replied,
those who lived beside
puked their guts and died.

As it happened, Buckthorn himself was sleeping one off in Chiloquin and remained unapprehended.

Over the years Buckthorn had bided his time, sharpened his skills. When MegaMax bought up the land surrounding his little plot, it served as catalyst, offering the opportunity which, fondled by lunacy, propels the artist onward to glory.

Buckthorn's plan came to him in a dream induced by an evening at the Pour House topped off by a 3:00 a.m. ravening attack of the munchies with a larder empty save for his sister's fruitcake (ca. 2007) in the bottom compartment of his refrigerator. The last details fell into place as Buckthorn hugged the porcelain the next day. Out of his cliff face he would carve a colossal Johnson. It would be the Washington Monument, the Grand Canyon, the Barbra Streisand of Johnsons, rising as a fertility symbol for the McKenzie Valley and as a tumescent ensign (long may it wave) looming over Rancho Rio like a visitation out of the Old Testament.

All is now in readiness. Buckthorn has completed the sketches and has read every scrap of literature available at the MegaMax University Learning Resources Arcade on their Bicoastally-Linked Info-Tracked Heuristic Electronic Resource, an alternative internet funded by Microsoft (formerly inter-library loan), on Gutzon Borglum and Mount Rushmore. He has resolved the circumcised/uncircumcised dilemma in favor of the natural look. He has also taken three correspondence courses in geology and has watched thousands of hours of things being blown up on television. Buckthorn has worked his way over every inch of the cliff, mapping out fissures and crevices, noting geomorphological anomalies of igneous intrusions in the metamorphic strata. Using single jack and star drill, he has punched a penile series of bore holes. Buckthorn knows that he will have but one shot to unsheathe the Great Johnson out of mute stone before the full majesty of civil and criminal law falls upon him like a ton of bricks.

All that remains is to load the holes with the plastic explosive even now on its way west with Stanley. Buckthorn has acquired two tons of the stuff through Easy Ed's connections in New Jersey. Alas, Buckthorn has not heard from Stanley since he left Quagmire some weeks past. Conceding the likelihood that Stanley is cartographically challenged, he is still seriously overdue even by

Buckthorn's least hopeful estimates. Buckthorn cannot know, of course, that at this very moment Stanley is boogying past E. E. Everclear on U.S. 285 Alt. on his way to El Paso.

To allay his anxiety concerning Stanley, an epicure of disaster, Buckthorn turns to his favorite author for sustenance. He has read the corpus of Larry McMurtry many times, but he wolfs it down again: *Terms of Engorgement, Noshing Cheyenne, All My Chins Are Going to Be Strangers, The Eats of Laredo, Broasted Dove,* and Buckthorn's favorite, *Pot Roast, Pass By*. He wonders if anyone ever sent Larry McMurtry a fruitcake.

– XXI –

In her office, Juggernaut broods at her Cray over the recent turn of events. By running OuijaWorks, the Cray has identified the Gang of Five (± Six) as the likely perpetrators of the debacle at the fair. The Cray has offered no solutions to the problem, however, and now cannot be bothered as it has entered into a series of checkers matches with a cunningly programmed Apple IIe in Slush, Minnesota. At her feet, Chuck Wepner, feigning nonchalance, sizes up the rubber casters on Juggernaut's chair. Chuck has a patch of fur shaved off his rump where an implant of one-hundred-proof East Timor latex has been inserted by the vet in hopes of weaning Chuck from his increasingly global appetite. Chuck himself is still shaking off the effects of the coma in which he was recently found, lying next to a partially devoured skidder tire.

Bakersfield is not amused. Negotiations with the state for unrestricted zoning at Rancho Rio are at a delicate stage—that is, the money is now on the table. Eyeclueless News footage of the Herbert Walkers dropping trou in an impromptu best buns contest as Loraine and the Lumberjills played "Cheek to Cheek" (even if the Herbert Walkers did lose in the finals to a euphoric Sheila Wallop) was not the sort of publicity MegaMax needed at this particular juncture.

Vexed, Marta works out on the light bag, then flips ball bearings into the air and drives them into the knotty pine paneling with her jugs. After showering, she motors upriver to the Pour House. In dove leather jeans topped by a muscle shirt, Juggernaut unfolds from her furiously red Miata in the Pour House's parking lot. The only other rig in the lot is a bronze Jimmy six pack, the ConCo TurboSaw sheathed in its bed gleaming like a gangster's wet dream.

Inside, Juggernaut swivels onto a stool at one end of the bar. At the opposite end, the Fell Faller sips from a silver flask his signature drink, absinthe cut with saw gas. On the bar in front of him stands a chaser, a glass of habanero juice. Juggernaut orders an Around-the-World, and Sheila consults her records; few customers are permitted the drink. Those served are logged in: date, time, and consequences. At the nether reaches of the William Burroughs's Scale of Toxic Exotica, nip and tuck with a neuromuscular paralytic favored by the Yanomami of the Amazon and FDC Yellow Dye #6 in Puffy Cheddar Diesel Cheetos, the Around-the-World, working off a gin base, incorporates a jigger of liqueur native to each country admitted to the United Nations since 1964 with a population less than that of Tulsa, Oklahoma. The resultant beverage fills most of a quart mason jar. Any residue must be shipped to a toxic waste site in Sheepdip, Utah ever since Sheila poured some down the drain, killing all aquatic life eight miles downstream and resulting in a stiff fine from the Feds.

Sheila's records indicate that Juggernaut hasn't had one in seven months and that she paid all damages, including medical expenses for those involved in the parking lot and rooftop brawl attendant on her previous Around-the-World.

Juggernaut swirls the mix, inhales deeply, and takes a long swallow. A little residue of vapor, as if from dry ice, seeps around her immaculate orthodontia as she turns to face the Fell Faller.

"So?"

Sheila looks from one to the other; then comes around the bar, locks the door to the parking lot, and disappears into her office. The clock ticks above the register. The ice machine cycles on and off again. In the corner beside a wooden bust of Ezra Taft Benson, the bar philodendron drops its antepenultimate leaf.

The Fell Faller rolls his hump in a massive shrug.

"So what?"

"Are you with us on this one?"

"What's in it for me?"

"Moby Fir."

"What's in it for you?"

"The Gang of Five and an autographed photo of your hump."

"You got yourself a deal, little lady."

The Fell Faller raises his flask in salute and knocks the last of it back. Juggernaut returns the salute and takes a long draught from the mason jar. The Fell Faller stuffs a fistful of Root Wad in his cheek and rises to leave. On his way out, he gives Juggernaut a comradely punch on the arm. She responds by delivering a great whack to his hump with her right tit.

In the parking lot, a gas chamber-green Forest Service rig is parked next to the Jimmy.

"Mr. Faller?" A Forest Service employee sits up straight to speak through the window, which is rolled down maybe two inches.

The Fell Faller adjusts the wad of tobacco in his cheek. "Who wants to know?"

"Bart Bevel, Timber Management Officer, Stumpage Ranger District, Cut-and-Run National Forest, United States Forest Service, Department of Agriculture."

"So what?"

Bart draws himself up to his full height behind the wheel. "It's come to our attention that you intend to remove a tree from federal inventory without bid, bond, contract, environmental impact statement, congressional approval, district court injunction, and note from your mommy."

The Fell Faller moves the Root Wad to his other cheek and spits a long, brown stream across the gravel. Then he walks to his truck, draws the ConCo TurboSaw from its sheath, and fires it up in a single motion balletic in its grace and precision. He moves around to the front of the Forest Service rig, revs the ConCo to a Wagnerian pitch, and slices decisively through the hood, grill, and radiator.

The Fell Faller returns to the window and looks in where Bart Bevel has shrunk down in the driver's seat. "If you're up for a little action, sweetcakes, stop by sometime when you're off duty and I'll show you my collection of bars and chains."

The Fell Faller winks, holsters his saw, and drives off, the lavender scarf on his left biceps flaring in the wind.

– XXII –

"Yes. Yes. Yes. Yes, I understand. Yes, of course. Yes. Yes. No. No. No. No, certainly not. No, I understand. No. No."

President York hangs up the phone and reaches for his bowl of Tums, which is empty. He roots with growing panic through his drawers and is about to strip-mine the floor under his desk where a stray Tum has been known to turn up when he recalls a partial, linty roll in his suit coat pocket. Alas, the pocket is empty, but a telltale lump in the lining and a little prospecting with his index finger reveal a hole through which the Tums—he estimates perhaps three or four—have slipped. Laying his jacket across his knee, President York grasps the lump and maneuvers it carefully upward. On the verge of success, the phone buzzes again and President York loses the ground he has gained in lurching across his desk to punch the "No Calls" button. Again he seizes the lump, and after several false stabs, succeeds in bringing it to the very edge of the hole in his pocket only to discover that the Tums have lodged on the wrong side of some silky inner lining. After some inconclusive diddling, President York rips the seam from his pocket and takes a letter opener to the lining, revealing at last a partial roll of cherry Lifesavers matted with microscopic debris. A sob of despair breaks from his lips as his digestive tract prepares to run away to join the circus.

Sensing that his avidity for antacids had assumed unseemly proportions, President York has taken the pledge, sort of. That is, he has given Marsha strict orders that he is to be locked in his office from 8 to 5 (off-campus, his craving vanishes at once). No matter how he wheedles or threatens, like a man chained with rabies in an old movie, he is not to be let out. Anyone who insists on seeing him in person must be strip-searched by Marsha to ensure that President York has not inveigled the visitor to smuggle in a stash.

This is the second day of the program, and Marsha has taken to her role with what now strikes President York as alarming relish. He recalls in dismay that years before he had asked Marsha to shoot him if he ever grew so portly he started wearing Guayabera shirts. He'd meant it as a joke.

On the verge of duodenal delirium, President York's eye alights on the blackboard where he had been playing tic-tac-toe with himself earlier in the morning. In a felt box at the far end of the tray lie four pieces of unused, just off-white chalk. The chalk represents a bequest to the university of Professor Hardy Hawthorne Howells. Not to put too fine a point on it, the chalk is, in fact, Professor Howells. A member of the English faculty since the school opened and mindful of increasing budget constraints, Howells had arranged for a cremation with his ashes pressed into chalk and donated to MegaMax. There had been some fuss raised by the family, but in the end the bequest was honored. With trembling hands, President York grasps a piece of the chalk, fingering for a moment its HHH monogram before wolfing down the calcium-laden cylinder.

His gastric sea becalmed, President York reviews the precipitating phone call from Bakersfield. Marketing had gotten wind of his recent hiring of Professor Wolfgang Glockenspiel as director of choral music. Glockenspiel, previously of Transkiester University in Bad Zeitgeist, had washed up at MegaMax on an American tour with the women's *a cappella* choir from the Dudermeister Axle and Drive Shaft Works. The collapse of East Germany had left Professor Glockenspiel awkwardly situated. An unfortunate incident in early adulthood involving a codfish casserole, two pneumatic corkscrews, a dachshund of uncertain gender, and a video of Princess Margaret had rendered Glockenspiel unable to register sounds below middle C. He did not think there would be a place for him in the choral life of the new Germany. When President York offered him a visiting appointment for room and board, Glockenspiel accepted at once.

Arrested by the name, Bakersfield had seen an opportunity to establish market separation between MegaMax and competing colleges such as Our Lady of Perpetual Dysfunction, a small Catholic school in Cataleptic, Kentucky; Comatose State (motto: "The Harvard of Hammer-Toe County, Alabama"); and Dyslexia Institute of Technology in Chronic, New York. Surveys had established that no other school in MegaMax's market niche (Q: What do you call MegaMax freshmen with an IQ in three digits? A: A dorm wing) was highlighting its faculty in a promotional campaign with the exception of Dyslexia Tech (motto: "Write It Your Way"), which featured Professor Otto Toot. The Conglomerate Relations Division had been trying to unload a minority interest in MegaMax U. to Übermensch, a Siemen's subsidiary that manufactured inflatable athletic supporters, and thought a more Teutonic faculty might cinch the deal.

It falls to President York to apprise the faculty in question that they can either remain at MegaMax under legally changed names or find work elsewhere. Marsha had slid the fax under his door earlier in the day, and the call from Bakersfield confirmed the contents. President York scrapes the chalky residue from his tongue on his teeth and reads the list again:

Dr. Wolfgang Busters, Professor of Criminal Justice
Dr. Wolfgang Green, Professor of Public Health
Dr. Wolfgang Tackle, Professor of Linebacking
Dr. Wolfgang Plank, Professor of English (In a gesture of intercorporate goodwill, Professor Plank would also hold the Kmart Folding Chair of Deconstruction.)
Dr. Wolfgang Way, Professor of Psychology and Director of THE ASSERTIVENESS INSTITUTE
Dr. Wolfgang Bang, Professor of Military Science and Aberrant Sexuality
Dr. Wolfgang Fang Li, Professor of Mandarin (Bakersfield's Chinese subsidiary, MegaMao, had turned up Dr. Li in the Beijing phone directory and had already brought him on board before hitting on the happy expedient of name changes.)

President York sighs and begins to draft a memo to the affected faculty. He is interrupted by a furious ruckus in the outer office—thumps and shrieks accompanied by the wafting aroma of *eau de pasta* with a hint of maraschino, Lunelle Johnson-Bender's signature scent. The bolt to his door is thrown back, but then the struggle eddies away. Cautiously, President York cracks the door and peers out. Marsha has stripped Lunelle to her girdle. As he watches, transfixed, the girdle, too, is catastrophically gone. No glutton for punishment, President York feasts his eyes momentarily on the cornucopia of cellulite before drifting in scholarly reverie to a recollection of Elizabeth Taylor's Fifth Law of Gravity: "What porks up must sag down."

President York shuts the door, wedges a chair under the knob, and returns to his memo. Before he begins to write, he moves his desk against the door as well, adding both filing cabinets for good measure.

— XXIII —

While not at the end of her rope, Sarah Trip is long out of sight of its beginning. ⚥, her book of poems from On the Rag Press, is out of print and a second collection is not forthcoming. Shifting cultural tides—presaged by a National Endowment for the Arts New Realities Assistance grant to performance artist Wallace (Beau) Shith to execute illegal aliens from Haiti, Mexico, and Puerto Rico in the infield during stock car races in Obese, Rotting Carp, and Condom, Alabama—have led to a Pulitzer Prize in poetry to Thom Judd for his paean to family values, *Thirteen Ways of Looking at an Assault Rifle*—a major stage-shaker recently at Bumpstock, a music festival for fans of automatic weaponry. Clearly, this is not the time for poems with detectable estrogen content.

Clad in J. Crew tatters, Sarah ponders her options as she trudges woodsward in the complex and elegant light falling between late-afternoon showers. Inexplicably, she has just received a letter from John Shine, a one-night stand from her past who figured unpleasantly in a poem from ⚥. Touching modestly on his cinematic career, Shine has gone on to chronicle his transit to Booty Books, publishers of romance novels whose list is distributed at freeway rest areas in the mid-South, flea markets, and truck stops, with excerpts available online at muffdvr.com. He has offered Sarah $2,500 for a fifty-three-thousand-word manuscript featuring a poetess who moonlights as a topless dancer and ends up marrying a doctor who comes in for a bachelor party and ends up curing her of chlamydia so that they can have 2.5 children named Faith, Hope, and Tra[vis]. All she has to do is supply the words, fifty-three thousand of them, none containing more than two syllables. Format constraints, Shine regrets, force him to reduce payment by one dollar for every word over or under fifty-three thousand.

Sarah assesses her rope burns. On the Rag Press has been bought out by the Methodist Women's League of Catatonia, Indiana, which now publishes Christian self-help books under the imprint of Magnificent Monthlies. The money she has tucked away from her post-college years as a compliance monitor for Title IX NCAA intercollegiate Division II poetry slam programs is nearly exhausted. Her amorous options—a sweet, furtive Japanese suitor who leaves white gastropodal casseroles on her doorstep and the beefy but harmless window peeper—offer at best wretched surcease, were she even inclined to be suited. Clearly, her options have dwindled to fewer than the number of functional genes on the Y chromosome. Sarah wonders if articles and conjunctions count towards the fifty-three-thousand-word quota.

– XXIV –

Following the debacle at the fair, Mark Neighbors has been recalled to Bakersfield for consultations. It is the first blemish on an otherwise spotless career with MegaMax, Mark Neighbors having first come to corporate notice as student body treasurer at Cal State Merlot, where he pocketed a nice chunk of change for booking the student senate on a MegaMax-packaged leadership retreat to Puerto Boracho. In fact, he had cooked the books with such aplomb that MegaMax stepped in to provide legal assistance when the retreat went awry at a bar, *Todo el Mundo y Yo Tambien,* where an incident involving a codfish casserole, three pneumatic corkscrews, a video of Princess Margaret, and two donkeys of certain gender resulted in an incendiary cultural misunderstanding, and Mark Neighbors, having fled back across the border disguised as a cocaine smuggler, was facing extradition along with revocation of his Sexual Continence and Hands across the Hemisphere Boy Scout merit badges. Since then, Mark Neighbors has proven a paragon of corporate discretion, screwing competitor and compatriot alike but never caught out unzipped.

Alarmed by media accounts of events at the fair, Bakersfield now faces Mark Neighbors across a trestle table in the banquet room at Luby's Cafeteria where the Nooners Rotary Club has just adjourned. Bakersfield holds all luncheon meetings here in keeping with company policy to maintain a folksy corporate profile in the neighborhood. After a little tussle with the accordion divider that separates the room from the rest of the cafeteria, Bakersfield hitches up its pants and speaks in a collective voice.

"So?"

Although no window graces the room and the building itself is relentlessly single story, Mark Neighbors, fearing defenestration, casually shoots his cuffs before responding to Bakersfield's unmistakable raising of the sash."Did you hear the one about Ralph Nader and Harvey Weinstein?"

Everybody has.

Mark Neighbors draws the ivory Mont Blanc from his jacket pocket, snaps it in half, passes the jagged implement across the table, and tugs back his collar, proffering a jugular imperfectly deflated by Inderal.

"Next time," says Bakersfield.

After Mark Neighbors returns from the bathroom, Bakersfield clues him in. The Estates at Rancho Rio are, in fact, merely an artifice, the sleight of hand necessary to acquire mineral rights and a state-chartered independent municipal utility district. Once this is accomplished, MegaMax will drill what promises to be North America's largest geothermal field. The 5 million-kilovolt generating plant, with its acres of turbines, clouds of mucosal, sulfury steam, shrieking bleeder vents, three-hundred-foot towers peeling off in every direction bearing transmission lines thick as a man's waist, and sludgy settling ponds for cooling the three-hundred-degree water before it is pumped into the McKenzie will render Edenic if not Paradisal the Weyerhaeuser pulp plant in Springfield (Motto: "The site that broke the Superfund"). The usual fuss will be raised, of course, but Oregon law gives MUDs absolute autonomy in developing renewable power. Besides, Oregonians are currently diverted by a nasty squabble about whether Hynix should be granted a $2 billion tax abatement for hiring unemployed mill workers to fabricate silicon wafers for $6.50 an hour. The debate centers on whether $6.50 an hour will skew the local wage scale alarmingly upward.

Mark Neighbors is to see to it, then, that Rancho Rio moves forward on schedule. Bakersfield is especially anxious that the remaining plots be bought up to satisfy the MUD requirement of at least twenty-five hundred contiguous acres.

Given the noxious emissions, the four-hundred-decibel background operational sound level, and the electromagnetic radiation, the upper McKenzie will be uninhabitable by all save seasoned habitants of metropolitan statistical areas of a least 2.5 million people. At which point the villagers can be expected to come looking for Mark Neighbors and other MegaMaxers with torches and pitchforks, foiled at the last by the Gulfstream, which will pluck them from the McKenzie airstrip as if from the roof of the Saigon embassy. Plan B calls for Mark Neighbors to make a run for the California line disguised as a basketball prospect.

Bakersfield sets about finishing its Frito Surprise casserole while Mark Neighbors digests the genius of the central concept and its peripherals. Rancho Rio property owners will be bought out for pennies on the dollar or offered discounted lots in a sluggishly moving MegaMax development in Metamucil, Wisconsin. Since the acid compounds percolating out of the plant's steam clouds are especially toxic to conifers, MegaMax has bought up speculative salvage rights from the Forest Service for all surrounding timber at 2 cents a board foot. MegaMax hydrologists estimate that permissible discharge into the McKenzie will not raise ambient river temperature to levels that will finish off the native trout and salmon runs, but that a little diagonal drilling could vent enough waste steam in the river bottom to turn the trick. MegaMax would then be positioned to establish an environmental theme park (through a wholly owned offshore subsidiary, MegaMuck) highlighting the ravages of environmental degradation.

Bakersfield pushes back from the table and lets out its belt a notch. Mark Neighbors squelches a notion that Bakersfield was originally from Arkansas and offers around a roll of Tums in a walnut, myrtle, and silver case. In a startling display of diversity, several accept while most fire up Havana CIAS (Assasinos Cubanos Internacional). A seepage of blue smoke wafts under and above the accordion divider, raising hackles but no hubbub since Luby's has posted a sign reminding diners that the banquet room is a federally designated tobacco sanctuary purchased by R. J. Reynolds the way the Nature Conservancy buys bogs.

Back at Bakersfield Field, waiting for Wally and Tice, Mark Neighbors idly thrums his suspenders and wonders how best to steer this turn of events to his advantage with Juggernaut. Disclosure is out of the question, but the modified limited divulgement he recalls from an old management textbook might serve his purposes. When the geothermal plant supplants Rancho Rio,

Juggernaut's 4 percent stake will be worthless. Poverty, Mark Neighbors knows, will not, alas, drive Juggernaut into his arms. Running his laptop through the corporate Fujitsu, Mark Neighbors calls up the Federal Tax Code and discovers that an unrealized capital gain donated to an institution of higher education north of the 44th parallel and west of the 122nd meridian and owned substantially but not entirely by MegaMax generates a 700 percent tax credit, doubled in the event that the donation comes from a MegaMax employee or subsidiary.

Wally and Tice sashay into the terminal followed by their bearer, Gunga Gin, a Sikh they picked up on summer vacation when they flew for the Kashmiri Liberation Front. Gunga bears a case of Everclear for the flight north. Mark Neighbors wonders if Wally and Tice might have been the couple disguised as Curtis LeMay and Amelia Earhart featured recently on Hard Copy flying air cover on alternate weekends for Patriot Guild maneuvers outside Aryan, Idaho, and for Graham's Crackers, a militia group in South Carolina.

– XXV –

Because he has unfinished business in El Paso, Stanley has chosen the southern route from New Jersey back to Oregon. Before Oklahoma City, the Twin Towers, and that spooky guy from Montana who proved that the Postal Service really can deliver, Stanley, as a payback for his eighteen months in federal prison, had intended to blow up the statue of Wellington Snark, founding father of the Bureau of Customs, depicted at the Juárez Crossing seizing the undeclared foreskin of Jesus who thought he'd take a second run at things without going through channels. Also, while held in the Hudspeth County jail pending transfer, Stanley had borrowed a book from the city library and had inadvertently neglected to return it. He had it still—*The Britches of Madison County: One Woman's Quest for Boxers in Brief Country*—and now aimed to bring it back, though he no longer thought it prudent to expunge Snark's statue as it seemed likely that authorities would get pretty hacked off these days at anyone blowing up public structures and might overreact by catching him.

Stanley rolls into El Paso, as fortune would have it, on Sunday morning. The library is closed, but closer inspection reveals a drive-through book drop. The drive-through, passing, in fact, exactly through the center of the building like a tunnel, was a nifty little add-on during construction when it was discovered that twenty thousand square feet of shelf space had to be deleted for the building to qualify for federal funding under a special congressional initiative to close thousands of libraries across the country in order to collect books at a limited number of sites so that a closer eye could be kept on them, this oversight falling to the division of the Department of Energy that monitors nuclear waste.

As quarterbacks playing in the Sun Bowl have discovered, the surreal skyscape and Florentine light of the high desert play chiaroscuroesque tricks with distance and perspective. Later, Stanley will swear he saw a Volvo station wagon pull through ahead of him, assuring Stanley's truck ample clearance.

As Reverend Endwell toils in the pulpit across the road, Buckthorn spins quarters with Sheila to see who'll buy the next round. They're watching the semi-finals of the World Championship Tractor Pull on ESPN7 from the county fairgrounds in Bovine, Nebraska. During a break in the action, the network cuts to live coverage of an ongoing feature, "Truck Stop: Selected Shorts." Flaco Dominguez is on the scene in El Paso where an apparent garbage truck has lodged itself decisively in the middle of a library.

Buckthorn sits transfixed, as if he were watching his nightmares broadcast coast to coast. Though the truck is wedged well inside the drive-through, the citron and lavender of the rear end, while masked in shadow and shading towards vermilion on the Pour House's ConCo TurboTube, resemble alarmingly the heraldic colors of a garbage truck that should be—a half-formed prayer rises wholeheartedly from somewhere deep in Buckthorn's bowels—the better part of a continent away from El Paso.

Then Stanley himself fills the screen, chatting amiably with Flaco Dominguez. Sheila sets a bottle of Stupefaction in front of Buckthorn and pats him sympathetically on the wrist where veins are beginning to bulge as he gets a grip on the bar top.

Stanley has just finished recounting the plot of *Britches* and is now expanding on a range of cultural interests, citing his artistic and business partner, Harley Buckthorn, for whom Stanley is transporting the fixings, as he understands it, of a groundbreaking piece of environmental art. He also wants to say a special hidy-ho to Pearly Gates, an old girlfriend who said he'd have to get shot or vice versa to ever be on television. In the background, a wrecker from Ace Towing rears up on its hind wheels in a futile attempt to winch out the truck.

From Bovine, the ESPN7 anchor breaks in. "Taco? Taco, this is Chris. Can you ask Mr. Jeebers where he would locate himself on that old Bell Curve we've all heard so much about lately?"

"That's 'Flaco,' Chris."

"Whatever."

"Mr. Jeebers, my colleague in Nebraska wants to know if, as a person of color, you have trouble steering and chewing gum at the same time."

Stanley wonders how they found out about his little deficit.

"Hold on there, guacamole breath; that's not exactly what I said."

"*Tú madre.*"

"Previs, did you hear that?"

The color commentator in Bovine steps whitely (that amalgam of all colors) into the breach. "I sure did, Chris. And you know what, my mamma always said that if English was good enough for Jesus it ought to be good enough for everybody else."

Bristol pulls the plug. "Thank you Chris, Previs, and Flako. We'll return with axle-to-axle coverage of the World Championship Tractor Pull after these messages."

As the camera pulls back from an obscenely gesturing Flaco Dominguez and theme music swells, Buckthorn can see an acetylene torch being fired up on a hastily rigged scaffold next to the garbage truck's scrunched roof.

Buckthorn can watch no more. The plastique is probably safe enough unless Stanley gets involved in the salvage operation, in which case El Paso will make Oklahoma City look like some kid fooling around with firecrackers that used to be called lady fingers but are now, Buckthorn supposes, known as ms(ing) digits.

As Buckthorn trudges across the parking lot to his truck, Chuck Wepner scoots out from underneath where he has tucked in out of the spotty rain. In his haste, Chuck drops something near the driver's door. Buckthorn stoops and retrieves what is either a badly made *faux* cucumber or some sort of sexual implement.

– XXVI –

Buckthorn pulls into Devaney's to pick up a few things and drop off Chuck's latest rubber fix in the community lost and found. Buckthorn carries the object gingerly, holding the dry end up and hoping what appears to be the gnawn lower extremity is slathered only in Chuck slobber.

Devaney recognizes the dildo at once. "Chuckie snuck in here yesterday when my back was turned and filched it out of the mail bag. He tore up the wrapping so I can't make out any address. I guess I can put it in the lost and found, but I don't expect anyone's going to claim it. It's just not the sort of thing someone is likely to come right out and own up to."

"Unless it's Juggernaut's."

Devaney arches his hirsute adornment, the absence of which sunk Richard Gephardt's presidential bid. "When I was with the Bureau of Weights and Measures, we ran a little analysis for an inter-agency strike team from the Department of Commerce and the Postal Service. Some outfit was selling porcine sexual aids by mail, and we were asked to verify the advertised dimensions and materials involved. I believe the Department of Agriculture was responsible for verifying the actual efficacy of the products."

It occurs to Buckthorn that a public service video starring Devaney talking about sex would drive thousands of teenagers out of carnal embrace and into the bedazzlement of watching paint dry.

"If Chuck didn't nibble a little off there at the end, I'd say—just an estimate, mind you—that this is an xxxx model, that is, 8¼–9⅛ inches, of foreign manufacture, probably Semitic, given, you'll notice, the treatment of the prepuce."

Buckthorn hadn't really noticed, truth be told, his artistic vision for the cliff face over Rancho Rio having driven all competing

Johnsons from his perceptual field. Holding the device up now for closer scrutiny, he happens on a trademark circling the blunt end in slightly raised letters: MegaShlong.

Magically, a carton of Tums topples from the shelf, reminding Buckthorn of Stanley. "You wouldn't have any idea how long it would take someone to drive out here from El Paso?"

"Funny you should ask," says Devaney. "Man was in here this morning, drove straight through, he said, from New Mexico. Took him a day and a half, I believe."

"He must have been popping little whites ones all the way."

"One might think so, except that the gentleman in question is a federal air traffic controller."

"Big white ones," says Buckthorn.

He did mention an inter-racial hallucination somewhere in New Mexico, but the rest of the trip was uneventful."

The door jangles and Sarah Trip walks in.

Buckthorn turns, and though he does not speak he clearly stutters.

Sarah takes in the vaguely gray, gnawn, dog-drooled dildo Buckthorn clutches like a rosary. "Your sex life is even more predictable and pathetic than I thought," says Sarah with a ripple of aesthetic pleasure at the percussive, alliterative *p*'s. "Mr. Devaney, I understand you're plugged into the internet."

"That's correct, Ms. Trip," says Devaney, glowering at Buckthorn, who simultaneously ratchets and swivels his eyes, looking for shelf space where he can ditch the dildo.

"I've entered into a publishing arrangement where there's going to be a lot of quick back-and-forth."

"'Quick back-and-forth,'" Buckthorn repeats, he hopes to himself.

"And I was wondering if—"

"Ms. Trip, I'd be honored. I once calibrated Carolyn Forché's angst when she was being considered for Poetry Consultant to the Library of Congress. If I may say so, you far surpass her in poetic dimension."

"Mr. Devaney. You. Read. Poetry!?"

America, of course, having more lottery winners, Little League players struck by lightning, mule farmers, and popes than poetry readers.

Devaney ducks his head modestly and nods. Buckthorn, taking advantage of the exchange, stuffs the dildo down his pants.

Having made arrangements with Devaney for digital transmission of her Booty Book manuscript, Sarah strides out past Buckthorn, pausing to rap the submerged dildo smartly with her index finger. "Next time you window-peep, you better hang onto the tree with both hands, because if I catch you on the ground you're going to be strapping on this baby"—she raps the device again—"where your pecker used to be."

The second blow dislodges the dildo, which plummets down Buckthorn's pants leg, lodging against his boot top. This was not exactly the context Buckthorn envisioned when he fantasized Sarah Trip first taking notice of his Johnson. On the brighter side, however, now that they have been introduced, maybe something will come of it.

The door rattles behind Sarah, and Devaney claps a knobby arm around Buckthorn's shoulder. "Harley, I'm going to speak bluntly, as I know your father would in these circumstances."

Buckthorn figures he has it coming.

"If you walk out the door with that dildo in your pants, Chuck Wepner's apt to take your leg off."

– XXVII –

Auditioning for a T'ang Dynasty landscape painting, wisps of fog thread the upper reaches of Naughty Girl Creek. As August supplants July and Oregon homemakers begin exchanging recipes for green tomato dishes, Tony Ten-Toes Jr. wistfully recalls the subscription he left behind when he repaired to the wilderness. Besides cataloguing the Cubs' annual collapse, the *Springfield Inquirer-Columbian* (formerly the *Springfield Union-Errata*) (motto: "A Newspaper Is the Compost of Its Community") ran a daily section devoted to rain. Even in Oregon—where the indigenous have more words for rain than the Inuits have for snow—such coverage is unprecedented and a source of considerable civic pride, even across the river in West Springfield, where civic leaders have otherwise abjured print culture in a desperate attempt to sucker some chip fabricator into locating there, such company having bought the pitch that remnant hippies who have ingested three decades' worth of every pharmaceutical known to man, beast, and vegetable would make dandy high-tech employees.

The *Inquirer-Columbian*'s rain section, presided over by whichever son or nephew is heir-apparent to the publisher, consists of Talmudic statistics: daily precipitation; annual precipitation to date; percentage of precipitation occurring as rain, snow, sleet, hail, graupel, mist, dew, fog, and slug slough; inches in excess of fifty-year average; days rained this date since 1907; percentage of saturation point of four common local soil types; feet above normal of Pucker Creek Reservoir; number of suicides.

The soft news in the section includes the forecast for tomorrow, the week, and the month; a rain crossword puzzle; a poem (haiku preferred) on rain; "Fun Facts about Rain" for the *Inquirer* in the Schools Program; Oregon record of the day for rain from the *Guinness Book of World Records;* a recollection from an old-timer about how it used to rain more and to greater effect than it does these days; a cartoon strip featuring Mildewman; Springfield's standing in the annual Oregon Municipal Rain Derby; a rain editorial and editorial cartoon; letters to the rain editor (specimen: "Dear Rain Editor: Having recently moved to the area from Quilcene, Washington, where it really rains…"; lyrics for the song of the day (specimen: "Raindrops Keep Falling on My Head," "Rainy Day Women," "Who'll Stop the Rain?" "Come Rain or Come Shine"; favorite rain fantasy (anonymous); an advice column written by a local hydrotherapist; homemaking hints by the section editor writing under the *nom de deluge* of April Showers; photograph (black and white only) of rain; classified ads for umbrellas, rain tires, rain slickers, rain gauges, roof repair, sun lamps, wholesalers of Prozac, Zoloft, and Paxil, anti-fungicides, slug and snail bait, cisterns, micro hydroelectric installations, windshield wiper refills, rain-proof bridal dresses, gutters, downspouts, caulking, basement and drain field pumping, white noise generators to override the sound of rain on the roof, getaway packages to Monsoon, Bangladesh, Hip Deep, Alaska, and High Sodden, East Anglia, rust inhibitor, anti-pucker cream, and galoshes.

Sacrifices, however, have to be made, and Tony has reconciled himself to *das ding an sich* rain unmediated by the *Inquirer-Columbian*. The upside is that rather than a daily blow-by-blow of the Cubs' misfortunes, Tony can only imagine their bungles, sometimes indulging the fantasy that the Cubs' curse of turning the diamond into a lump of coal has somehow lifted and they will return in befuddled triumph to the World Series, giving Tony the chance to reclaim his patch of ancestral turf by wagering on the outcome with Buckthorn.

A maniacal whine, as if from an ex-spouse, ruptures the perfect envelope of silence. The sole machine in all the fastness springs to life with Hiro Ishimatsu at the controls. The ultralight is tethered like a rocket being test-fired. Hiro winds the engine out and waggles the system of levers and pulleys that controls the aeronautics. After a thirty-minute run, he shuts the engine down and pronounces the ship airworthy. All that remains is the camouflage paint job. Hiro supervises as D. B. Cooper slathers all top surfaces

Doug fir green so that seen from above the ultralight will merge pigmentally with the dominant flora, unemployment checks, and October through June complexions. Everything underneath he paints gray so that those on the ground will be hard pressed to pick the ship out against the matching background of the sky.

That night, the Gang of Five contentiously lays their plans. An abbreviated launching strip has been cleared, running fifty feet back from a handy local precipice. A store of gasoline acquired from Orville Crease—whose progeny siphons it from cars parked at recreational trailheads—has been laid by. The source of contention is the precise nature of the mission to be undertaken. Public consensus has attributed the nitrous oxide episode to the Gang, along with the disappearance of 50-cent pieces, the election of a Republican county commissioner, and the account of a Forest Service employee in the *National Enquirer* of his abduction by Sasquatch. Carlos argues that anything less than a media-intensive appearance will undercut the stair-step publicity campaign he has crafted for the Gang. Hiro weighs in on this side of the debate with references to Pearl Harbor. Tony—calling to mind what happened to the Indians (formerly the Native Americans formerly the Indians) when they pressed their luck after Jamestown and again after the Little Big Horn—counsels caution. D. B. Cooper, asulk because the ultralight offers limited opportunities for skyjacking, sides with Tony.

Which leaves Sasquatch the swing vote. This is a tricky proposition. Prior to membership in the Gang, Sasquatch, though a Jungian who freely consulted his anima and shadow in all matters, considered himself a democracy of one. Subsequent to membership, while slipping nightly into Devaney's for Tums, Sasquatch has stumbled upon the *Manchester Guardian* online, discovering the sometimes-decisive role of minority parties in a parliamentary system. Sasquatch is also mindful of the fact that at one juncture or another each of the Gang has supported his ouster. Mounting the podium, whose woodenness reminds him of the *faux* bear he snatched from the Upper McKenzie Fair, Sasquatch lifts his voice in song: "Que sera, sera..."

– XXVIII –

Ordinarily, C. C. Fellows operates as a sole proprietor, but these are not ordinary times. A farmer, of course, is always subject to the vagaries of weather, critters, fluctuation in the futures market, etc., but C. C. is slicing mucho more dicily than, say, your ordinary soybean and milo raiser in Kansas (motto: "Not Even Almost the Next Arkansas"). The agrichemical industry has not done much for the average marijuana grower, so when Hemp Smut strikes or the Cannabis Canker Borer marches like Sherman through his patch, C. C. can't drop by Springfield Feed and Seed for a pest-specific remedy. There is no federal commodity support when Mexican growers dump product at ruinous prices to build market share. The county extension agent is of no use when C. C. has those nagging little horticultural quandaries like what kind of overstory planting will render pot plants least visible to aerial detection yet allow enough light through for optimum growth. He can never raise up offspring—if ever he had such—to grow and show the crop at FAA competitions. His local State Farm agent will not sell him crop insurance, and he can't write off any losses on his tax return. Mainstream media will not carry ads for his product; banks will not loan on it. Were he ever to stop using public lands and try to put down some roots, the State of Oregon would offer no agricultural exemption on his property taxes. A growers' cooperative, which once had seemed like a good idea to C. C. (the economies of scale in bulk purchasing of fertilizer, drip irrigation systems, and deputy sheriffs; a coordinated marketing strategy; more lobbying clout in Salem), never really got off the ground. The organizational meeting, held on a moonless night in densely woven woods, ran amuck when someone's police scanner fired up like a bad movie and everybody started shooting. C. C.'s bazooka didn't sound at all out of place; if anything, he thought he might have been a little undergunned. And that was that for the coop.

A recent Oregon ballot initiative legalizing marijuana had promised high times, but the measure's passage was overturned by the Supreme Court on grounds that it was invalidated by the Federal Schedule I Controlled Substances Act and had obviously been passed by the same stoned Democrats who voted for Biden. For good measure, the Court rescinded the voting rights of all who had signed the initiative petition. A subsequent Joint Committee of Congress, stricken by giggles and the munchies, nodded off without taking legislative action.

All in all, this has not been the kind of year C. C. had in mind when an article in *High Times* lured him to Oregon from his job as a lentil buyer for Holy Cow, a Hindu restaurant in deep L.A. Snow collapsed the plastic shield over his germination beds and a late frost wiped out most of his first planting. While years of selective breeding developed plants that can mature in boggish soil, the annual unprecedented rains have cost him his usual losses to root rot. Some hippie's trained magpie (the tie-dyed feathers and Grateful Dead stage pass fingered its ownership) snatched beakfuls of crop until C. C. erected a replica in the field of Sir Willis Wallis, notorious in aviary circles as the Scottish sportsman who brought down the last passenger pigeon. A pesky infestation of neon-white slugs ensued, and then the ball buster: hopelessly lost while marking a salvage timber sale, U.S. Forest Service employee Bart Bevel stumbled across C. C.'s drying shed. The subsequent raid by the Bureau of Alcohol, Tobacco, and Firearms, the Lane County Interagency Drug Task Force, the Oregon National Guard, exchange cops from Columbia here to participate in the BustAmerica Program, the Strategic Air Command, and Springfield Explorer Post 127 leveled 320 acres of forest, inadvertently knocking out C. C.'s shed when a SAC fuel-air bomb was dropped four miles from the coordinates Bart Bevel provided.

His cash reserves nearly exhausted, C. C. knows he must take on partners. And soon. He needs a drying shed for the incoming crop, an awesome but touchy hybrid whose TCP content depends on careful management of the seasoning process. His ConCo

TurboTiller is down to its last tines and will have to be replaced before the next planting. And the Gang of Five has been pressing him to deliver a promised sponsorship fee for the Springfield Parks and Recreation Horseshoe League.

C. C. arranges to meet Orville Crease at an inconspicuous table in the Pour House. Sheila Wallop has always been partial to C. C. He reminds her of a former husband, the expatriate Bolivian medicinal leaf buyer. From deep behind the bar, she brings out a special decantation of Cuervo Añejo; a scorpion drifts languidly in the lower amber sucking on a joint. Orville Crease is a different matter. Knowing he favors Kahlúa, Sheila assembles in a dusky bottle a base of Old Funerary bourbon stylized with vanilla, instant coffee, and Kiwi liquid brown shoe polish.

The deal solidifies as C. C. knocks back his tequila and Orville a Cookie Monster (Kahlúa and Oreos). Orville can supply operating capital from an unnamed Springfield source. He promises, too, a solution to C. C.'s most pressing problem—a replacement drying shed. What he wants in return is 97 percent of C. C.'s net or 2 percent of his gross and C. C.'s promise to take on Waylon as an apprentice.

"You know, the boy ain't exhibited much aptitude for the family trade. But I smack guarantee, he's a felon at heart. He just hasn't hit his stride." Somewhere in the nether reaches of his front pocket, Orville roots away at what C. C. would rather not imagine. "He's not cut out for the retail end of the business—not a people person like his old pa. So I figure getting him upside the production end is all it'll take to shake the cooties off his dick."

Always a fan of the well-turned phrase, C. C. asks after the etymology of the expression.

"Well, it's just the truth, that's all. Man got the cooties and goes to take a leak, he's so busy scratching and snapping them with his fingernails it don't matter if the seat is up or down, he's going to hear it from the missus with his pee going all over."

More deeply puzzled than ever about his role vis-à-vis Waylon's cooties, C. C. aims for a clarification. "So you're saying this could be your boy's first shovelful of dirt on the ladder of success?"

"Exactly."

The bar phone rings and Sheila answers. After a brief exchange, she puts the receiver down and comes over to C. C.'s table. "Stanley is just up the road from the state scales at Burns. He wants to know if two tons of plastic explosive weighs more than two tons of garbage. It sounds like a trick question to me."

C. C. converts tons to pounds to kilos and figures it up. "It comes out pretty near the same, Sheila."

"That's what I told him, but I was never any good at those story problems. Besides, Stanley is still working through his rejection of African American matrilineal culture, so he wasn't going to take my word for it anyway. I'll tell Buckthorn he owes you."

"Tell him," says C. C. specifically, "that I'll add it to his tab."

After a couple more rounds, Orville and C. C. head out, crossing the highway to see Reverend Endwell. The reverend's portable sign, rust-streaked where bolts secure its frame, tilts noticeably, one wheel riding the perceptible slough of the sodden embankment down towards the ditch bearing the message "Hannibal Lecter: Honk If You Can't Stop." The sign might as well be Mayan hieroglyphics since Orville Crease can't read and C. C. Fellows hasn't been to a movie since *Cheech and Chong Meet the Mormon Tabernacle Choir.*

Orville raps feloniously at the door of the Church of the Doublewide. Buttoning the flap of his back pocket over his wallet, Reverend Endwell grabs a shepherd's crook left over from the Christmas pageant and pries open the door, which balks in its warped frame in rainy weather. He grips the crook tighter when he sees Orville Crease. Orville introduces him to C. C. and explains how Cash Crop is in quite a pickle owing to the loss of his drying shed, jeopardizing his sworn commitment to prove that American-grown herbs can compete with foreign imports, never mind their NAFTA advantages.

Ever alert for opportunities to engage the unchurched, Reverend Endwell shows C. C. the furnace room and vestry. C. C., having no remotely prudent option, accepts the offer.

"No strings attached," the reverend croons, palms up. Along with his classmates at Antepenultimate Bible College, Reverend Endwell understood that his pastoral career—before, that is, he landed a syndication deal on cable—would offer none of the fiscal advantages available to his establishment colleagues. No spiritually entrepreneurial collateral education complex where, say, relational singles volleyball and presentations on Dow Jones predictions from the Book of Revelation might induce the heathen into the neighborhood so that if they didn't return to her parents' church for marriage and christenings they might end up feeding the most convenient ecclesiastical coffers. Reverend Endwell's few secular inducements—praying over lottery tickets and writing letters of reference to probation officers—didn't seem to be putting many people in the pews. If a prominent local businessman like C. C. got churchy, the reverend might hope to graze in higher fiscal clover as other supply-siders followed.

"Of course, the church has always held a special silo in its heart for farmers abiding in their fields," says Reverend Endwell, stacking the biblical deck in God's favor since all Oregon shepherds were Basque Catholics. "I would be remiss in my office, however, were I not to admit that bringing in the sheaf, as it were, encompasses the hope of bringing in the sheafer." Reverend Endwell fixes C. C. with his best spiritual gaze, a look reminiscent of a Vegas slots player with a dwindling stack of quarters.

"Whoa there, padre." C. C. moves crabwise, angling for the door. "Like Spinoza said, religion is the opiate of the people. I appreciate your offer, and I know abetting others is your look-see. And it's not that I don't expect competition in my line of work, especially from the opiates. But I can't be giving an edge to them what is out after my livelihood."

"I'm afraid I don't understand," Reverend Endwell says, puzzled by the misattribution of Marx.

Orville Crease cuffs C. C. casually on the back of his skull to get his attention and gives him the Arkansas squint, honed on home ground to stop rabid hogs in their tracks.

"What C. C. was meaning, Reverend, is that he's just been so puke sick with worry he can't see straight, let alone talk straight. Soon as that crop is tucked in, he'll be regular again in no time."

Reverend Endwell clasps his hands pastorally on his lower abdomen and nods agreeably. C. C. manages an anemic smile of assent, the afterburn of the Arkansas squint blurring into his memory of an unpleasant visual from a misconceived horticultural junket to Sinaloa.

"God's bounty is welcome here," the reverend says, gesturing vestryward and speaking his best King James in case C. C. turns out to be an unchurched Episcopalian.

"You got it, dude," says C. C., in case the reverend happens to be a Presbyterian. "I mean Your Reverence, Father Dude," C. C. adds, carved by another Arkansas squint.

– XXIX –

Little suspecting the chicanery afoot in Bakersfield, Juggernaut is reading the most recent issue of *MegaMaxims*, the weekly journal of the corporation. Makeover of the Month features Emily Dickinson's house, a medium-slow mover for high school librarians and, inexplicably, Paraguayan apiarists, neither group a notably big spender at the gift shop. A junior executive named Marley Squab, fresh from his success at MegaMorph, a body-shaping salon in Anorexia, Connecticut, tripled the upside in less than a year by converting the house into MegaMort: A Museum of Literary Devices. Squab had not merely acquired literary artifacts, he had assembled them into an integrated tableau that was enjoying considerable success, even among nonreaders.

MegaMort features a living room with Hemingway's shotgun hanging above the hearth. In the study, the last bottle Dylan Thomas drank from rests on the desk, along with eighteen other receptacles—decanter, jug, carafe, flagon, jarl, vat, pot, tank, magnum, tub, flask, crock, firkin, carboy, cruet, decanter, stoup, and aftershave dispenser—which provided Malcolm Lowry his last imbibement. In the kitchen, of course, is Sylvia Plath's oven, on top of which is the bowl of ill-cooked okra and grits that fatally clogged Faulkner's lower digestive tract. Because visitors—especially men—keep trying the oven's knobs to see if it is really hooked up to a gas supply, Squab has installed a section of the railing from the S.S. *Orizaba* that Hart Crane vaulted over to hold customers back. Outside, the Oldsmobile that Randall Jarrell strolled into—retrofitted with Anne Sexton's exhaust pipe—is parked in the driveway, which is set off from the lawn by the Minneapolis bridge abutment from which John Berryman took the plunge. Squab hopes to inaugurate an international section with Mishima's harikari sword, but Japan has declared it a National Cultural Resource, so the exhibit awaits the conclusion of back-channel negotiations to exchange the sword for DNA from the crew of the *Enola Gay* along with MegaSoft Resurrectionist software, licensed so far only to Pope John Paul II and Disney.

Juggernaut sails the magazine across the room and sighs, popping the buttons off her Henley. Chuck Wepner stirs, then settles back into snacking on a box of ink erasers filched from Ms. Mucilage's classroom at McKenzie Station Elementary.

Juggernaut has long resigned herself to the likelihood that she lacks the imagination to screw the American public on a scale that would add market value to MegaMax's standing with international bankers. Bakersfield, she understands, sees her as a manager, nothing more. Nor less, thank heavens, her application for summer employment at Hooters, rejected because of overqualification, never turning up in her MegaMax personnel file. Her sole entrepreneurial excursion, rounding up venture capital for Czechmate, an enterprise that vetted prospective central European émigré brides, ended in an out-of-court settlement when the company failed to screen out formaldehyde junkies from the portfolio assembled for Hugh Hefner.

Juggernaut fears that her management style, state of the art in the Bush years and now again, could be precipitously superseded in the next paradigm shift by the wimp, wuss, or weenie styles—disarming the customer rather than dismantling him—already issuing from forward-looking MBA programs. Considering her future, Juggernaut wonders if Mark Neighbors is as inept in as he is out of bed.

– XXX –

Far up Wapiti Road, athwart a cashmere blanket on the northeast flank of Horsepasture Mountain amidst an hysterical eruption of wildflowers, Amanda Pennypacker sucks reflectively on a lemon tart, her full skirt, twinkling like escaped wardrobe from *The Sound of Music,* spread about her, its top laced in the style favored by 1950s Hollywood milkmaids or 1920s Berlin cabaret dancers, couturesque proof that fashion happens first as sadism and then as masochism. Farther along the slope, the meadow is adorned with musky plumes of bear grass, giving way higher up to the clustering firs and blue-gray hemlock where no one goes.

Amanda strokes the silky throat of a tiger lily, considering her future. A husky chill springs up as the sun hunches behind a cloud, and Amanda clutches the lily's diminutive and disturbingly hairy stem, thinking of her past.

After her conversation with Reverend Endwell, Amanda has spent weeks tracking down Miss Timber Topper, finding her at last in a West Springfield group home for beauty pageant runaways. As it turns out, Miss Timber Topper, while a delegate to Girls' State, had shared an elevator with Bob Packwood and thus was, of course, no longer a virgin. That Senator Packwood groped a Danish modern coat tree, a water cooler, and newspaper rack in the rotunda when they emerged left Miss Timber Topper deeply confused about her sexuality, though very clear about her political orientation.

It is, Amanda understands, up to her. As the only apparent near-virgin on the McKenzie (West Virginia had, in fact, come twice but only in transit—once as she tugged at his stuck zipper and once at the sight of her Rabelaisian muff—and Arkansas had come once, also *in principio res,* as she unscrolled a prophylactic on his emergent member), who could she really ask whether

Arkansas's only Lincolnesque appendage, an unusually long middle finger—that might, now that she thought about it, appeal subliminally to women voters—applied vaginally was really the same thing as, well, the real thing.

Amanda sucks the last of the tart and casts away the shell. Gray jays, the petty gangsters of the high country, elbow each other aside as they peck the pastry. From far down Wapiti Road a whine and its rounded echo surge and drop on the wind, then steady into a rising shriek. Except at the candle-passing ceremonies at her sorority, especially the three times Brenda Bendover announced her engagement, Amanda has heard nothing like it. More annoyed than alarmed, Amanda gazes down the switchback curves of the Wapiti grade as a silver blur emerges and disappears.

It is—though she will not know it for some minutes and then only imperfectly—Beau Zipp in his super stock Camaro, the White Flight, formerly sponsored by the Republican Party of Klandestine County, Georgia, currently sponsored by a Sun City social organization, Grand Arizona Geezers. Beau, a contemporary of Cale Yarborough and Richard Petty—in fact, they still get together whenever their schedules overlap to knock back some prune brandy and swap stories about their prostates—is tuning up for the annual Pike's Peak Climb. Beau has been racing himself back into shape after an increasingly unsuccessful retirement by driving the Northwest county fair circuit. He was on his way from Burns to Albany when he swung into the Pour House for a quick one. After he and Sheila emerged from her office, Beau decided to stick around and train locally. Wapiti Road had been recommended so here he is, blasting the straightaways and choreographing the corners in improvisational skids—now like Meryl Streep's South Dakota accent in *Buffalo Chip*, now like a Big Pharma attorney—tweaking the sheer cliffs and sheerer drop-offs, steeper than the precipitous downturns of Sarah Huckabee Sanders's mouth.

As the White Flight nips and tucks on up the ridge, some deeper rumble vibrates the air, a complex bass line rolling down from higher up Wapiti Road. Before Amanda can imagine what to expect, Stanley heaves into view, having slalomed the Peterbilt up the backside of Wapiti to avoid the DPS scales on the highway between Mill Creek Road and the South Fork turnoff. Down the hill he rambles, the El Paso Library-creased roof lowing a throaty bugle above, the brakes smoking furiously below as the Peterbilt loses altitude like a wounded B-24 in *Twelve o'Clock High*, five gears beyond prudence, two beyond sanity.

"Oh, my," says Amanda, gathering her skirt and tripping fetchingly toward the road, thinking to rip a revealing though not obscene strip from her bodice to flag down the errant drivers. Before she can reach the road where her Acura is neatly tucked into a turnout, both vehicles are face-to-face on the miniature straightaway. Stanley, having driven for thirty-seven hours, assumes the Camaro is an hallucination, like the Virgin Mary who appeared in hour twenty-nine in a Coors display at a 7-11 in Nip and Tuck, Nevada, and rumbles on, curious as to whether contemporary usage mandates an "a" or an "an" before "hallucination." Beau Zipp, accustomed to head-on collisions only with the wall, spins the Camaro like a roulette wheel, climbing the bank above the Acura, doffing his Australian bush hat to the stricken Amanda as he plows past through huckleberries, rhododendron, and sundry saplings, regaining purchase on the road still turning six thousands rpms and smoking on up Wapiti as Stanley recollects that the hallucinations he has enjoyed lately are typically female, so perhaps the feminine progressive article—what was it, aunty, anna, anima?—was called for.

Amanda, nearly aswoon athwart her ruffles, thinks that Beau Zipp looks like Kris Kristofferson if he'd had better luck with steroids. She must ask Reverend Endwell whether Mr. Zipp has any standing as a local shaman. If not, perhaps there is a community college course he might enroll in.

– XXXI –

Like a sulking Samurai in a Kurosawa film, the Fell Faller mopes about in his room at a downriver motel, the Inn and Out, an establishment featuring room rentals by the hour for honeymooners on a budget, county road workers with the afternoon to kill, interstate truckers logging their mandatory two hours of bed rest for every three weeks on the road, and Forest Service management working on their mid-life crises with Springfield barmaids.

As never before, the Fell Faller has been smitten by love. He no longer sleeps with his ConCo TurboSaw. The jilted implement lies as if in a heap in the corner, sprocket grease smeared on its housing, bar stippling with rust wherever Oregon air touches raw metal. Ever since the McKenzie Fair, the Fell Faller's dreams have been haunted by the shapely ecclesiastical neck he so cavalierly behickied when the lights went out. Reverend Endwell has come to occupy his days as well, driving all thought of Moby Fir from his mind. While the Fell Faller cannot exactly bring himself to attend church, he hides in the woods each Sunday to watch the reverend help his congregation down the makeshift stairs from the doublewide. The Fell Faller lingers after the last parishioner has left, hoping for another glimpse of the reverend, who sometimes reemerges with pipe wrench and sewer snake, crawling beneath the trailer, if Orville Crease has used the bathroom during services.

The Fell Faller has had his flings, to be sure, but this is different. This is someone he could imagine restoring an authentically neglected Victorian on the coast with, converting it to a bookstore, bed and breakfast, and studio for the design of ecclesiastical ensembles for gay clergy—the kind of guy you could take home to Dad. That Reverend Endwell might share these feelings he dare not hope. Still, there was, in the general squalling and ruckus the reverend kicked up mid-hickey, an undertone of delight the Fell

Faller thought he detected, a sort of suppressed pre-squeal that left the question fractionally open. Then, too, the reverend does serve as scoutmaster for an upriver troop.

If the Fell Faller watched PBS, he might have invoked Eros, recently featured on the PBS special *Aphrodite in Omaha*. PBSless, the best he can do is try to remember whether Rock Hudson ever played a clergyman in one of his movies.

Splayed in despair on his bed, the only Rock Hudson movies coming to mind those featuring Doris Day, the Fell Faller is roused by a puny but persistent hammering at his door. It is Chip, the faithful choker setter from the Pour House. The Fell Faller, not recognizing him at first, growls and flexes his hump to ward off a misguided pizza delivery or presidential candidate.

Chip flinches, but holds his ground. "It's me, Mr. Faller—Chip, the faithful choker setter from the Pour House Tavern."

"So what?" says the Fell Faller, but his heart's not in it. He no longer cares what unless the what is a who and the who is Reverend Endwell.

"You said I was to find you if I was to find Moby Fir so I found you because this guy found Moby Fir and I found him."

At mention of Moby Fir, the Fell Faller is surprised by an old pornographic stirring in his groin, the reflexive curl of his trigger finger, larger by a third than the other digits on his right hand from years at the throttle of the ConCo TurboSaw. But it is not enough. His work, so recently his life, means nothing now. He is, he realizes, pining away. The awfulness of the pun, its pathetic irony, deepens his malaise.

The Fell Faller shakes his head gravely, mournfully. "I can't do it, son."

Chip gulps and rubs his nose furiously with the back of his hand. He scuffs the toe of his boot at the edge of a stain in the carpet. The stain bears an uncanny resemblance to an aerial view of the municipal landfill in Gasbag, Ohio, or the spinster aunt of Rutherford B. Hayes.

"But you got to," says Chip.

"Do not," says the Fell Faller, poutily.

"Do too," says Chip, pluckishly.

"Do not," says the Fell Faller, his legendary squeak rising an octave.

"Due to?" asks Chip.

"Do wah do, tell me who, who, who wrote the book of love?"

As if cut off at the knees by the ConCo TurboSaw, Chip is stumped. He can't think of any books except *Chilton's Guide to Auto Repair,* let alone who wrote them. Rifling through his memory, Chip lights on his high school English class. Never much of a reader or writer, Chip was allowed to graduate by reciting from *1,000 Great Thoughts of History.* In this fashion, during his senior year he produced the 5,267 grammatically complete sentences the Oregon Department of Educational Uniform Remediation prescribed as the requirement for a high school diploma. Chip sees now that all along they had been right—someday he *would* be glad that the D8 Cat he once on a dare took for a joyride from a road construction site had sunk into the school's septic drain field as he was lining up for a run at the administration annex. As a class I misdemeanor, abuse of a septic system allowed his judge the latitude of sentencing Chip to one more year of high school or two years in the slammer. As the old quotations come bubbling up—Chip thinks, emboldened by his clever turn of phrase, from the septic tank of memory—he draws himself up to his fullest oratorical height.

> As a determinant of anxiety, loss of love plays a role in hysteria similar to that of the threat of castration in the phobias and of dread of the superego in compulsion neurosis.... The task of subduing so powerful an instinct as the sexual impulse, otherwise than by giving it satisfaction, is one which may employ the whole strength of a man.... After long doubts and vacillations we have decided to assume the existence of only two instincts: Eros and the destructive instinct. (Sigmund Freud 1856–1939).

Chip adds: "This noble precept is often cited by Plato: 'Do thine own work'" (Montaigne 1533–92).

The Fell Faller is struck squeakless. He opens his mouth several times: breath rushes out, but no sound issues. His duty, he sees, is clear; his folkloric stature compels it. Casting aside—O bitter moment—all gauzy dream of tumbling Reverend Endwell into the sack, the Fell Faller strides to the ConCo TurboSaw, slings it across his hump, turns to the open door through which his Jimmy six pack stands, steadfast and steed-like, in the August Oregon mist. "To strive, to seek, to fell / and not to yield," says the Fell Faller, his voice resumed.

"'Find,' I think you'll find," Chip says pedagogically. "Alfred Lord Tennyson, 'Ulysses,' ca. 1867."

Flint returns to the Fell Faller's thousand-mile gaze. With his free hand, he grasps Chip by his britches, inverts him, raps his noggin smartly against the floor, sets him back on his feet.

"Let's get after it."

– XXXII –

Stanley wheels the Peterbilt triumphantly past Devaney's, tootling the air horn in greeting before turning up Hack Creek Road to Buckthorn's. Devaney rushes out in time to wave Stanley around the corner. Though keeper of the great seal of the Perpetual Order of Oregon Phlegmatics (motto: "Just Don't"), Devaney is moved to gestural affect by Stanley's return, more precisely, by Stanley's truck's return. The local garbage situation has reached crisis proportions since the Forest Service started issuing swipe cards to campground visitors, allowing only card-carrying recreators and modestly dexterous bears access to the newly configured dumpsters. It has always been an article of faith with Devaney that the benchmark of a civilization is how it handles baseball free agency and garbage. *L'methode d'nuit* currently in favor consists of McKenzians driving around after dark pitching sacks of trash from the back of one's own pickup into the bed of someone else's, ideally when the other party isn't around, though some of the more athletic can sling a sack on the move into a passing truck, ConCo Carborundum Sacks being essential for this maneuver. In such manner, trash is passed from household to household, accumulating here and there in trucks of the unobservant.

Buckthorn's Chevy is piled high. No one, not even the Creases, would dare litter since the State of Oregon, home of progressive legislation such as the first bottle return law, public beach access, the recently quashed reefer referendum, and assisted suicide has instituted environmental *Hudud*, which provides that anyone caught littering has to eat whatever he pitched. *Trashiers* are held in custody until they have gormandized their felony. Repeat offenders (they aren't many) are hobbled and left to graze the right-of-ways for litter left by Californians. Devaney's rush and wave are indeed heartfelt.

Arriving at Buckthorn's, Stanley is more circumspect, idling the Peterbilt alongside the house where its metallic bulk interferes with Buckthorn's afternoon TV reception. Sure enough, Buckthorn comes shambling out, resembling a man who would still be in his jammies if he wore any.

"Hey," says Stanley, resembling a man who would be full of trepidation if he knew what the word meant.

"Hey?" Buckthorn says, swinging up on the running board and thrusting an arm through the window across Stanley's shoulder. *"Hey?"* he repeats, clutching Stanley's right trapezius in a death grip. "I trust you with my truck and have to bail you both out from the Mafia; you disappear for weeks with the goods; the next time I look you're on ESPN inviting the Feds to drop by after coming within a flick of static electricity from blowing El Paso into southern Sinaloa and what I get is *'hey?'"* Buckthorn tightens his grip.

"Yipes," says Stanley, wholeheartedly.

"That's more like it," says Buckthorn. "'Yipes' is just a whole lot closer to the essential nature of our situation here."

"Buckthorn, holy shit, turn loose of me, will you?"

"Closer still," says Buckthorn. "'Holy shit' in fact fundamentally hits it right on the old noggin." Buckthorn gives Stanley a parting squeeze. "Let's get this sucker unloaded."

Stanley's right arm dangles and he rubs at the shoulder with his other hand. "Can't," says Stanley. "I'm disabled; I think you wrecked something."

"Do you know the difference," says Buckthorn sweetly, "between disabled and dismembered?"

Stanley doesn't like the drift of this, but he can't tell whether he's better off knowing or not—purely an academic anxiety since he doesn't, in fact, know the difference.

"Dis," Buckthorn says, tapping Stanley's trapezius, "was your able shoulder. Dis," he says, giving Stanley's crotch a smart rap with the back of his hand, "is your member, up to this point."

Stanley blanches, a neat trick of pigmentation he learned from the secret mojo decoder he got for joining the Colin Powell Fan Club. Stanley pats his arm. "Good as new. Must have been a little crick or something. You want me up back or on the ground?"

After the plastique has been stacked in Buckthorn's bedroom and Stanley has driven off, taking with him, at Buckthorn's insistence, a partially gnawn fruitcake—a characteristic McKenzie gifting of food at life's defining moments (birth, death, Christmas tree shopping with a spouse, paying off your bar tab, release from jail, a run-up in the value of the Togoan *pizzle* against the dollar, a currency futures holding where a sizable chunk of the pension fund of the Brotherhood of International Loggers and Knockabouts is invested)—Buckthorn returns to the TV, his choices for the rest of the afternoon consisting of an Eyeclueless News special featuring four Oregon women who have not been groped by Bob Packwood; a local light metal band, *The Kervorkians Unplugged*, on Springfield Cable Access Microchannel; and, through the vagaries of reception, three PBS channels whose programming reflects public broadcasting's commitment to the new political reality of having to appeal to advertisers and audience. Buckthorn slaloms down the PBS channels: *Beets as You've Never Tasted Them*; *Masterpieces of British Punctuation: This Week, the Ellipsis*; and *Community College Librarians Work the "New York Times" Crossword Puzzle.*

– XXXIII –

President York tugs with all the hope a lapsed Presbyterian can muster at his office window. The sash, he assumes correctly, has warped beyond Schwarzeneggering. Even were he to force the issue, the drainpipe just within reach is rusted beyond likelihood of bearing the weight of his presidency. With a last obligatory tug, he turns, Tumless, to the thrumming door upon which Lunelle Johnson-Bender announces herself.

"Walden," he hears her say, "you cocksucker, open up."

President York's lower member shrinks into his scrotum, but his heart leaps up. A complaint filed with the Oregon Coital Orientation Commission or perhaps the Oregon Prohibited Mean Speech Bureau might rid him of this woman. Rushing to his desk, he activates the whole-room recording system installed by MegaMole, the corporate security arm.

"I beg your pardon?" he says, speaking faintly to invite a forensically recordable response.

"I said your lock's stuck here, open up."

President York switches off the system and indulges in a moment of transcendental inter-American administrative bonding with Salvador Allende. Then, heaving and thrusting, he wobbles the filing cabinets away from the door. "Just dusting," he pants as Lunelle sweeps in. "If you don't keep after it, well, you know—"

"What I know," says Lunelle, swiveling past the cabinets and squeegeeing into a chair, "is that Professor Waxwroth has unspeakably defiled the good name of this university."

Eyeing the revolt of the provinces south of the Empire waist on Dr. Johnson-Bender, President York makes a preliminary shuffle in his throat, waiting for the unspeakable to be spoken. He quickly reviews his menu of presidential responses from a book he has just finished: *Boss/Unboss: The Tao of Management.*

"We're paying Waxwroth more than our football players to engineer a few buckets of Albino Banana Slugs. And do you know—do you have even the dimmest idea—what he's doing?" Lunelle surges forward in the chair, which crackles alarmingly deep in its architecture.

"Where the osprey stoops, there the fisherman baits his hook."

Lunelle cuts President York a sharp glance. "Slugs, Walden. We're talking about slugs here."

President York nods sagely. "I see."

"There had been unconfirmed sightings of Waxwroth in the classroom. Naturally, I was inclined to dismiss these reports, but I felt it my duty to check them out."

President York's upper intestinal tract unkinks one revolution. Whatever mischief Waxwroth is up to, it cannot have anything to do with teaching. Virtually nothing at the university does anymore.

"But sure enough, there he was down in the utility tunnel, blatantly lecturing some students—lecturing, mind you—with no student access to our Digital Online Tutorial System. He was just—" she barely suppresses a shudder—"talking. When I demanded that he explain himself, Professor Waxwroth said something smart-alecky about not being a philosopher, a psychologist, or a memoirista so that, incapable of accounting for himself, he was explaining mitochondria."

"The wise man is the foolishness of God."

"What?" Lunelle's dulcet tones ring out like a ship's horn signaling a breach below the waterline.

"I see," says President York.

"Walden, forgive me for saying so but I believe you need help. Frankly, I have believed this for some time. Let me arrange a consult with the university therapist." Should Walden wonk out, Lunelle fears that MegaMax might bring in a real president who could thwart her upward mobility like tin snips applied to her underwire Lily of Bulgaria.

President York—who recalls that the current university therapist specializes in aligning the body's polarity by coating the top of the head and soles of the feet with Vaseline and passing an electric current between the analysand and a brass, pyrite, and procrustean statue of the corporate paradigm, currently Vlad the Downsizer, who reduced the population of Transylvania while stoking the kingdom's coffers—pulls it together. "We'll appoint an ad hoc committee," he says decisively. "I must say I don't understand how we could have a football program the existence of which I was unaware. Controls must be established to prevent this sort of oversight. Imagine how our student-athletes must feel knowing that a professor is making more money than they. I simply won't stand for it."

Lunelle rises and edges towards the door. "Actually, Walden, we haven't had a football team in seventeen years. We're talking about annuities for players from the '80s and '90s."

"I see," says President York, anxious to press his advantage as Lunelle backs away. "I appreciate your candor. We're all in this together. I'll get back to you. Have Marsha schedule us next week. The plum's secret is the worm's—." President York claps a hand over his mouth but Lunelle is already beyond hearing, in the outer office tussling with Marsha, who has broken free from the office ficus to which Lunelle had bound her with red tape on her way in.

– XXXIV –

E. E. Everclear drifts reluctantly out of his reverie, brought round by an unprecedented outbreak of sunshine striking him flush on the toot of his adult beverage of choice, Everclear (motto: "The Official Drink of Controllers, Radarfolk, and Sundry Hangarpersons"). He has sweated through his nearly green polyester shirt, which is now fused to the back of his wooden chair. The smell of sweat, man-made fiber, and varnish—cheeselike and faintly fungal and, lacking only the tincture of Pine Sol, high school cafeteriaesque—has provided the olfactory bridge from reverie to duty.

E. E. relinquishes the misty recall of a blind date at his previous FAA posting with a woman who modeled plus sizes at Mucus Couture and Radiator (motto: "You'r Steamin' and W'ere Seamin'"). The complex bouquet of LaVerne—or was it Larue or Lanelle?—has magically wafted up here to docks even more boonish than Louisiana. And a good thing, E. E. thinks, providential, even, as he peers out the tower window and sees, as through a scrim of Vaseline, several pairs of approaching wings. No moving point of light appears on his radar screen, but E. E. registers scant surprise. According to the transfer manifest, his radar system has been passed down from O'Hare—where it routinely crashed during power fluctuations—to Austin—where it malfunctioned in high cedar pollen counts—to Billings—where it blanked out daily from boredom—to McKenzie Station, where its performance has ranged from mercurial to protean ever since E. E. toppled a snifter of Everclear down the console.

Raising the perceptual ante, E. E. takes another look out the tower window to see the approaching craft has multiplied—oh, Christ!—but veered—thank God!—into a holding pattern that does not remotely conform—oh, poo!—to FAA regulations concerning separation by altitude, airspeed, and heading, leading to the likelihood—oh, shitfuckscrew—of a Multiple Aircraft Incident: Main Event. E. E. tries heroically to raise the airships by radio, but he has shut off the system so as not to interrupt his nap and cannot just now recall how to turn it back on. He thinks to go out and wave them off like carrier pilots, but he cannot remember the correct flagging from *Hellcats of the Navy*. Bracing for the carnage to come, E. E. knocks back the last of an open bottle and focuses in with the tower's ConCo TurboVisioners ("For Use in Media-Intensive Emergency Only") on a fraternal circle of turkey vultures.

As the vultures laze downwind, E. E. considers the likelihood that he has indeed seen an aircraft, that the plane has crashed, and that the buzzards have gathered like a bosky lunch rush to feast on the remains. But the vultures drift on, catching a thermal and spiraling up. Bad for business, even if there isn't any, thinks E. E., chalking up his lucid reflection for the day. The gulls at Kennedy, the migratory waterfowl at Bismarck, and the pileated woodpeckers at Mucus clogged engines like gumbo and exploded against a fuselage like avicular kamikazes, yet passengers were oblivious unless, of course, the plane itself actually crashed. But vultures (an obituary, a dirge, a morgue, a threnody, a wake, a Buncombe?) circling a field was hard to put a positive spin on, even by the FAA, which has managed to convince millions of Americans to keep flying on turboprop Brazilian Malaires, veritable airborne rummage sales whose parts periodically fall off here and there in transit.

Truth be told, E. E. is a little deflated. There will be no incident, toward or untoward. There will be, he understands, no aircraft. The last flight he brought in (or hadn't, as the case may have been) was a Forest Service DC-3 returning three weeks ago from a Confederate Air Show in Impetigo, Mississippi. E. E., mistaking the flight for an apparition, had refused to respond to radio pleas for wind speed and direction and landing clearance. In his last weeks at Mucus, E. E. had been reprimanded by the tower supervisor for talking down phantom planes and he is determined to get off on the right foot at McKenzie, even if the only oversight is a bimonthly query from the regional FAA traffic center in Seattle confirming his pick in the office pool selecting the date by which air traffic controllers will surpass postal workers in the application of automatic weaponry to colleague and supervisor downsizing.

We may imagine, then, E. E.'s anxiety as a mechanical drone, as if from a committee heard through poorly taped and floated sheetrock, inserts itself into the afternoon. After scanning the room for insects and popping his temple sharply several times with an open palm, E. E. checks the radar. Sure enough, a wavering blip creeps onto the screen. Shifting the resolution to short range, E. E. picks up *Oprah* and then reruns of the semi-finals of the World Championship Tractor Pull from Bovine, Nebraska, before smacking the console on what he has always assumed to be the mechanical equivalent of its temple and bringing in an anomalous shape. At five thousnd meters, the shape dips to avoid, E. E. surmises, the holding pattern of vultures, but comes steadily on, dropping below the radar's sweep, whose lower range grazes the tops of the old-growth Doug fir. Rummaging through his laundry basket for a minimally unstained pair of briefs, E. E. buffs a clear spot in the tower window and looks west as a time warp from Kitty Hawk hauls into view slaloming out of the treetops.

But for the radar blip, E. E. would have chalked up the ultralight to the hallucinogenic properties of Everclear. For once, however, the screen and his eyes corroborate. Bearing down on the center of the runway, the ultralight cuts loose a cluster of canisters. Having eaten his way through trade school on macaroni and potted meat, E. E. recognizes at once the tins of Spam. As they hit the grass field, several of the tins seem to explode, raising dusty little eruptions of soil ranging in volume from a shovelful to a pitching wedge divot. Banking and climbing, the ultralight peels past the tower and E. E. can see the man at the helm, a Nipponese International Pilot who shoots E. E. the international digit.

No sooner does the ultralight vanish like Kris Kristofferson's certificate of airworthiness than the MegaMax Aerocommander barrels in for a landing, flaps down and engines reversed before E. E. can warn them about the bombing run. Sure enough, the Aerocommander catches one of the miniature craters, blowing a tire and skidding diagonally on collapsing landing gear, two more Spam bombs going off as the craft bellies over them.

When the dust settles, Mark Neighbors and the Herbert Walkers tumble off the plane and appear to kiss the ground in a gesture of papalesque homage. Closer examination through the ConCo TurboVisioners, however, clarifies the act as that of tossing not only themselves but their cookies. Wally and Tice saunter out as E. E. rushes onto the runway with a fire extinguisher and an emergency carton of Tums. Wally yards out a Colt .45, the likes of which E. E. has not seen since they dropped *Terry and the Pirates* from the comics page. For a moment, E. E. thinks he's going to put the Herbert Walkers out of their demonstrable misery, but instead Wally unlimbers on a Spam canister down the runway, detonating it with his fifth shot.

"God, Tice," he says, fingering his cobrahide belt, woven through what appear to be assorted shrunken ears, "I'll never forget the smell of Spam and saltpeter."

"Yeah," says Tice. "Reminds me of my third marriage."

– XXXV –

"Marta," Mark Neighbors says earnestly to Juggernaut as they stuff the last of the whimpering Herbert Walkers into the back of the Land Bruiser, "I must speak with you privately."

Juggernaut, still mulling her provisional future with MegaMax, having high-beamed the potential paradigm shift away from her dominatrix management style to that of a limp Johnson, takes in the tattletale off-yellow seepage at Mark Neighbor's crotch. Not so incontinent, she thinks, as the mewling pile of Herbert Walkers wedged in the Land Bruiser nattering on about the little episode with the Gulfstream. Not so incontinent, she supposes, may be the best a girl can hope for these days.

After offloading the Herbert Walkers at Rancho Rio, Juggernaut drives back upriver to the Pour House. As they near the bar, a silver Camaro accelerates out of the parking lot, a rooster tail of gravel in its wake. Smoking four tires and fishtailing in and out of both lanes, the Camaro catches traction at a speed shift to third and the driver pours it on, touching the brim of his Australian bush hat in salute as he peels past.

"Jesus," says Mark Neighbors, thankful he hasn't refilled his bladder since landing.

"Must be Sheila's new prospect," says Juggernaut, hoping Mark Neighbors hasn't refilled his bladder since landing.

Inside, Sheila Wallop drifts behind the bar in a gauzy daze. "I had no idea," she says dreamily, "that a super stock Camaro displaced 480 cubic inches and cranked 500 pounds of torque at 4,000 rpms. Well, you kids help yourselves; I need to tidy up." Sheila turns toward the office, not entirely disheveled but not exactly sheveled either, trailing a suspicion of erotic disarray as she wafts officeward, humming the chase theme from *The Dukes of Hazzard*.

Mark Neighbors and Juggernaut settle in, pour themselves drinks. Juggernaut hoists her glass in salute. "To MegaMax, stacks of jack, and the flat tax."

"Actually," says Mark Neighbors, rubbing manfully at his Hugo Boss stubble, "that's what I wanted to talk to you about."

Juggernaut considers and dismisses her slant rhyme and modified iambic as the topic at hand, settling on money instead. At 89 percent pre-sold, Rancho Rio has borne Juggernaut to the threshold of bonus. Enough, she hopes, to send Chuck Wepner to the Hazelton Clinic for the cure that, according to the website of Latex and Leather: No More Devices, has been so successful with J. Edgar Hoover, the Duchess of Cornwall, and Giancarlo Cardinal Fetishini, though less so with Lindsey Graham.

"How much?" Juggernaut asks, an involuntary quiver of the right breast belying her flat tone.

"Everything, I'm afraid."

Off balance, Juggernaut surreptitiously clasps her breast in both hands to still the quiver. *Everything*? Could her excellence have moved MegaMax to such largesse? Not likely. *I'm afraid*? That must be it. Bakersfield had recently engaged a Prussian Manager of Extraordinary Compensation. Herr Tschirt, who had studied economics at Heidelberg with Hegel's gardener's nephew, subscribed, she knew, to the historical inevitability of the dialectic and to cutting your nuts off occasionally to help you focus. Since Herr Tschirt's arrival, all bonuses have been subtracted from the salary of MegaMax employees assigned to the same enterprise. Her bonus has come out of Mark Neighbor's hide, and he is here to buy her an insincere but politic congratulatory drink, to get some tips, to float a loan to cover a margin call.

If MegaMax sees her as a comer, Juggernaut exalts, it doesn't matter whether Mark Neighbors is a comer or—the trouser stain reinserting itself—a goer. No need now to consider coupledom.

"So," says Juggernaut, stretching luxuriously, "let's talk about the numbers."

Mark Neighbor's loins fax a wake-up call to his Johnson as Juggernaut's 44s jut above the table. Heroically, he steers the hard facts past the enticing possibilities. "A complete scam. Rancho Rio is sitting on top of the largest geothermal field in North America. As soon as the MUD is approved, MegaMax taps the field and bye-bye, bucolic idyll. A geothermal power plant is pretty much a total insult to the senses—think Roseanne singing Christmas carols at a Wal-Mart in Anencephally, Alabama. Nobody who bought in, not even a Republican environmentalist, is going to find this very amusing. Somebody will have to take the hit for not pointing out the geothermal fine print to Riotarians. Guess who Bakersfield has in mind?"

"So," says Juggernaut, demurely retracting her bosom but shifting so that her torso stands out in profile against the bar's single window, "let's talk about us."

Past the panoramic foreground, Mark Neighbors can see through the window a derelict pickup, sagging to its springs under a load, headed downriver with Buckthorn at the wheel.

– XXXVI –

Returning upriver from an interdenominational prayer service for the West Springfield City Council, which had recently voted to convert to Shintoism if Suzuki put the city on their short list for shooting a commercial, Reverend Endwell passes Buckthorn's truck as it splays down the highway. The sight of the truck triggers in the reverend an associational spiral that corkscrews to Amanda Pennypacker and thence his Johnson, the invariable terminus these days of associations prompted by Chocolate Sugar-Frosted Marshmallow Bran, rain falling or not yet falling, the Book of Leviticus, etc.

Amanda has brought the not unexpected news that no virgin or near approximation thereof is to be found on the upper McKenzie save Amanda herself. While Amanda searches Ford Foundation guidelines bearing on *pro bono coitus*, Reverend Endwell promises to round up the requisite local shaman. Wrestling with his conscience, the reverend wins two out of three falls, leaving him free to make one-third of an honest effort to contact Tony Ten-Toes Jr. through a help wanted ad in the *Springfield Inquirer-Columbian*. Absent any response, the reverend prepares to make the ecumenical stretch. In the trunk of his car he carries selected items of shamanesque couture: Tonto, Dennis Rodman, and Miley Cyrus costumes rented from Easy Ed's Pawn and Appliance.

Ford Foundation policy, it turns out, fudges Amanda's query, leaving her free to donate her neo-virginity to the community. Amanda demurely but resolutely works out the details with Reverend Endwell over coffee and frozen yogurt in his living quarters (more properly his one-sixteenths, given the configuration of the doublewide).

"The actual, the actual, uh…"

"Event?" the reverend offers helpfully.

"Yes, the event. It will actually involve, the, uh, *actual*?" Amanda dandles her spoon in the sugar bowl.

"Qnxtqkl ritual would seem to require so. Of course, you should feel free to concentrate on the symbolic character of the act. The physiological is merely the apparatus by which we reach higher planes."

"Like Richard Gere."

A spasm of coughing overtakes the reverend. "Coffee went down the wrong pipe," he says, patting his throat. "So here's the arrangement. You must follow the instructions precisely. Any deviation and the ritual is kablooie."

"Well, I'm certainly not going to do anything deviant and I hope no else expects to either." Amanda punctuates her position with a dainty but emphatic snort.

The reverend scampers to reassure her. "The standard orifice and organ, missionary position, foreplay strictly limited to maneuvers described in the Explorer Scouts *Handbook*."

"Well," says Amanda wistfully, ever the good sport and not wishing to seem obstructionist, "I suppose a little something out of the ordinary would be okay."

"Oh, I'm sure there'll be a surprise or two—a *good* surprise," the reverend hastens to add.

"Speaking of surprises, a girl certainly doesn't want to come away from her first experience with a bun in the oven or one of those sexually transmitted diseases that used to be on the cover of *Time Magazine*. That would be just a major bummer."

"Not to worry," Reverend Endwell soothes. "I've been checked out—that is, I've checked out this shaman pretty thoroughly. I dare say," the reverend goes on expansively, "that I know him as well as I know myself. For instance, he's had a successful vasectomy and Qnxtqkl custom compels strict celibacy between ritual deflowerings. After each deflowering, the shaman's pric—that is, his dic—er, coc—his, well, thingamajig, is boiled in nettle oil for purification. As you may imagine, a shaman undertakes such an event only given the utmost necessity."

"Yikes," says Amanda, remembering her mother tonging hot dogs from a rolling boil. And that was only water. Amanda's maidenhead seems now a small sacrifice in comparison. "How did you find all this stuff out, anyway?"

"As it happens, our shaman once applied for credit at Easy Ed's Pawn and Appliance. Easy and I have an arrangement. I could tell you things about the shaman he doesn't know about himself."

A sudden thrumming on the roof from a passing downpour turns the doublewide into something like a clothes dryer with a load of marbles. The reverend elocutes above the din.

"So here's the deal. Thursday night, at 11:15 on the dot, come to room four—"—a clap of thunder is followed by a protracted burst of applause from the wild gray yonder—"—teen at the Inn and Out. You know the place—that *faux* Motel 6 on the right just past the mustache factory. The door will be unlocked. The lights will be off, but as a further caution you must put on the blindfold that will be hanging on the inside doorknob. If the defloweree catches sight of the shaman, her eyes must be plucked out by ravens. Likewise, the shaman cannot speak or his tongue will be fed by his former mother-in-law into a ConCo TurboPulper."

"There's a lot more to this shaman business than people let on. No wonder you don't run into them in your, like, daily or really even yearly life."

Amanda's fetching naïveté so inflames the reverend that his Johnson embarks on a yeasty rising, bulging his trousers at first, then poking the fabric up between his thighs after he crosses his legs. Reverend Endwell casts desperately about for something to lay in his lap, but his books, papers, and other impedimenta are across the room on his desk.

"Behold!" the reverend commands in his best Old Testament voice.

"What?"

The reverend faces a monumental choice: what, indeed, should she behold? His Johnson thrums along his thigh, straining against constraint.

"There." With a sweeping gesture the reverend indicates the window behind Amanda. As she turns to look, he scoops a handful of yogurt from his dish, tugs out the waist of his trousers and shorts while sucking in his stomach, and glops the slushy raspberry lo-cal on his rampant member.

"I'm afraid I don't—"

"Holy hollyhocks," says the reverend, puckering from the chill.

"Are you all right?"

"No," says the reverend. "An old affliction, I'm afraid. I must be alone with it."

Amanda, concerned, rises to leave. The reverend rises as well, stooping slightly to disguise the diminishing lump in his pants.

"I'll see you on the—that is, I'll see you to the door."

Amanda waves him back. "Please, I can find my way," as indeed she can. Three steps and she's out, repeating aloud as she walks to her car: "Thursday night, 11:15, the Inn and Out, room number four."

– XXXVII –

Carlos Castaneda scuffs pensively through the forest. The bombing run has thrown a scare into the Herbert Walkers, but MegaMax won't be caught napping again. Not long after the Spam surprise, Carlos spent a night in the Pour House disguised as J. D. Salinger. Wally and Tice came in to knock back a few and let it be known that the Gulfstream had been retrofitted with gear and armaments sufficient to make it a match for any Third World and several Second World air forces.

Clearly, another approach is called for. Something bold, certainly telegenic. Something to turn Rancho Rio into a public relations hairball that MegaMax finally would have to cough up.

Carlos's ruminations are interrupted by a notable tussle coming from a rhododendron thicket just ahead. From the sound of it, something has gotten snagged in one of C. C.'s booby traps. Carlos pushes cautiously into the thicket until he espies what appears to be a badly articulated scarecrow. Perhaps, he speculates, he's stumbled across C. C.'s R & D facility where he tries out new tactics to thwart his *bête noire*—more strictly, his *bête Pica pica*—some hippie's magpie who filches C. C.'s crop like a pro, flapping off with beakfuls of bud and leaf, leaving seed and stem behind.

A closer examination reveals the figure to be that of an actual man, thrashing about to little apparent effect as though his limbs were being manipulated by some schizophrenic puppeteer. Closer still, Carlos can see that the outdoorsman in question (outdoorsy given his L. L. Bean ensemble, from mukluks to Patagonian bush hat and pendant with turquoise and silver; in question given that he has managed to snag both arms and one leg on the sinewy and volute, not to say cochleate, limbs of at least one but possibly several rhododendri) is in something of a pickle, having somehow contrived to thrust the woody perennial up one sleeve of his

Filson; it exits at the collar, where it crosses another limb entering at the collar and traveling the length of the opposite sleeve. A third limb—no, a third and yet a fourth—have thrust up the right leg of his britches. Neither has yet emerged at the beltline, but either the outdoorsman finds a rhododendron assault erotic or at least one of the limbs appears to be probing alarmingly near the fellow's Johnson and related gear.

"So," says Carlos, transfixed by the improbable physics of the configuration, "what have we here?"

The thrashing figure wheezes to a stop, squinting Carlos into focus as he steps forward.

"Barry Buncombe."

"Carlos," says Carlos. "What brings you up this way?" he asks warily, the apparently global ineptitude before him leading Carlos to suspect Buncombe to be a federal agent of some sort.

"Actually, I'm more or less lost. Really don't get out much. No time for it. Mostly on tour."

"On tour?"

"Books. I write them. About all this." Buncombe essays an inclusive gesture with his right arm, driving another six inches of rhododendron above his collar line.

"All this?"

"Gaia, the wild kingdom. That sort of stuff. I'm a nature writer."

"Well, you've turned up in the right place. There's hardly anything but nature for miles in any direction."

"I know. Live here. Downriver, actually. Milepost 42?"

"That must be around the Santini Brothers equipment yard."

"Correct."

"Isn't that a lot of racket for a writer?"

"Can't say. Gone mostly. Believe my wife has complained of it."

"To Santini?"

"To me."

A breeze ruffles the rhododendron patch and Buncombe bobs on the limbs like a rookie sailor in medium chop. In fact, Buncombe is turning a little green at the gills.

"I suppose the highway noise drowns out a lot," Carlos concedes, "especially all the wrecks."

Buncombe's house, like an out-take from Hansel and Gretel, is far enough back from the highway to be smothered in dank firs but close enough and slightly uphill so that the road noise beats against it. A seductive straightaway lies in front of the house, terminated at either end by wicked S curves. Known to locals as the Icebox, this particular patch of road traverses a frost pocket and is often glazed with ice when the rest of the McKenzie highway is only wet. A logger bar in Springfield runs three yearly pools where you can bet on how many forest visitors will expire on the down-river curve, the upriver curve, or the combo. It occurs to Carlos that he would rather live in Forest Service housing—created by the same design team that produced the visitation rooms at federal penitentiaries, the Alan Greenspan 87-cent piece, and Bill Clinton's running shorts—than abide in the house of Buncombe.

"Study's around back. There mostly. Also play CDs while writing. Windham Hill recording of moss propagating. Really sets the mood."

"So lay a couple of your titles on me. I've been out of the reading loop lately."

"Not, in fact, read upriver. To my knowledge. More of a national author. Actually, international."

"I'm not really a local myself," says Carlos, "so you could slip me one of your international titles."

"I suppose."

"Sure, what harm could it do?"

"Well, then. *Arctic Swoon.*"

Somewhere above them, a nighthawk booms out of its plummet through the insect nations. Buncombe recoils violently, setting the rhododendron limbs and, perforce, himself, awobble.

"Was that a wolf?" Buncombe's greenish tinge blanches to a phobic hue.

"No," says Carlos. "That was a bird."

"Thank God," says Buncombe with some fervor, going green again as the rhodies continue to pitch him about. An unfortunate episode early in Buncombe's career as a nature writer had left him unstrung by so much as a picture of a wolf. In fact, photographs of wolves produced hysterical spasms in Buncombe. The very word, he decreed, was not to be uttered in his presence. He had been compelled to fire one of his researchers when it turned out that her middle name was Lupe, an altogether too evident mnemonic for *lupus*. Buncombe also sent cash (untraceable and therefore not jeopardizing his environmental *bona fides*) to Alaskan legislators who supported aerial hunts and to stockmen's associations opposed to the reintroduction of the timber wolf into the northern Rockies.

"*Arctic Swoon*. So you're a romance writer."

"Gosh, no. Way too much testosterone in those books. Ruination of nature, that stuff. Wolves full of it, even the females."

"So what is it, then?"

"Barry Buncombe's meditation on man's place in the natural world, up northish."

"Barry Buncombe. That's you, right?"

Buncombe looks confused. "Of course."

"I mean, you just talked about yourself as somebody else."

"Chronic modesty. First person a big no-no."

Carlos assumes what he assumes to be a coy expression, the subtlety of which is largely lost on the bobbing and weaving Buncombe. "I know a little something myself about laying low as an author."

"Award for it, in fact. The Walden Puddle Prize. For self-effacing sensitivity at greater than ordinary length. Committee singled out my conversion of first-person singular to second-person rural."

"Can you make money off that stuff?"

"The books, actually, no. But they set up the collaterals."

"Collaterals?"

"College circuit is big. Schools converting their women's studies programs to environmental science. Long-term deal with MegaMulch. My remaindered books recycled as organic garden material. Personal appearances, of course. Here and there: annual Ozonefest in Zodiac, Colorado; ribbon-cuttings at new franchises of ConCo TurboTours. That sort of thing. Also consultant on several Hollywood projects. In turnaround, as we say. Great green name, you know. Think about it: holly wood."

Carlos thinks about it and recalls a doubleheader at a club in

Juárez featuring Holly Wood and Candy Barr. He'd had to haul Don Juan down off the stage just ahead of the steamed-up donkey who was not being a good sport about the prospect of a foursome.

"—and product endorsements." Buncombe apparently is still speaking. "A major revenue stream. Plucking the heron, as we say in the nature biz. Most recently a four-figure deal with MicroSponge for software that biodegrades after ninety days. Love the slogan: 'MicroSponge Words: Writ on the Wind.' Use it for all my books."

By now, Carlos has grown queasy watching Buncombe pitch about. Seizing the man by his ears to steady him, then bending Barry in turn this way and that so as to extract the deviously articulated rhododendron branches, Carlos frees Buncombe from his arboreal entrapment.

"I was wondering," says Carlos, maneuvering a last stem past Buncombe's cuff line, "how you ever managed this." He releases the stem, which springs back into ambush like a hooded cobra.

Buncombe stumbles about, trying to get his land legs under him. "Don't get out much into the tall timber. Buncombe mostly a home boy. Though we do love to frolic in the McKenzie in our hazmat suit in the moonlight, listening to the thrum of migratory catfish whiskers."

"Hazmat suit?"

"Gosh, yes. McKenzie full of arsenic or asbestos or transfats. Comes from the lava, upstreamishwise from here. Suit also handy in foreign travels. World full of germs, actually."

"So how do you get the rich effluvia of nature's outthereness into your books all suited up like that?"

"Field personnel. Hire them for research. Also PBS specials and the Discovery Channel. Plus collection of *Boy's Life*. All the way back to Baden-Powell. Great stuff there. Maybe a little heavy on self-reliance and the practical. My readers prefer the collaborative and metaphysical; doesn't take much of a twist. Also make up a fair amount."

Carlos's stomach rumbles as Hiro's Spam Stir-Fry drops a notch lower, working its way south to a rendezvous with Carlos's intestinal tract.

"Was that a wolf?" Buncombe plucks at Carlos's sleeve, eyes swiveling wildly.

"No," says Carlos. "That was potted meat product."

Further conversation reveals Carlos's own literary history and current circumstances. As it happens, Buncombe has recently lost his publicist, who was hired away by Larry Lopez, Buncombe's bitter rival in the nature writing biz, who had landed a ten-book deal with Chrysler Corporation for a series on four-wheel wilderness adventures promoting the Jeep Ground Pounder in conjunction with Chrysler's "Tread Widely and Shift with a Big Stick" campaign. Carlos agrees to think about signing on to represent Buncombe. On the spot, he sketches out a campaign where Buncombe's Native American ancestry is discovered, blunting Lopez's multicultural edge and enabling Buncombe to be repackaged as a shaman. Alternatively, they could go the Anglo-Celtic route, reconstructing his Druidic origins and marketing him as a wizard of the ecult. In either case working in mention of Corn Goddesses, etc. to touch base with Buncombe's female readership and emphasizing Darwinian species rightsizing to position Buncombe for corporate tie-ins.

To sweeten the pitch, Carlos googles "nature writers" in the latest census figures to discover that they now outnumber memoiristas, romance novelists, and cookbook authors. Noodling with the categories, Carlos turns up Dick Crass, a fusionist whose 137th book, *Yaakety Yaak: Table Talks with Really Famous Writers*, a nature writing/gastronomy undertaking, had rocketed up to 4,648,233 on Amazon, narrowly edging out *Grooming Tips* by Rudy Guiliani. Carlos sketches out for Buncombe the dazzling prospect of his own nature writing/motor vehicle fusion project: *ROADKILL: Critters in the Soundless EV Future.*

Buncombe is smitten. How could this gentleman know that whenever Buncombe traveled by private conveyance, he brought copies of his books so that if he came across roadkill he could stop to track down a grieving relative who might want to purchase a personally inscribed tribute to their recently smooshed?

"How could you know this? Did you have to swerve to miss me?"

"Certain kinds of folks I can read pretty well. I figured this was right up your alley."

The afternoon darkens as a second layer of clouds—known to Oregonians as the undercast—slides in beneath the upper gray. Carlos sets out for the trail that will lead Buncombe back to his car. Scarcely have they trucked a few hundred feet before Buncombe, huffing heavily, sags against a tree trunk for a breather.

"Whew. Tough. Not so hard coming in. Can't figure."

"Well," says Carlos, "we *are* walking uphill."

"Uphill. Right. Must be it. Really don't get out much. Uphill, you say?"

Carlos sets out again and Buncombe struggles to follow, tugging himself free with some difficulty from the tree where his L. L. Bean chamois shirt has stuck to an oozing pitch pocket.

– XXXVIII –

The Fell Faller fouls off two Scenic Byway signs before uprooting a third with a mighty whack as he swerves down the highway in his Jimmy six pack. The Fell Faller is not a happy lumberjack. Chip had arranged a secret meeting with his Moby Fir source. The source, insisting on strict anonymity, exchanged a map for half of a torn thousand-dollar bill. Chip handled the swap, money and map coming and going through an imperfectly patched hole Juggernaut had punched through the outside wall into the Houdini-sized stall of the men's restroom at the Pour House during the brawl fueled by her first Around-the-World.

As it turned out, the tree in question was a doddering cottonwood, oversized largely because of an accumulation of decades of conky fungi circling its trunk. Few think to trifle with the Fell Faller, who is thus inclined to attribute the foul-up to a magnitude of arboreal incompetence found chiefly among agents of the Forest Service. Which lightens his mood not a fraction, though clear-cutting ten acres adjacent to the cottonwood levels him out enough to drive away with some sense of equity.

Back at the Inn and Out, it develops that the owner—who has locked up for the afternoon while he drives in to Springfield to buy bathmats and bedding from a nursing home shut down by the Department of Health—has rented out what until 11:00 a.m. that day had been the Fell Faller's room. Having checked out to make short work of Moby Fir, the Fell Faller now needs to check back in to make short work of Chip's explanation. Novice shadows—gathering like bashful nieces as the sun blows through town like a bachelor uncle headed elsewhere—creep over the Jimmy, where the Fell Faller sips at his flask, then dozes, waiting for Mr. Patel to turn up. Mr. Patel, alas, has been caught up in Springfield's new Synchronized Online System, a real-time traffic control program for the municipality's seven stoplights. The system, of course, is hackable from Royal portable typewriters in the Ned Lud Middle School Business Communications classroom, locking down all traffic for hours at a time.

What turns up instead is night, which the Fell Faller wakes to, crabby and disinclined to spend in the cab of his truck. Scratching in all the requisite places, the Fell Faller scans the lot. Several cars are scattered throughout, none near his old room. Scrunching across the gravel the Fell Faller grasps the knob of number fourteen, intending to pull the entire assembly out. The knob, however, yields at his touch and the door falls open. Unable to get the light to work, the Fell Faller decides against a shower, peels his clothes into a heap, and launches himself into bed, from which the voice dearest to his heart exclaims, "Holy hollyhocks!"

Meanwhile, back at room number four, Amanda timorously nudges open the door, holding a variety pack of Trojans demurely behind her back.

Half visible in the bathroom, a man is applying a ConCo Turbo-Blaster to his several hairs.

"Goddamit, Everline, just because they pitched me out of the Senate doesn't mean you can barge right in without knocking."

As Amanda stumbles back in confusion, Chuck Wepner blazes past, nabbing the Trojans like a conductor snatching the mail sack as the night train sparks through.

– XXXIX –

Having offloaded the plastic explosive and stuffed some of his drill holes, Buckthorn calls it a day and shambles on up to the Pour House, where Sheila and Devaney are propped on opposite sides of the bar.

"Lookee here," says Devaney, "the tie-breaker just walked in. Now I ask you, Harley, if you were to open a weight control spa, would it be The Last Resort or Fat Chance?"

Buckthorn looks to Sheila, who continues to buff her nails. "He's got it in his head that he's going to win this contest in *Entrepreneur* for naming a new business. I think—"

"Now, don't be influencing the boy. He's—"

"—that a man who has some serious competition for a lady's favor just might pay some attention to what *she* wants to talk about instead of nattering on about some cockamamie scheme."

Devaney hitches one eyebrow, then the other. "Cockamamie. Sure, that's it. Cockamamie Calories. Now that would grab your attention."

"Uh, Mr. Devaney, I don't think that's exactly what Sheila had in mind. I mean, about conversation."

"Well, I've never been much of a talker, that's for sure. You folks just go on ahead with it and I'll just sort of tag along."

Sheila holds her nails out for inspection, then raps one smartly against the rim of Devaney's glass. "Not that you're much of a doer, either. I've had better talks with my philodendron; more action too, come to think of it."

Devaney offers a one-and-a-half-shoulder shrug.

"That's *exactly* what I'm talking about."

"Come on, guys." Buckthorn makes a surprisingly adept conciliatory waggle of his hand.

"Not till I hear one—mind you, *one*—interesting string of words out of his mouth. Either that or he makes good on his promise to ravish me before the week is out."

"Whoa," says Devaney with real alarm.

"Gotcha."

"I don't know what's got into her."

Sheila leans towards Buckthorn and stage whispers, "Beau Zipp."

Buckthorn adds a second hand and both elbows to the conciliatory waggle. "Guys, come on."

Devaney registers Sheila's whisper with his signature tweedy snuffle. "Just to keep the peace, here's something. This morning a guy comes in and wants to buy some Cajones with 39/64ths of a thousand dollar bill."

"Cajones," says Sheila. "Now we're getting somewhere."

"A new finger food from Frito Lay. Aimed principally at the Hispanic market, I believe; produced by the Frito de Dolores Division."

"39/64ths?" queries Buckthorn.

"Exactly," says Devaney. "As if I didn't know that the Department of the Treasury requires no less than 5/8ths of a bill for redemption."

"Exactly what I'm talking about," says Sheila. "Here we've got balls and bucks and a mystery man and what do we end up with?—fractoids."

"Fractions," says Devaney.

"Aarrugh," says Sheila.

"So who was the guy?"

"Well, Harley, I'd never laid eyes on him, to my knowledge. But given the mode of dress, the rhapsodic though derivative engagement with my dried floral arrangement depicting the Treaty of Ghent, and his difficulty in finding his way back to his car, I'd venture to say that he was some kind of nature writer."

Just then the door to the Pour House flies open and through it strides Reverend Endwell. Sheila brays in triumph. After years of carnal challenge on her portable sign, she had snuck in a quasi-literary dig: "RUM DOES MORE THAN REVELATION CAN / TO JUSTIFY GOD'S WAYS TO MAN." It had, apparently, turned the trick.

Walking purposefully to the bar, nodding distractedly in response to Devaney's and Buckthorn's greetings, Reverend Endwell places both hands flush on the burnished wood.

"Whiskey," he says in a voice whose tone is just a shade off that of Moses calling for schnapps at the Sinai Roadhouse.

Sheila carefully pours a shot of Old Funerary, ready for trouble. Reverend Endwell knocks it back, makes an electric gargling noise that begins high in his throat, trailing off down his gullet.

"Another." The drink and electric gargle repeat.

The reverend nods again to Devaney and Buckthorn, rises, and strides with a purposeful wobble out the door.

– XL –

Walloped by the future, Juggernaut toys with the past to avoid the present. She thinks of Chuck Wepner as a lad, gnawing fetchingly on furniture, houseplants, and boyfriends, a Norman Rockwell puppyhood with no hint of the dark obsession to come. To prolong the memory she decides on a gambol through the property and calls for Chuck, who bounds into the room with an enthusiastic if muffled woof, flashing what appears to be either a canine dental device or a condom ensnared in his teeth. Before Juggernaut can snatch it out, Chuck swallows hard and pants openmouthed, albeit with telltale latex breath.

"Oh, Chuckster, will we ever have the money for Hazelton?"

"Ralph," says Chuck, mustering up a bark that most nearly covers his rolling belch.

"And I love you too, Chuckums. We loves him gigabunches."

Chuck knows what comes next and flops on his back for the belly rub, hoping he hasn't picked up any tummy tread marks while sprawled on the highway licking up panic skids at either end of the Icebox.

Their amble takes them along Naughty Girl Creek, which meanders through Rancho Rio before flowing into the McKenzie at the property's eastern boundary. Chuck Wepner trolls hopefully for scraps of inner tubes or hip waders of clumsy fishermen come to grief. Marta idly juggles a noggin-sized stone from tit to tit as she strolls along, straining the high-tech machinery in her bra by MegaMams, the corporate lingerie division. Ahead, in a minor backwater, a glistening white glob catches her eye. Chuck's too. Who hurls himself headlong into what streamside had surely seemed the legendary White Rubber Glob of Qnxtqkl lore. It turns out otherwise. As Chuck discovers, scrambling out of the water trying to shake free segments of glob that have attached to his lips, nose, nuts, Johnson, and general fur with some kind of mucosal adhesion. Rushing up, Marta tries to flick one off, but the glob latches onto Juggernaut like snot moving from one finger to another. After a brief but disgusting tussle, Juggernaut manages to scrape off most of the goop with bark and scour the residue with handfuls of duff.

In the creek, the parent glob has reformed, pulsing in the current. Looking closer, Juggernaut can almost make out what seem to be melting configurations in the transcendental goo, shapes dissolving into shapelessness. Bringing to mind the Herbert Walkers. And then something else, as the stream delivers into the backwater a thing made of the glob's plasmodic soup, held tenuously intact by a glutinous membrane. It is, beyond quibble, an Albino Banana Slug. The slug eddies into the phlegmy pod, oozing away until it becomes indistinct in the general swillage.

Juggernaut shudders in disgust. And shudders again to the not unorgasmic contraction of fiscal advantage. Somewhere upstream lies the slug source. Found, it offers Juggernaut leverage to float a golden—even a platinum—yacht from MegaMax in which to cruise off ahead of the McKenzie's geothermal douche. Marta twirls in glee, lopping the tops off several saplings as her jugs, exceeding the MegaMams' centrifugal force capacity, fly out of control. Chuck joins in the celebration, leaping up to plant an immoderate smooch, leaving behind a smear of saliva and slug dissolve that Juggernaut wipes away with her sleeve, swiping it carelessly across her lips where a reflexive tonguing registers the flavor of Spam teriyaki.

Juggernaut turns thoughtfully towards home, while on the upper reaches of Naughty Girl Creek Hiro Ishimatsu wades his rice paddy, shaking drops of soy sauce on the backs of grazing Albino Banana Slugs. The slugs, writhing and melting in the briny solution, hump themselves from paddy to creek, whose icy waters retard but do not arrest their salt-soaked transmogrification.

– XLI –

Long ago and far away, President York reminds himself, he had escaped the embrace of one whose institutional ball busting was to Lunelle's scrotum strum what Godzilla was to Tinker Bell. Of course, he had been more agile in those days, shrewder too, truth be told.

Hulga Hamhocks chaired the department at his first teaching position, a state college with not one (caution) nor two (red alert) but three (academic meltdown) directions of the compass in its name: Southwest Central State University. The chair was a strapping six-footer with gray hair going orange and the calves of a piano mover. Hulga exuded the forthrightness and bulky good cheer of a major kitchen appliance. She was, President York remembers, everything you'd ever want in a man.

Looking at her you thought big. And slumpage. Though not her breasts. Big, that is. Certainly slumpage. And frump. Dress and hairstyle out of a 1950s ad in *Parade* for orthopedic inserts. Except sometimes spookily just off-frump. Sometimes Hulga resembled a cross-dresser, Camilla Parker Bowles as turned out by Fredericks of Waco. Clattering down the hall in her low heels, listing as though badly stacked, a maniacal whinny the only hint of her true insanity, Hulga Hamhocks bestrode the department like a panzer.

The faculty spoke of her among themselves as Der Warden. Perhaps it was the automatic closing doors with reverse peepholes installed in faculty offices and the loop of keys worn on her belt or bulging from her clutch. There was also the penal-gray Mercedes she drove. The two most junior of the faculty were expected to arrive each day early enough to bracket the chair's designated parking spot with their own cars to prevent door dings.

At weekly faculty meetings, attended by her Minions—the Coordinator of Academic Technology, who replaced bulbs in the overhead projectors, ramrodded purchase orders for exotic new decantations of duplicating fluid, and had written a grant co-funded by the Goldberg Foundation and General Entropic that provided electric page-turners for all freshman texts; the Coordinator of Resuscitative Studies who, having once read the introduction to Aristotle's *Soporifics* while himself a freshman at St. Mediocretus, now patrolled the remedial curriculum, ensuring that all instructors administered similar tonics; and the Coordinator of Coordination, who was chiefly noted for developing an interdisciplinary course in Medieval Eastern Civilization and Kinesiology: "Movers and Shakers of Pretty Old Oriental History" and for stuttering for days after closed-door meetings with the chair (they must have had names but President York can no longer recall them; collectively, they were known as Sucks R Us)—Hulga would often touch up her rouge as the Minions groomed their achievements for the edification of their colleagues. The meetings closed with the two most senior members present leading faculty in singing the departmental alma mater, "Sixteen Tons," while a male professor selected at random engaged in a frisky little interlude with Hulga modeled on Pin the Tail on the Donkey: the Lorena and Dwayne Bobbitt Game.

Though President York had made good his breakout to a university that solicited students with ads on matchbooks, he had seen Southwest Central colleagues' careers rendered into bars of soap and lampshades. Those who survived spoke obliquely of certain devices strapped in leather cases in Hulga's office closet. So far as President York had been able to ascertain, Hulga's position was apparently firmly secured as a result of a long-standing ambiguous relationship with a local funeral director who served as a university regent.

No, Lunelle is no Hulga Hamhocks, but President York knows he cannot afford complacence, especially with Bakersfield in the mix. He must find a way to diffuse her concerns lest the cucumber she has detected in his presidency turn into a full-fledged pickle.

President York resolves to divert Lunelle by widening her sphere of power, assigning her the responsibility of chairing a working group to review the university's three-thousand-page policy manual on the heraldic display and licensing of the university colors, currently beige and gray with rust highlights.

– XLII –

For some weeks following her discovery of the Albino Banana Slugs, Juggernaut has thrashed her way up Naughty Girl Creek seeking their source, pounding a path through the streamside entanglements with her breasts. Now, bruised (despite strapping on the cast aluminum Demi Moores she purchased by mail from Fredericks of Renton, a franchisee that specialized in custom work on the nose cones of Boeing 767s) and slugless, Juggernaut turns reluctantly to Mark Neighbors, proposing a limited (not-to-exceed-the-lifespan-of-a-subatomic-particle-only-three-physicists-believe-exists) partnership to turn up the slug source.

"Here's the deal," says Juggernaut, crafting a plan that would require Mark Neighbors to risk all appendages save one. "We find the slugs and you swap them to MegaMax for a cash-out of my 4 percent of Rancho Rio, which I have transferred *tempus bogus* to your intestate father. You invest these proceeds in an IRS futures contract you take out on my 2018 tax return. By way of backside, we hedge the contract with a lose-lose Chapter 7 real estate derivative, a Haynes Asset Portfolio: Leveraged Extrapolation of Slum Stuff, modeled of course on the classic Scamford Stables sale of partial interest in a three-legged Thoroughbred, Due Diligence, to white-collar parolees with a taste for irony so that they could check in with their parole officer from the stables and assert that they were presently exercising Due Diligence. Then you sell the whole sordid Rancho Rio story to Semi-Tumescent Copy, Eyeclueless News' investigative public interest program. The Eyeclueless payment is made to my unnumbered account in Santo Madoff while you transfer your liquid assets into my stateside accounts, the interest from which I declare on my 1066Q, letting me sell short my IRS futures contract and picking up, needless to say, a sweet bundle." Juggernaut shivers with the erotic stirrings of a new business plan.

"Needless to say," says Mark Neighbors, flinching as fourteen of his seventeen fiscal neurons short out.

"Of course," Juggernaut adds sympathetically, "there's some risk to you—death, jail, confiscation of your collection of scratch and sniff sports cards."

"There it goes! There it goes!" Mark Neighbors ejaculates.

"What?" Juggernaut queries, fearing stress-induced hallucinatory redundancy.

"My last appendage."

"I believe I read that poem in college. Browning, wasn't it?"

For weeks, Mark Neighbors and Juggernaut push up Naughty Girl Creek deep into the Three Sisters Wilderness through vine maple and alder thickets, devil's club and rhododendron thickets, cedar and fir thickets, Oregon grape and Arkansas gropeweed thickets and finally even beyond a dam site proposed by the Corps of Engineers (motto: "A River Runs: Screw It") at a point where the annual flow of Naughty Girl averages 103 cfs. From time to time, a swirling scrum of slugs eddies past, offering renewed promise of the slug lode somewhere upstream.

Clumsy but willing, Mark Neighbors batters forward gamely, flagging from time to time but lunging on as Chuck Wepner sinks his canines into Mark's Florsheim vibrams whenever the pace slackens. Still, it is fiendishly, even federally, slow going. Despite her resolve, best instincts, amatory history, and OuijaWorks query, Juggernaut finds herself strangely moved by Mark Neighbors's mewling every time something goes awry: say he gets poked in the eye with a sharp stick or Chuck's nip lands a little north of his Florsheims or he cannot recall whether his father's deathbed advice was to avoid the jug at all costs or that a jug in the hand was worth two in the bra. Since he fully expects MegaMax, the IRS, the SEC, the McKenzie *polis* and/or his old fraternity to catch him out and do him in, he supposes all his travail to be utterly irrelevant, which sets off a fresh round of mewling, prompting a sharper motivational nip from Chuck Wepner.

Late one afternoon Juggernaut has lagged behind to tinkle while Mark Neighbors forges ahead under Chuck's watchful eye. Juggernaut is arrested mid-squat by inarticulate shouts and barks indicating that the clumsy chump and cunningly entrapped dog are dangling upside down from some sort of snare. As indeed they are when Juggernaut arrives, herself now, too, under the appraising shotgun of C. C. Fellows.

"The Code of Cannabis requires that I give you thirty seconds to convince me not to cash in your chips," says C. C. as Chuck Wepner makes eyes at the rubber butt plate of the Browning. "But seeing as how you are all operatives of the Evil Empire, I believe I could make a twenty-five-second exception."

"That's terrific," says Mark Neighbors, his enthusiastic tone, reserved heretofore for reports to Bakersfield and finding an extra piece of bubblegum in a scratch and sniff sports card, emerging upside down and loopy, striking everyone's ear as if a 78 record were played backwards at 33 rpms. "Fifty-five seconds."

Whatever fractional compunction C. C. may have felt is washed away in the tidal stupidity before, above, and a little to the left of him. He will at once safeguard his crop and advance the human genome. Overhead, a magpie flaps providentially past with something in its beak and C. C. unlimbers both barrels skyward, bringing down a shower of needles but no bird. "Oops," says C. C., patting his pockets for extra shells.

Whereupon Juggernaut steps forward, swipes the gun from his grasp with a slick Maraca move, and then, clasping the barrel between her breasts, bends the Damascus steel obliquely.

"Bet you can't do acute," says C. C., stalling for time.

Juggernaut inhales deeply, her breasts shifting like tectonic plates. Between them, the barrel folds again like the Seattle Mariners two weeks into the season.

"I don't suppose I could interest you in a position, uh, partnership, uh, tell the truth I was fixing to retire and been looking for someone to hand the whole shebang over to?"

"What I'm interested in," says Juggernaut, "is Albino Banana Slugs."

"You mean them damn gastropods that been working over Hiro's rice paddy?"

"That wouldn't be Hiro Ishimatsu of the legendary Gang of Five?" The foreplay of a new plan sets Juggernaut aquiver.

"So," says C. C. in shrewd appraisal, his years of pedaling oregano to garage bands in the Dakotas looking for killer pot turning to current advantage, "maybe we could do a little deal after all." Instantly, he finds his neck snugged uncomfortably between Juggernaut's breasts.

"I don't expect," says Juggernaut, "that we have anything like Damascus steel here." She gives C. C. a playful little flex, sending him into spasms of coughing. Juggernaut fixes on C. C. what, if she were old, male, and bald, could be characterized as a Jack Nicholson smile and unflexes.

"Two and one-third miles upstream, left at the beaver dam bearing 281°, eighty-seven baby steps plus fourteen giant steps and you'll bump smack into the 'Gangs R Us No Girls Allowed' sign."

"Since you know the way," says Juggernaut, "I'm sure you won't mind tagging along."

"Yes, I mean no, I mean—"

"Good, then we're all in agreement." Juggernaut turns her attention to the thrashing pair suspended behind her. Having set his rope aswing, Chuck Wepner has managed to pendulum over to Mark Neighbors where he has gnawed the heel off one Florsheim and is making considerable headway on the second.

– XLIII –

For Reverend Endwell, partway through a family heirloom recipe for stewed *pescado* when the power goes out, courtesy of the local electrical cooperative, McKenzie Up-River Kilowatts (motto: "If You Wanted Reliable Service, You Shouldn't Have Moved to the Country"), it is truly a dark night of the sole. Making a grim meal of the raw though soggy fish, he considers his predicament. The episode at the Inn and Out with the mysterious stranger was not the sort of sexual dalliance congregations had come to expect of their pastors. No, this was something far beyond the routine ecclesiastical grope, fondle, boink, slather, and toe suck. For one thing, there was the question of gender—that is, not one of each. For another, there was the pitty-pat of his heart whenever he recollected the smallest particular of the stranger. The hard fact was that the most his heart had been able to muster for Amanda was a pitty-pitty, though his Johnson had lobbied mightily otherwise.

From his desk drawer, Reverend Endwell withdraws the silk scarf the stranger had thrust to his bosom in the pitch black as he left the room. He inhales deeply, savoring the aroma of Armani and saw gas. The Free Will Apostolics had made their denominational position pretty clear some years previous when they excommunicated John Wayne on the grounds that a best boy was right there in the screen credits of his movie *He Wore a Yellow Ribbon*. Reverend Endwell resolves to check out the Metropolitan Community Church and the Episcopalians.

Not to be imagined, Reverend Endwell imagines, is the possibility that the stranger, whose body he knows better than Leviticus but whose face he has never seen nor voice heard, passes by unacknowledged in daily intercourse up and down the river. Or worse, has moved on to more convivial environs such as Coos Bay, often characterized as the San Francisco of Oregon. Worse yet, that the one and a half encounters (the reverend, dazed on nitrous oxide, is fuzzy about 50 percent of the details surrounding the hickey at the McKenzie Fair) have left the stranger with no available means of identifying him except in the dark. Since he can't exactly run a personals ad in *Magic Moments on the McKenzie,* Reverend Endwell hits on the happy expedient of his portable sign. Laboring through the night over Holy Writ and circumstantial nuance, wondering in passing why the furnace room of the doublewide smells increasingly like his freshman dorm at Brown, he crafts the message that appears the next day: "WHOsoeveR laYeth with his Own kind shall sUck saw gas."

For his part, besotted though he is, the Fell Faller hardly dares hope that the fickle knuckle of fate has punched the reverend's name next to his own in the Book of Love. True, by the end of the evening the reverend had been an enthusiastic, even inventive partner (who would have thought the Gideons could be put to such good use). And he had taken the scarf. Too, there were precedents for a relationship between a man of breeding such as the reverend and a rough tradesman such as himself. Sustained by these tokens, the Fell Faller resolves to focus on Moby Fir, taking *Dear Ellen*'s advice that love happens sometimes when you're just rummaging around in your closet, being, in this instance, the woods.

– XLIV –

Sheila is gazing dreamily at an article in *Mature Bride*, "Incontinence at the Altar: How to Tell—What to Do," when Devaney walks in, checking, as always, to be certain that the door has latched firmly behind him. What had once seemed to Sheila charmingly attentive now strikes her as an exact for-instance of Devaney's anality, not to say constipation. But no matter. Let him calculate the total squares of toilet paper he unscrolls, factoring five for the primary wipe and three for the follow-up (ts = [5 + 3] × hs where hs equals the hardness of the stool). Sheila is moving on.

Bestirring herself to mix Devaney his usual, the Geezer (Ovaltine with a splash of prune rum), Sheila slides it across the bar along with a blurry photo of someone in racing gear landing a looping right to the nose of someone who might have been Beau Zipp. "A. J. Foyt," says Sheila proudly, tapping the pugilist. "Last year on the Senior Circuit after Beau squeezed him into the wall on Turn Three in the Prostate 200."

Devaney examines the photograph, which looks as though it had been carried for some time in the wallet of someone who exerted more than the usual pounds per square inch on his patootie. "This is only a rough estimate, mind you, but statistically the incidence of y as the penultimate letter of a surname is, to be perfectly frank, so rare as to be anomalous. I can well understand the exquisite thrill such an artifact must provide."

"If you understood as much as one phoneme about exquisite thrills, I might be assembling my trousseau for you-know-who instead of for the Paul Newman of the Senior Circuit."

"Now that you mention it, I don't recall seeing Mr. Zipp recently."

"That's because you haven't," Sheila says, doodling away on a bar napkin. "He's off qualifying for the Myrtle Point 87."

“Didn’t someone say that he had managed to do irreparable harm to a critical component of his engine?”

“Which is why I sold that little patch to MegaMax at twice what it’s worth. We dropped a new Robert Yates Aurora into the Camaro and laid in two back-ups. You might as well know that I’ll be joining Beau on the circuit as soon as he’s broken the new engine in. Unlike some, Beau finds me too much of a distraction when he’s involved in all that technical whatnot of setting the car up.”

From his side of the bar, Devaney can see that Sheila’s doodles resemble upside-down Johnsons. “I gather, then, that MegaMax now controls the entire Rancho Rio parcel except for Harley’s little holding.”

“Whatever,” says Sheila, beginning to doodle what resemble upside-down circles.

Although not ordinarily subject to something as whimsically unquantifiable as misgivings, Devaney reconsiders the letter that arrived only this morning for Buckthorn. Devaney is pretty sure that the IRS doesn’t send out tax refunds by registered mail. If Rancho Rio goes forward, a MegaMaxMart on the property will pretty conclusively cook his goose. He’d read in *Entrepreneur* how a general store in Turgid, Louisiana, owned by the same family since 1817 and serving a parish where 93 percent of the residents were related was run out of business in three weeks when they couldn’t compete with a new MegaMaxMart run by a native of Toe Jam, New Jersey, on the price of okra meringue pie, deep-fried earthworms, and copies of Heisenberg’s *Uncertainty Principle* translated into the native tongue, *Merde Happens*.

Troubled, Devaney returns to the store, where Buckthorn has just picked up his mail and is opening the IRS letter as if the return address read T. Kuzcinski, Mutant Springs, Montana.

“Yessss!” cries Buckthorn, jigging around the store in what even Devaney recognizes as clumsy stepping, even taking into account the dominant Anglo-Saxon dufus gene. “Missed me again.” He thrusts the letter at Devaney, who reads thoughtfully.

“Right there,” says Buckthorn, jabbing his finger at the salutation on official stationery the vague gray of a bachelor’s undies. “*Harvey* Buckthorn. They got the wrong tax evader.”

"Let's see," says Devaney. "They got your address."

"Right."

"Your Social Security number?"

"Right."

"The two thousand, six hundred, and seventy-eight dollars and forty-seven cents paid by WalArt for seventeen of your sculptures—"

"I only shipped sixteen; they never noticed."

"—none of which appeared on your 2014 federal return?"

"That must have been the year I had Stanley's brother file my taxes."

"I'm not an accountant," says Devaney, "but I believe the applicable professional phrase here is 'deep doo-doo.'" Devaney reads on to discover that in fulfilling its pledge to Congress to become a more user-friendly operation, the IRS now conducts audits without involving the taxpayer since these proceedings had been consistently fingered in exit surveys as traumatic. Similarly, the IRS was sparing Buckthorn the embarrassment of a public auction of his known assets. As these assets consisted exclusively of real estate, the IRS had solicited bids from all contiguous property owners, that is, MegaMax/Estates at Rancho Rio, which had offered $1 more than the taxes, plus interest, plus penalties. Buckthorn was free to bid against MegaMax, but Section 139¶28.27[73]609±π4286-6b≥c{lx}1/8 of the Tax Code stipulated that if he tendered an offer he would be charged with the felonious application of encumbered funds—that is, money the Feds would seize if he had any of it.

"Crimenentlies," says Buckthorn, reverting at moments of crisis to the linguistic comfort of his grandma's lap.

"Well, no use shutting the barn door after the milk's been spilt," says Devaney consolingly. "Let's catch some sports."

Devaney punches up ESPN7, which not coincidentally is broadcasting the award ceremony of the Myrtle Point 87. Beau Zipp, clutching the trophy in one hand and what must have passed in Myrtle Point as a bimboette in the other, is interviewed leaning against his car, which prominently displays the MegaMobile logo.

"I'd like to use this occasion to let all my fans know that Beau Zipp has been picked up on a five-year sponsorship by the

MegaMag Racing Team. I'd also like to thank Roxie Rae here—" Beau does something just out of camera range to Roxie Rae's tube shorts that elicits a shrieky giggle and hand slap—"for proving that you don't have to be in this town too long to get the lay of the land. I've also been authorized to disclose that we're in negotiations with Roxie Rae to serve as official Team MegaMag mascot for the rest of the season."

"Double crimenentlies, I mean, that slugfucker is two-timing Sheila." From a standing start, Buckthorn goes ballistic faster than you can say "postal."

"And apparently with something other than slugs," Devaney opines.

"I'm telling," says Buckthorn, steaming towards the door.

"You'll do no such, Harley." Devaney latches onto the scruff of his neck with a grip of iron, honed from years of crunching numbers on a thousand calculators. "I'll deal with this."

On-screen, Beau Zipp plants an immoderate smooch on Roxie Rae. "You boys have been covering Junior Johnson; well, the press is about to catch the rise of Senior Johnson." Beau winks and flicks a forefinger off his zipper.

"I'll take your Johnson," howls Buckthorn, "and knot it in a double reverse sheepshank."

"Remember, Harley," says Devaney, loosening his grip and patting Buckthorn paternally, "I'm taking care of all this."

– XLV –

Sarah Trip's first manuscript had been turned down by Booty Books. While she had hit the word count right on the wazoo, far too many of those words, John Shine explained, contained more than one syllable. Still, Sarah had shown a real gift for the tonier sort of loin-stirring tale that Shine was looking to expand Booty Books into, not, mind you, forsaking his core readership based on the demographics of bars in the Southeast where women wore bass plugs as earrings and still believed in true love. His projected new division, Puss 'n Books, was aimed at romantically hapless single women from eighteen to fifty-three, who bought 94 percent of all mainstream fiction. The focus was emblazoned in the neon motto Shine had mounted over his acquisition editor's desk: "A Harlequin Romance for Women with BAs." Having read all first novels and memoirs (a distinction that had long since evaporated, as far as Shine could tell) by women over the past decade—and enough second and third novels to see that he need read no more—Shine had abstracted the formula for Puss 'n Books, which he passes along to Sarah Trip.

Heroine must fit the following profile:

1. Age eighteen to fifty-three
2. At least a college grad (if graduate or professional degree, must manifest correspondingly more self-loathing)
3. A dysfunctional family with
    - A. A mother who
        1. Abandoned her
        2. Competed with her
        3. Tried to live her life through her
    - B. A father who
        1. Abandoned her
        2. Never took her seriously

        3. Molested her
    C. A brother who
        1. Molested her
        2. Molested her
        3. Died of AIDS
    D. A sister who
        1. Is more attractive
        2. Married a lawyer/doctor/accountant
        3. Has kids and/or breast cancer
4. A rich inner life characterized by
    A. Sophisticated psychological insights
    B. Proustian particularity of memory, especially of all amatory disasters
    C. Lavish sexual fantasies
5. Lavish sexuality unfolded with
    A. A seasoned, nurturing older man
    B. A hot, educable young stud
    C. Discovery of amatory appliances
6. Discovery of self initiated by moving to
    A. The country
    B. The city
    C. Back home
    D. Detox
7. Administration of various psychotherapies that
    A. Changed everything
    B. Changed nothing
    C. Made it worse
8. A smart mouth
9. A history of boyfriends who were
    A. Assholes
    B. Assholes
    C. Assholes
10. Having pretty well mucked up her own life, resolves to pass on this expertise by means of
    A. Stepchildren
    B. Adoption
    C. A sperm bank

11. A commitment to third-generation feminism—that is, a firm belief that while men would never get it, they could be induced to behave as though they got it
12. A yearning for something more

Beyond this bedrock aesthetic, Sarah is free to embroider as she sees fit, bearing in mind that all the target readership really wants are legs and a life like Taylor Swift's.

Sarah sees the formula as far from formulaic, in fact, as an astonishing act of empathetic grasp she had thought to be multiple reincarnations beyond Shine's reach. He has laid out the virtual configuration of her very own life. Sarah takes out her journals and begins to transcribe.

– XLVI –

Bakersfield, of course, knows that Juggernaut and Mark Neighbors have crossed over even as Marta unscrolls her plan, MegaMole having implanted a microtransmitter in the heel of Mark Neighbors's Florsheims. Directly post-plan, the transmitter seems to be picking up principally the sounds of canine digestive processes and subsequently the gormandizing of either pill bugs or political consultants, MegaMole—in the process of hiring NSA analysts who interpolated electronic intelligence from the microtransmitter in Recep Erdoğan's ConCo TurboClearEarShears as well as a clutch of mothers who can tell unerringly what their toddlers are up to through one ceiling, three walls, and the whine of the Electrolux—as yet lacking the expertise to distinguish between pill bugs and political consultants grazing on dog doo-doo.

But no matter. Bakersfield knows all it needs to. For a half pittance, they have signed Beau Zipp on the contingency that Sheila Wallop sell her strip of land interrupting the Rancho Rio holdings. Within thirty days, they will have Buckthorn's as well. The only hitch has been the Albino Banana Slugs. So far, Freddy Waxwroth has managed to develop an Albino Plantain Slug, an Albino Banana Thug, and an Electric Banana. While there are intriguing commercial applications of Waxwroth's research, Bakersfield can now pull the plug, moving Waxwroth's funding to the Athletic Department for scholarships for premier computer gamers, Bakersfield having decided to follow the model of Stanford and the North Dakota School of Mines to establish MagaMax U's academic reputation via athletic success.

Once the property is replete with slugs, the municipal utility district application will be a lock and the geothermal plant will go forward, subsidized at 80 percent by a two-hundred-year 1 percent loan from the State of Oregon under authorization of a recently passed state referendum to establish a tax on assisted suicide and use the proceeds to support the state's alternative energy initiative: Utilization of Renewable Resources Project.

Of course, an example will have to be made of Juggernaut and Mark Neighbors. In lieu of turning them over to the McKenzie *polis,* MegaMax will arrange for Juggernaut to manage a tire recycling facility while Mark Neighbors will man the MegaMax dunking booth at the annual Sierra Club picnic.

Even as plans for the MUD ooze ahead, MegaMax is dickering with Indonesian interests to purchase 49 percent of Rancho Rio so that they can bring in a shadow management team to learn how Indonesia might yet turn a profit on a white donkey of a development they are stuck with in Tarwater, Arkansas. The current marketing plan of selling only to unindicted co-conspirators, probationers, and those with a Presidential pardon has produced lots of prospects but not much cash flow. (A recent ad featuring Michael Milkin, Anthony Levandowski, Henry Cisneros, Paul Manafort, Philip Esformes, and Martha Stewart shot at the Aspen Minimum Security Federal Correctional Facility had produced a barely discernible uptick in sales.)

Although Bakersfield rarely ventures north of the Kern County line, Oregon statute requires that corporate principals be present to kiss the earth whenever a new development is approved (prior to Rancho Rio, the last development green-lighted under provisions of the Native Oregonian Preservation and Enhancement act was approved in 1978 when Mother Teresa was authorized to cobble together a half-story bark hovelment to house retired sisters from her order). Bakersfield arranges to meet with state officials on the afternoon of the morning they buy Buckthorn's parcel at IRS auction. They also invite Indonesia to the occasion so that they may consummate their deal as well.

In Karma, New Mexico, a registered shaman putters through alien entrails he bought as Air Force surplus in 1947 while a rinse of blue smoke rises from his pipe. The entrails arrange themselves in the shape of a $, a mobile home, and an emergent male member.

– XLVII –

Deep in their forest fastness, the Gang of Five has just concluded its weekly colloquium (today's topic: Spam exports and the impending trade imbalance with Uzbekistan) when a squabble breaks out about whose turn it is to go into town to renew the group's Forest Service Wilderness special use permit for gangs. Sasquatch, who scored a case of Polident from Devaney's loading dock and having applied it like cologne now smells approximately like a change of shift at the nursing home, begs off because of that erotic species misunderstanding with the *faux* bear at the McKenzie Fair. Hiro is off the hook because he can't read English. Tony Ten-Toes Jr. refuses to sign another treaty with the Federal Fork-Tongues. D. B. Cooper is pretty much out of the question for anything involving human contact, though government employees are one of those borderline calls.

"Which leaves *me* again," Carlos Castaneda snivels. "I don't see why I'm always the one who has to take care of this kind of stuff."

"Because," says Tony, "you are the warrior of bamboozlement. Also, if you don't, we'll turn you over to the appropriate academic authorities who will make you write a doctoral dissertation."

Carlos quivers abjectly. His left hand contracts into a writer's cramp, incapable of producing so much as a titular colon. Visions of footnote fetishistas pucker his Johnson.

"Fee, fi, fo, fum…" says Sasquatch.

"Ready or not, here they come," concludes D. B., gesturing verbally downstream where C. C. Fellows emerges from a copse of bonsai sequoia, yellow miasma, and pestiferous.

Shirt ashred and bobbing along on two Florsheims with one heel between them, Mark Neighbors follows C. C., attended closely by Chuck Wepner. Juggernaut brings up the rear, though this is not at once apparent as her bazooms emerge from the copse at some considerable interval in advance of the rest of her.

It is a delicate moment. Somewhere, a B-movie's town clock ticks towards noon while a stray citizen scurries off Main Street. In the bar, Jack Palance knocks back the last of his whiskey while in the Marshall's office the old coot deputy cocks his Walter Brennan signature shotgun and the quivery son of the young widow, the Marshall's romantic interest, wears the face of one who knows he will be wounded but not shot dead. The Marshall himself is wondering how soon his pension from the Screen Actors Guild will kick in so he can move to Petaluma and raise begonias.

Calling on not inconsiderable reserves of smooth, honed by his early years of specialization in widows, orphans, and charitable trusts, Mark Neighbors pees his pants; sniffing the air, Chuck Wepner follows suit down the inseam of Mark Neighbors's bark-brown L. L. Beans. At once, Tony Ten-Toes Jr. recognizes the conciliatory gesture and signals Sasquatch, whose bladder resembles the Hindenburg, to reciprocate. As the Sasquatchian stream gullies its way towards Naughty Girl Creek, Mark Neighbors is reminded of part of a junior high joke involving a book, *Yellow River*, by I. P. Freely. If he can remember the rest, he will tell the joke to Chuck, hoping to curry some favor.

With it thus established that neither party means the other any immediate harm, the two groups settle in warily on opposite sides of the campfire. Given his precarious position, C. C. does introductions all around, mightily sorry he left his stash at home. Having revealed the gang's hideout—and at that to MegaMaxers—C. C. is awkwardly situated, to be sure. A little palaver, perhaps.

"So, big guy," he says, addressing Sasquatch. "How's tricks in the old *Australopithecus* line?" Sasquatch winks with one eye—an adaptive development mistakenly attributed to *Homo erectus*—and wiggles his opposable thumbs. "Maybe later on you could show our off-forest guests your Elvis impersonation."

Sasquatch, always a trouper when it comes to audience requests, at once dedicates the number to Chuck Wepner and breaks into "You Ain't Nothin' but a Hound Dog," his hip swivel tumbling Hiro down the slope and into his rice paddy where the Albino Banana Slugs graze—it must be said—sluggishly.

Juggernaut waits until Sasquatch finishes; applauds politely so as not to invite an encore. (For enthusiastic applause, Juggernaut claps her breasts together, producing a sound not unlike Big Ben *prestissimo.*)

"I believe our mutual interests may be served, improbably enough, by congealed white slime." Juggernaut imagines the stir this sally will produce when she is invited back to Wharton to model a case study in hostile negotiations for students in the MBA program.

"I don't see how former Senator Packwood and Harvey Weinstein fit into the picture," says Carlos.

"The lady," says Tony, "is obviously referring to the Bureau of Indian Affairs."

"Actually," says Juggernaut, "I'm referring to those." She gestures towards the rice paddy, where Hiro is dousing himself in soy sauce to the metabolic distress of the slugs, who arch up like a McDonald's logo and peel off his body.

Juggernaut explains to the Gang why MegaMax covets the slugs and sketches out her plan. She points out to C. C. and the Gang that once the geothermal plant is operational, not only will no one else move to the upper McKenzie but most current residents will be driven off, leaving lots of room for indigenous gangs and progressive herb farmers.

After some further discussion the Gang signs on, and everyone sets about slug plucking. As a Cub Scout, Mark Neighbors had once toured a hot dog factory. This is worse. Nevertheless, by nightfall a glutinous mound of Albino Banana Slugs oozes to and fro in an old washtub. Plans are laid for the slug transport while Hiro whips up a celebratory dinner of Spam Soufflé.

Meanwhile, back at Bakersfield, the MegaMax corporate law firm, Nasty, Brutish, and Short, has just added a unilateral rescission codicil to Juggernaut's contract and, invoking the codicil, splits her 4 percent of Rancho Rio between their snack food division, MegaMunch, and their adult club in Puerto Borracho, MegaMuff.

– XLVIII –

The Fell Faller stares straight ahead and then obliquely into the bathroom mirror, trying to decide whether he should grow a mustache. With the question still unsettled, he throws in an obligatory flex and recoils in alarm. While his lats, pecs, and abs respond as always, his hump makes a sad little preliminary bulge before sinking back into flaccitude. He flexes again, producing no more than a retrospective twitch. There can be no mistake; love has turned him soft as well as dotty. He curves his lip into a clear-cut sneer, only to watch it leak away into a contoured partial cut of a sneer, feathering at its edges into a simpery smirk. A chill rising from his bowels, he endeavors to call to mind his mandala, thousands of acres of stumps. What appears instead are truck-decorating tips he picked up last month in *The Gay Logger: Out of the Closet and into the Woods.* It has been weeks since he last felled a tree. He must sink the ConCo's chisel bit teeth into substantial biomass soon or he will surely fade away like Minnesota in the playoffs.

And not just any biomass, either. The Excalibur of chain saws, the ConCo TurboSaw had been claimed by the Fell Faller when he drew it forth from the General Grant Sequoia, pissed into its empty tank, fired it up, and dropped the General flat in his tracks. With that act, the Fell Faller understood that he was sworn to fire up the saw only in heroic enterprise, seeking out the most egregious carbon dioxide junkies. As a myth, an exemplum, a way cool gnarly machine, the TurboSaw had grown faint from disuse, having in consequence acquired a more than passing resemblance to Buckthorn's Johnson, referred to unkindly in some circles as Mr. Microsoft. The Fell Faller must turn up Moby Fir. Which means turning up Chip.

Which he does, in the parking lot of the Pour House where

Chip's pickup has been mired for three days in the Challenger Deep, a regionally notorious mud puddle formed in the precedented September rains.

A little post-structuralist reconstruction of the torn thousand-dollar bill's appearance at Devaney's fingers Barry Buncombe as the probable yentzer. Although sheer arboreal incompetence is the likeliest explanation for Buncombe's attempt to fob off a cottonwood as Moby Fir, the Fell Faller fiercely figures fobbing feigned facts foments fulsomely fractious forestry. A visit to Buncombe is clearly in order.

The Fell Faller turns up as Buncombe is trying to correct the tilt of his V-frame cottage, his architectural firm, Moore or Les (motto: "Less Is More") having persuaded him that a conventional A-frame made a retro sort of statement for one who had won the Four-flusher Prize, an award even Carlos Castaneda had never pocketed, though he was a finalist the year judges Stephen Ambrose, L. Ron Hubbard, and Rue Paul gave the award to the Democratic Party's National Platform Committee.

So that Buncombe won't mistake his intentions, the Fell Faller drops two totem poles arrayed on either side of Buncombe's driveway. The Fell Faller wrinkles his nose at the resultant debris, which smells like an untended terrarium in a first grade classroom during summer vacation, the papier mâché and toad turd totems having been trucked in only last week from British Columbia as a token of the eternal esteem of the Qnzxtqkl for Buncombe's revelation in his book *Gaia: You Go, Girl* of the sacred, unspeakable (not to say unpronounceable) name of the Great Juggler who keeps all celestial spheres in motion; named, He drops the ball.

"I've come for Moby Fir."

"Too bad," says Buncombe petulantly. "Not telling."

"I don't know what your problem with pronouns is, bub, but that's going to be the least of your worries in just a jiffy here." The Fell Faller unshoulders his saw, switches to the lupus manifold, and fires it up. As the rpms build, a rising alpha male howl issues forth; throttled back, the saw idles at a throaty growl.

Buncombe's bowels and tongue let go simultaneously. "On the other hand, autopoetic ecosystems manifest a self-corrective function (if one subscribes to the Santiago Theory, of course) that rewards dissipative structures through a feedback loop that would, in the instance of this instance, flexibly accommodate the butterfly effect resultant on the insertion of a 35mm extraction of the sacramental image of what has been dubbed familiarly Moby Fir." Buncombe had recently discovered the tree's location when he profiled Sasquatch for *Parade Magazine.*

"What I'll be inserting," says the Fell Faller, "is 1,524 mm of ConCo TurboSaw."

"Right," says Barry Buncombe, his bowels evacuating like Dunkirk. "Township 16, Range 20, Section 3, the southeast of the southwest, more familiarly known as the headwaters of the south tine of Fork Creek."

– XLIX –

With most of the plastic explosive loaded in the holes, Buckthorn slips into McKenzie Station High School one night to simulate the detonation and consequent sculpt on one of the Kaypros in the computer science lab. Entering the explosive specs and factoring in 2,137, which has always been his lucky number, Buckthorn punches up the post-kablooie cliff face, turning up 139¶28.27[73]609±π4286-6b≥c{lx}1/8. Buckthorn smacks the Kaypro upside its cybertemple, a tonic he has seen E. E. Everclear apply to the air traffic control radar. The Kaypro screen darkens, then belches forth something that resembles Robert De Niro's Johnson auditioning for the role of Gandhi. Close enough, Buckthorn figures, though he is troubled by a subsequent unease prompted by having fuzzed the image with a simulated local drizzle and watching it morph into a simulacrum suggestive of Buckthorn's former brother-in-law, Rafe Fines (pronounced Ralph Fiennes), a Johnson of the first magnitude, Buckthorn reminds himself.

Buckthorn repairs to the Pour House, where Sheila is watching the motor sports segment of the Grammy Awards. Three-Wheel Drive, a trio from Loogie, Missouri (motto: "Home of the Tri-State Wedgies Championship"), has just waltzed off with a Grammy for Best Acoustical Instrumental without Drums and Guitar at Quarter-Mile or Shorter Dirt Tracks in Southeastern Tennessee. Buckthorn bites his tongue—more precisely, clamps down on his tongue like a pit bull—as Sheila takes the occasion to rhapsodize about Beau Zipp.

At length, she notices Buckthorn in some apparent state of discomfort. "Bucky, what is it? Did you get stood up for another date?"

"My thung hurs," says Buckthorn, turning loose his bite and reaching in with thumb and forefinger to massage the throbbing organ.

"I don't know how many times I told you this was going to happen if you kept on with those Puffy Cheddar Diesel Cheetos."

Buckthorn nods meekly. With his tongue in its present state, he probably should lay off the Cheetos for a while. Their uncanny blend of adhesion and abrasiveness is legendary; McKenzie motorists keep cases of the stuff in the bed of their pickups to scatter for traction when they get stuck in mud or snow. Also, the Yellow Dye #6 melts ice like magnesium chloride hexahydrate.

Fearing a conversational lull that would turn the topic back to Beau Zipp, thereby inviting the blurted truth, Buckthorn strikes out obliquely. "Remember after the Olympics when the women's hockey team got to meet with the President and had their picture on the Wheaties box and the men's hockey team got to meet with Dennis Rodman and had their picture on Scott institutional grade bathroom tissue?"

"How could I forget? For a while there we had customers who wouldn't wipe unless we stocked Scott Olympic Commemorative half-ply."

"Right," says Buckthorn.

"And?" says Sheila.

"And?" says Buckthorn. "Oh, *and*. And it kind of reminded me of a guy I went to school with who's driving for Greyhound. Last I heard, that is. He dropped out of high school because he couldn't pass driver's ed. But he was a whiz in geography. You know how some people can recite all the state capitals? Well, Wayne could name every county seat in the country. His sister's name was Ann or Pam or Florence or something like that. She had blond hair that we knew was all hers because Wayne was blond and that was before men dyed their hair."

Sheila looks at Buckthorn with genuine concern. "You were saying about the hockey team...?"

"The hockey team, right. I think some of them were blond too." Despite his swollen tongue precluding oral consumption, Buckthorn musters a shit-eating grin.

"I think, Harley, that you should either start drinking a lot less or a lot more."

"I'll go for door number two, except you'll have to extend my tab."

"No can do. And I'll tell you why." Sheila's gaze locks on like a Sidewinder Missile. Her pupils configure momentarily into an 8 and a 6, a shape Buckthorn has seen them assume whenever she has to throw someone out on his—or, from time to time, her—ear. "I've been given to understand that you've paid down your tab with C. C. into four digits while I'm left carrying you at figure approximately equal to the national debt of Guinea-Bissau. And with about the same odds of repayment."

Buckthorn's ingratiating grin wobbles off sideways. "I've got something big in the works, Sheila. When this comes through, the Dia Foundation is going to be all over me with money like the Russians on Trump."

"For crying out loud, Harley. Everybody knows that Dia got stiffed in the will when Dominique de Menil died. And now that Halliburton and Dresser have merged, Slumberger stock has been heading south. In fact, Dia's been subject to credible buyout rumors involving Up against the Wall. I understand that *Art Forum* is going to report in their next issue that Dia has been forced to freeze funding for Terrell Crisco's invisible band-aid applied to the financial district of Ulan Bator. I don't think they're going to be taking on any new patronage projects."

"Cool. I've got an in at Up against the Wall," says Buckthorn, calculating that if that doesn't pan out maybe he could hustle a stipend from Anthony Weiner.

The Pour House's door opens a crack and someone backs in, taking a stool at the far, dim end of the bar.

"What'll it be, stranger?" says Sheila, trying to place the man.

"Green mixed with something clear and an amber chaser anything you got that's."

"Don't I know you from somewhere?" Sheila queries.

"Sure you don't I'm."

"Wait a minute, it's coming to me..."

"My luck just."

"That's it; I've seen you on America's Most Wanted. You're Otto Toot, the man who designed microwave turntables so they always stop with the cup at the back and the handle facing away from you."

"As easy as you think not," says the stranger, backing out the door, whereupon he leaps into his Studebaker and speeds away, recalling happier times when he held the Palindrome Chair of Mechanical Engineering at Dyslexia Tech.

"Poor guy," says Buckthorn, whose familiarity with kitchen appliances does not extend beyond pushing "low" for the right rear burner of his range, the only button that works on the only element not burned out.

"I wouldn't waste my sympathy," says Sheila. "Semi-Tumescent Copy also fingered him as instrumental in the development of voice mail."

– L –

Having settled back into the routine of his McKenzie route, Stanley misses the high adventure of hauling a load of plastic explosive across the country. His current ventures in living on the edge—using spot remover on his carpet without first trying it out on an inconspicuous swatch; serving as Lane County liaison in Bob Packwood's comeback campaign for a seat on the Oregon Board of Commercial Blow Drier Regulation; going partners with his brother, who has ditched Merrill Lynch for the Nebraska franchise of Magic Johnson, a post-Viagra small jones boutique featuring QuickDick™; accepting Buckthorn's standing invitation for a home-cooked meal—while not without considerable chanciness, don't really stack up to watching Doc feed the deck card by card to Doll, who had been dealing when Stanley filled his inside straight. Not to mention the notoriety from his ESPN7 interview. He is still getting general delivery letters from old friends in the hood, threatening mayhem if he doesn't make good on the funds he'd borrowed here and there. Also, his fourth grade teacher, Mrs. Muscatel, has written to correct his grammar. Then there is the marriage proposal from Rihanna, though Stanley thinks her handwriting looks suspiciously like Buckthorn's when he signs up on the Pour House's blackboard for next up at pool.

In short, Stanley is not at all sure that his daily rounds approximate in any useful way the Journey of the Hero. Maybe if Buckthorn has some plastique left over when he's done with the cliff, he'll hire Stanley to haul it back to New Jersey. He is also going to ask E. E. Everclear if he can fill in for him on his days off.

Fate, however, operating as a wholly owned subsidiary of MegaMaze, has something else in mind.

— LI —

Amanda is disconsolate, the moral and logistical anguish of offering up her deflowerment all come to naught, or naught to come, or whatever. Having failed in her last-ditch effort at community development, she fears nothing remains save the gruelish consolation of graduate school in Urban Affairs with a specialization in Community Development. She recalls tardily the advice of her father, proffered upon his transferring the operations of Haverford Coil and Capacitor to a maquiladora in San Dioxin, Mexico, in advance of a vote on the Brotherhood of General Utility Servicemen's bid to become the bargaining agent for his employees: be sure to sell out late enough that you're worth something but soon enough that somebody's still buying.

Following the debacle at the Inn and Out, Amanda sought out Reverend Endwell to ascertain what had gone wrong. Alas, the reverend had seemed utterly uninterested, as he was devoting his complete theological attention, he said, to whether the biblical injunction to be fruitful and multiply was not, in fact, a divine solicitation of homosexuals, especially those who could work the times tables.

Not knowing where to turn, Amanda turns into the parking lot of the Pour House, swerving around the Challenger Deep where the local Explorer Scout troop is in the process of lowering a bathysphere. Although she has never patronized the Pour House, Amanda has shared some giggles with Sheila Wallop at the bi-monthly video club and sing-along at Loretta's Curl Up and Dye.

"Honey, you look like shit," says Sheila sympathetically. "Let me make you a Roseanne Wallbanger."

"Goodness," says Amanda, "what's that?"

"Goodness doesn't enter into it. You knock back a couple of these, you may still look like shit but you'll feel like a million."

"Oh, I so hoped to find such succor here."

"You want some succor, I could make you a Bill Clinton."

"A what?"

"Crème de shlong with a dash of bubba."

"Gosh, I don't think so, thanks," says Amanda, puckering at the prospect.

Sheila suggests that they divert themselves by watching the qualifying trials for the Pit Bull 500 in Jerkoff, North Carolina. "My fiancé is a contestant," says Sheila. "I'll be joining him on the circuit as soon as his engines are broken in."

Amanda gestures at the screen. "Isn't that Mr. Zipp now?"

Strolling into the Pit Bull infield comes Beau Zipp, a jaunty bow tie affixed to his racing duds. At the center of the oval Roxie Rae, arrayed in white tube shorts and a white quarter tank top, carrying a spray of white malphasia teased into the shape of Champion spark plugs, awaits, rubbing her knobby ankle bone subtly against the corresponding ankle of the adjacent preacher.

The ESPN7 announcer explains that the Reverend Bobby Backslides of the Jerkoff Free Will Apostolic Church will be hitching Beau Zipp and Roxie Rae before the race. He invites viewers to stay tuned following the checkered flag when Beau Shith, in the grand finale of his NEA grant, assisted by his brother, Bull, and in his only North Carolina appearance as a tribute to Jesse Helms, will incorporate a crowd vote in his performance art piece, soliciting local opinion on whether to execute in the infield a member of the media or a politician who believes in big government.

— LII —

Since no one can hazard a guess how long the Albino Banana Slugs might survive outside their habitat, it is decided that Hiro will fly them in, landing on Rancho Rio's single straightaway, most of the streets being cul-de-sacs, circles, coves, eddies, roundabouts, mazes, corrals, spirals, or box canyons. Juggernaut and Mark Neighbors will broadcast the slugs hither and thither across the property, having first swapped them to MegaMax for a cash-out of Juggernaut's 4 percent position in Rancho Rio. When the slugs are implanted, Mark Neighbors will call the Fish and Game people for an on-site slug audit that will secure full-steam-ahead development rights for Rancho Rio.

The aerial drop-off goes smoothly, but as the slugs are salted—scratch that; let's say peppered—throughout the property, they rear up, antennae weaving as they catch the irresistible scent of plastic explosive. Scrunch by scrunch, they creep away toward Buckthorn's cliff face as Mark Neighbors frantically works his way through voice mail at the State Department of Fish and Game:

> For the catchable number of Chinook salmon before the population of Chinook salmon reaches the point where addition, much less multiplication, is indistinguishable from subtraction, press 13.
>
> For the number of exemptions year-to-date to the ban on automatic weapons in bear hunting, press 2. For automated approval of an automatic weapons exemption, press OK. For tanks or artillery exemption, press !!!!. For tactical nuclear weapons exemption, press .
>
> For information on the Texas Plan for deer harvesting pending before the Oregon legislature (provisions include laser sighting devices, mobile elevated hunting blinds, corn

feeders and salt licks, banding of bucks with satellite tracking devices accurate to ten feet, and fitting trophy bucks with hobbles), press 3.

For the address, phone number, employer, children's name and school, Oregon tax return, credit report, and medical history of members of the Animal Defense League, press 86.

At length, Mark Neighbors reaches an operator who rings the Endangered Species Coordinator who says callers should leave a message on his voice mail as he is currently in the field confirming unconfirmed reports that Sasquatch was sighted walking out of Walgreens in Springfield without paying for a case of Tums. Mark Neighbors rushes into town, hoping to catch up with the coordinator, while Juggernaut hustles to keep track of the migrating slugs.

Which she can until dark falls. But by morning, the slugs are long gone. In fact, they have clogged each of Buckthorn's boreholes and are busily gormandizing the stabilizing element in the plastic explosive. Without it, the explosive might well be set off by the static electricity generated by the removal of Roxie Rae's bubblegum-flavored panties from the dryer in a laundromat in Chigger Knob, Tennessee (motto: "Duct Tape Capital of the Mid-South").

When Mark Neighbors returns with the State Fish and Game agent, the slugs are nowhere to be found. The agent agrees to collect specimens of multiple slime trails for the state lab to see if DNA testing can confirm that they were deposited by Albino Banana Slugs.

With the agent so engaged, Juggernaut and Mark Neighbors huddle urgently. MegaMax has agreed cheerfully to cash out Juggernaut's share of Rancho Rio in exchange for the slugs, throwing in as a gesture of goodwill the bounty promised citizen slugnappers. The cash-out deal is contingent only on perfunctory state certification of slug numbers, the money already deposited in an escrow account at the Bancos Unitos Special de Timo branch in Santo Chimera.

"No slugs, no dough," says Juggernaut, peevishly whacking the top off a stout cedar sapling with a power Maraca move.

“We can do better than slugs,” says Mark Neighbors, flinching as Juggernaut’s 44s whistle through the foliage. “We can deliver Sasquatch.”

“Say what?”

“Figure it this way: if the State had any seminal vesicles, it would cream its pants to turn up a bunch of gastropods. Imagine what they’d do to lay hands on a species that not only is extinct but never existed.”

“I see your point.”

“Of course, this will require some delicate negotiations with the Gang of Five.”

“So they’d agree to sell out their fur-favored comrade?”

“I’ve worked out a multiple pitch: contribution to scientific advancement; gang rightsizing in these times of criminal bloat; appeals to greed (we’d fork over the MegaMax Slug Bounty); self-interest (I could have Professor Waxwroth turn out a study confirming that sooner or later Sasquatch is going to eat them). I’m pretty sure we can bring them around.”

“What about the S man himself? He’s certainly not going to sign on.”

“He’s got to have a pretty shaky self-image—I mean, how sturdy an ego can you have when only crackpots think you even exist? Also, I have it from a reliable source that he’s a Republican. I figure he’s so beholden to the rest of the Gang that he’ll rubber-stamp being sold down the river.”

Chuck Wepner perks up at the magic word, eyes brightening and great gobs of saliva rolling off his tongue.

“If you ever use that word around Chuck again,” says Juggernaut, “I will amend several parts of your anatomy, to their considerable disadvantage.”

– LIII –

The Fell Faller drops by Devaney's Mercantile to pick up a map of Fork Creek. He finds Devaney around back, crouched over a freshly spaded plot of earth, laser range finder in hand.

"Morning, Mr. Devaney. I was wondering if I could buy something."

"Let me finish out this row and I'll be right with you. If I stop in the middle, I have the Devil's own time finding where I left off." Devaney works his way on down the row, laser-ranging the space between each lettuce seed and nostalgically confirming depth with his retirement gift from the Bureau of Weights and Measures, a probe calibrated in microns.

Back inside, Devaney rummages through his map bin, finally turning up a USGS topo of the drainages south of Naughty Girl Creek: Found Creek, Geek Creek, Agua Blanca Creek, and Fork Creek.

"Mighty rough country, Mr. Faller, even for a woodsman such as yourself. Several parties have disappeared without a trace up there over the years: Jeb Bush's presidential campaign, the 2003 Oakland Raiders, Charlie Sheen's acting career, the Social Security system surplus. It's not my place to give advice, but if I were to place advice I would advise against that place."

"I appreciate the concern, Mr. Devaney, but as my daddy always said: 'Fell, you ever tell a living soul what I always say and I'll cut off your funny-looking little pecker with a rusty can lid.'"

"I can see where that might fix itself in your memory."

"Anyway, I know right where I'm going. And I won't be going more than once."

"May I infer from your steely tone of finality you have reason to believe you've located Moby Fir?"

"No need to infer, Mr. Devaney. Next time you see me I'll be packing a round from the butt cut." The very thought of it sends an old, familiar quiver through the Fell Faller's hump.

"Just a suggestion, then; not advice, mind you. Based on the most credible variant of the Moby Fir legend, the Secret of the Universe is inscribed around its base. Perhaps, before you begin cutting—"

"The universe can't put much stock in its secret if the best it can do is scribble it on some cellulose factory's arboreal manifestation of Marfan syndrome."

"Just the same," says Devaney, "if you were to jot down whatever might be so inscribed, it could prove of inestimable value to humanity, not to mention yourself."

"I don't expect it could do any harm," says the Fell Faller, having dozed through the paragraph on universal absolutes in philosophy class at Lumberjack Tech (since 1997 Lumberjack and/or Jill Tech) (motto: "Fall 'em All and Let God Sort out the Culls"), where U.S. Forest Service funds previously appropriated to subsidize road construction so that timber companies could buy stumpage at 5 cents on the dollar until prohibited by Ninth Circuit Court decision are now diverted to LJ/J Tech to train fallers, choker setters, buckers, scalers, etc., the money laundered through a National Endowment for the Arts program to preserve folk art.

Scarcely has the Fell Faller stridden out than Reverend Endwell minces in.

"Something wrong with your hips, Reverend?"

"No, no," says the reverend. "Ecumenical outreach. All God's Johnsons—that is, children—are welcome at the Doublewide. My gait is a public solicitation of congregants from, as it were, every walk of life."

"I'm passing this along," says Devaney, not wanting to pursue the topic, "because I see from your mail that you are an inveterate environmentalist."

"Gosh, yes," says Reverend Endwell. "Ever since my summer at Camp *Rhus Toxicodendron*. And I try to practice what I preach. Our church is currently involved in a project to encourage indigenous, organic agriculture, and I personally compost all of my sermons."

Devaney has heard other suggestions about what Reverend Endwell should do with his sermons, but it would be rude to say so.

"Apparently," says Devaney, "the Fell Faller has reason to believe he's discovered the location of Moby Fir. You are aware, no doubt, of what this portends."

"Holy hollyhocks," says the reverend. "It means we're talking Moby Stump."

"Exactly."

"But what can be done?"

"As I see it, our only chance is a firside appeal from someone of unimpeachable moral standing."

"We're sunk," sighs Reverend Endwell.

"Actually, I was thinking of yourself."

"Myself? Oh, right, of course. Myself. Sure. Slipped my mind there for a minute."

Devaney draws up a map that even Reverend Endwell might be able to follow. It requires that the reverend walk Fork Creek to the junction where its South Tine flows in.

"Just remember, keep the water in sight and walk upstream," says Devaney. "And hurry."

"Right," says Reverend Endwell, calibrating his voice to approximate the level and resolute Gary Cooper tone recommended at Antepenultimate Bible College when proclaiming the social gospel. The reverend strides purposefully to the door, which he tugs on at first casually and then wholeheartedly.

"Push," says Devaney, who returns to his office to resume a task he'd taken on as a favor to an old Weights and Measures chum operating on inter-agency loan as a fabrication enumerator at a redacted address on Pennsylvania Avenue, recently detailed under the impeachment clause of the Constitution to a redacted address in the 1100 block of South Ocean Boulevard in Palm Beach. The task involved ascertaining how many nations might be induced to enter into an irrevocable non-extradition treaty with the United States in exchange for construction of a **********!! casino/resort.

– LIV –

Reverend Endwell sets out up Fork Creek, struggling mightily until he espies across the stream what might or might not be right-of-way clearance for a projected interstate highway. Crossing over, he strolls on, noting the occasional swatch of lavender fluttering now and again from the brush. The color is hauntingly familiar, but Reverend Endwell can't quite lay his hand on the memory. In the sweet by-and-by, he arrives at the junction of Fork Creek and its South Tine. Towering over the commingling of waters is a tree so vast that the reverend's practiced botanic eye can discern at least three distinct biozones from its base to where its presumptive canopy vanishes in the Oregon undercast. Its girth is to the circumference of a Run-of-the-Mill™ (Weyerhaeuser company anthem), six-hundred-year-old Doug fir as Mariah Carey's girth is to fiber optic bandwidth. And at that girth stands the Fell Faller, legs spread, head thrown back, a creamy look of erotic arousal splayed across his features.

Reverend Endwell is diverted momentarily by the uncanny familiarity of the pose, eliciting in him a sort of *déjà* screw, but he recovers at once. "Woodsman, spare that symbol of man's puniness before the grandeur of nature!"

The Fell Faller starts out of his trance to behold his beloved. At once, he recalls the dilemma of Captain Vere in *Billy Budd*, torn between love and duty. But he can no longer recall how it came out, having quit reading when it became clear that Claggard and Billy were never going to get it on. Whatever that outcome, his obligation is clear. "Only two things are puny here," says the Fell Faller. "The Medicare prescription benefits the grandeur of nature and a thousand bucks will buy you, and your chances of diverting me from my sworn duty."

"Sworn to who?"

"That would be 'whom,'" says the Fell Faller. "As an objective case form, 'whom' must be used when the pronoun is a direct or indirect object or, of course, the object of a preposition." It wouldn't do to have the love of his life think him the Dan Quayle of loggers. Even if the upcoming topplement of Moby Fir promised the amatory equivalent of fulfillment of his daddy's old threat.

"Like, whatever," says the reverend, hoping to put the Fell Faller at ease by speaking as he imagines Dan Quayle might were he a teenager today. "The issue," says Reverend Endwell, lapsing again into revspeak, "is whether your allegiance to some pop culture-inflicted self-image hasn't placed at mortal risk your immortal soul, not to mention your standing in what in some quarters is still known as the human race." (Motto: "Twice as Many Genes as the Fruit Fly").

The reverend's words fall like honey on the Fell Faller's ears, which he immediately stops up with wads of sphagnum moss. Though the reverend gestures expressively, the Fell Faller hoists his ConCo TurboSaw and yanks the starter cord. Nothing happens. He yanks again, then again. Still nothing. On the TurboSaw's monitor a message appears: "Unable to complete your connection. Reason: ConCo system is down or insufficient combustion resources. Start saw later, you nincompoop. ConCo error type 6,497."

Without a cell phone to call technical support, the Fell Faller is, in a manner of speaking, stumped. He rends his garments, then picks up his falling ax, curling it back in a practiced arc learned now so long ago when he was just starting out on the Professional Fallers Circuit, working the Peckerpole Tour. At the apex of his back swing, the Fell Faller feels a gentle hand on his bare hump. He freezes in Bunyanesque tableau. As the hand massages his hump, a second works it way down his arm, lingering suggestively at his biceps before moving on at last to his fingers, each of which melts at a stroke from the ax handle.

"It's you," says Reverend Endwell, grasping the ax, then setting it aside to grasp something at first softer.

Later, plucking thorns from each other, a trifle of their carnal tumble, which wound up in a creekside blackberry patch, they try to construct different scenarios for a mutual future. Romantic haze notwithstanding, employment is the obvious nine-hundred-pound gorilla squatting on their bluebird of happiness. Having little beyond his ecclesiastical talents to bring to the marketplace, Reverend Endwell sees few options once he is defrocked. Perhaps he might hire out as a freelance spiritual consultant to local firms such as Easy Ed's Pawn and Appliance. For his part, the Fell Faller cannot conjure up an economic future once he has left behind the roar of the chain saw, as he has sworn to the reverend he will do.

Grudgingly, the boys rerobe so that Reverend Endwell can get back in time for Wednesday night services. Turning to leave, the reverend lays a fond pat on the flank of Moby Fir in appreciation for his fir-fetched matchmaking services. He withdraws his hand and gazes quizzically at the deeply ribbed, conch-encrusted fir hide. "I believe," says the reverend, "that a passage from the Book of Nature has been inscribed here."

"The Secret of the Universe!" exclaims the Fell Faller. "Devaney was right."

In the thinning autumn light, they squint intently at the oracular scrawl.

"The Mariners in seven," the Fell Faller deciphers skeptically.

"No, no wait," says Reverend Endwell, tracing out the last letters with his finger: "Index Funds."

"Meaning no disrespect," says the Fell Faller, hawking and swallowing. "The Universe has piss-poor handwriting."

— LV —

Word quickly passes up and down the river that Sheila Wallop and Beau Zipp are kablooie. No one dares broach the disengagement, however, even to tender oblique condolence or good riddances. Sheila is ferociously unapproachable. She has hired Iphigenia Crease to run the bar while Sheila herself remains day and night in her office, from which issue the strains of Monte and the Monotones, Beau Zipp's favorite group:

Well I got me a bottle
and I'm runnin' full throttle
and I got me a piece of your heart.
You thought I was foolin'
when I said I ain't coolin'
my heels long around these parts.

From time to time, Sheila orders out for petrified prefabricated sandwiches that have been in the display cooler so long even Buckthorn won't eat them. She washes them down with an Around-the-World.

Some days after Sheila repairs to her office, Devaney shows up at the Pour House with a large package wrapped in paper featuring Santa Claus and what may or may not be jolly elves.

"Evening, Mr. Devaney," says Iphigenia, getting three words out of three in sequence right for the second time all day.

"I've come to call on Mrs. Wallop," says Devaney, noting with dismay the haphazardly arranged beer mugs drying behind the bar, several bottles of liquor on the display shelf with the labels facing away from patrons, and bar rags folded in half instead of thirds.

Iphigenia makes an indescribable preverbal noise best described as the nasal equivalent of the Bhutanese nuclear arms program. "Like you don't know the only phone we got is in her office, but she ain't accepting no calls and anyway you couldn't very well call her up and her answer on the same phone, now could you?"

Not for the first time, Devaney wonders whether all McKenzie Consolidated School District teachers should be taken out behind the bus barn and shot or sponsored for sainthood.

"If you'd be so good as to announce me to your employer."

"*Good*," says Iphigenia. "You wouldn't be saying something roundabout about what I know is said about how I used to get about with the boys up and down the river?"

"I believe the conventional idiom is 'get around.'"

In a dark corner of the bar, someone who resembles a wanted poster of D. B. Cooper breaks into song: "Round round get around I get around, / Oh, get around round round I get around..."

As Iphigenia boogies out from behind the bar to join in, Devaney slips into the back with his package and knocks on the office door.

"Damn it, Iphigenia. I told you to ask the customers how to mix their drinks. The next time I'm interrupted better be on account of ESPN footage of you-know-who being carted off the track in a wheelbarrow like a jigsaw puzzle of a weasel with most of the pieces missing."

Devaney intuits at once that only his most burnished charm will turn the trick here. "Mrs. Wallop, I happen to have come by a spare ticket to the quarterfinal countoff of the Oregon Actuarial Federation. I thought perhaps you would accompany me."

What might or might not have been a muffled sob issues from behind the door.

Having taken his best shot, Devaney is stymied. He wishes now that he had paid better attention when his sister back in Grande Merde, Michigan had tried to explain why demonstrating the features of a glow-in-the-dark slide rule was not what a girl had in mind when she asked you to park on past her house where the streetlight was burned out.

Ransacking his neural filing system under "Trivia," he comes providentially upon a shard of gender wisdom: "No woman ever believes she is thin enough." He seizes the insight as a drowning man might seize a barbell, mistaking it for a lifebuoy. "You know, I could see about stocking those prefabricated sandwiches at the Mercantile. If you keep eating them, I'll bet you'll be thin enough in no time at all." To be on the safe side, he adds: "Besides, I've always admired how your triceps wobbles when you punch the cash register."

This time, the sound behind the door is unmistakable. "Boo hoo hoo."

Devaney, who last heard a woman cry in 1971 when the Arthur Murray instructor who had drawn him as a partner for the graduation ball ran sobbing from the room, is truly nonplussed. It just doesn't add up, he thinks to himself. Even his Boy Scout *Handbook*'s paragraph on girls indicated that they respond to flattery, flattery being a form of discourse along with fishing stories and golf scores that involve a different standard of Scouting candor best explained by your bachelor uncle. Nonplussation notwithstanding, something must be done.

Sucking in his chest and thrusting out his belly, Devaney flings open the door. Sheila lies prone on the office sofa, forearm pressed across her eyes, triceps dewlap quivering.

"I didn't mean that I expected you'd go to the Actuarial Count-off if you had another engagement on your calendar," says Devaney, backpedaling.

Sheila sits up, color returning to her cheeks. "You mean like scrubbing out the men's urinal?"

"Actually, I surmised that you might be spending a few weeks rearranging our living room. I've been given to understand that brides squander an inordinate amount of time on that sort of thing."

"Brides?" said Sheila, the color in her cheeks spreading to her ears, nose, forehead, throat, and triceps wattle.

"Well, yes. When we're married—"

"Billy, I know this will come as a shock to you, but most marriages, even in our meta-modern, post-millennial culture, are prompted by a proposal."

"Sure," says Devaney, "I knew that. Meant to mention it sooner. Must have slipped my mind."

“I can imagine,” says Sheila, taking note for the first time of the oddly shaped package Devaney has been imperfectly hiding behind his back, “how delivering Christmas presents in October might well be an index of mental slippage.”

“Oh, this,” says Devaney, thrusting the package into Sheila’s arms. “I figured you had plenty of wedding rings, and I noticed that you have a tough time with the cobwebs on the ceiling so I got you this instead. Go on, open it up. It’s a ConCo TurboSuck. Got it on special at Suck It Up, a vacuum store run by an ex-football coach. A mid-range model, but if it works out you can accessorize with a hair dryer and a septic pump.”

Sheila hurls herself back supinely on the sofa. “Oh, boo hoo hoo.”

Devaney sinks to his knees in dismay. “Aren’t you happy?”

“Of course, darling” says Sheila through her tears, planting an immoderate smooch on Devaney’s forehead. “It’s just that a moment like this is so emotional for a girl.”

Devaney is about to mention that after four times or so you’d think a girl would get used to it, but the barest flicker of self-preservation stills his tongue. He says instead: “Of course, if the TurboSuck is too much machine for the job, we have thirty days to trade it in on a cheaper model.”

— LVI —

One afternoon when he has finished his route, Stanley pays a call on E. E. Everclear. As Stanley pokes his head through the trap door into the tower, Everclear is pounding vigorously on the radar console.

"What's happening, man?"

E. E. looks in bemusement at what might or might not be a flabbergast from the past. "Sucker's fucked up again."

Since Stanley plans to offer to fill in for Everclear on his days off, he seizes the opportunity to hone his professional wherewithal. "I mean, you know, technically what's wrong? Go ahead and give me the whole electroaeronautical nine yards."

"Technically," says E. E., "your truck is fucking the sucker up."

"Jeeze," says Stanley, abashed. "I didn't know. I'll move it; looks like there's plenty of room out on the runway."

E. E. waves the suggestion off. "That's okay. Might not be your truck after all. The same thing happens every time someone makes a long-distance call from McKenzie Station to one of those 900 sex numbers."

Stanley tries to remember whether Buckthorn's at home this afternoon.

"I'll just power the system down," says Everclear, rooting around a tangle of extension cords and yanking plugs until the screen goes dark. "What can I do for you?"

"I was wondering," says Stanley, settling in on a crate of Everclear, "if I could fill in, you know, on your vacation or weekends or sick days or whatever."

E. E. tries unsuccessfully to squint Stanley into focus. He's pretty sure he's seen the lad somewhere before. "It's an awesome responsibility, son."

"I hear you, man. When it comes to responsibility, I wrote, printed, distributed, sold, read, and reviewed the book. Only recently I transported two tons of plastic explosive transcontinentally across thirty-four state lines without a permit. When you're talking Stanley, you're talking the right stuff."

E. E. tries squinting with one eye at a time. "You spend much time in hallucinations?"

"Hey," says Stanley huffily, "everybody's entitled to his or her flashbacks."

"I meant other people's hallucinations."

Stanley scrunches his neural cortex prefatory to giving the query a serious synaptic ride, but E. E. waves off a response. "Never mind. That wouldn't be any more than a periodic annoyance in this line of work. I'm curious, though, what prompted your interest."

"Well, I've been thinking about a career change for way long." Stanley shifts his position on the crate, clanking some bottles as he moves.

"Careful there, son."

"It's not like the garbage business doesn't have its satisfactions, but it just doesn't stroke my dick the way it used to. Not a lot of upside, if you get my drift. Also, there's the mess."

"The mess?" says E. E., shaking his head ruefully at how little the public at large—of which he assumes Stanley to be a periodic member whenever he isn't among the 87 percent of black men between the ages of nine and fifty-seven in penal situations—really knows about air traffic control. "The mess?" E. E. repeats. "Did you ever hear about how you should never tour a hot dog factory to see what goes into one?"

"Dig," says Stanley. "Same thing Buckthorn says about his sister's fruitcake."

"Well, you don't really want to know what goes into air traffic control, either."

"Maybe you could give me a little peeksie. You know, like a paradigmatic (Stanley has been reading *Annoy & Baffle Friends & Strangers with a More Preposterous Vocabulary in Thirty Days*) episode."

"I guess I could do that," says C. C., fairly sure by now that the visitor is not an hallucination. "Let's see. Back in '85 before I started my internship at O'Hare, I used to walk past the flight controllers' briefing room—."

Stanley jumps in, eager to complete the tale. "And you could hear that they was boogying down—loud music, them little carts full of airline booze rolling in and out, stewardesses shrieking."

"No," says E. E., "it was always real quiet. Sometimes just a muffled little tap-tap, like wood on tile. It's not what was behind the door that arrested my attention." He stops, shudders, pours out a wallop of Everclear. "There was a plaque on that door: 'This Facility Complies with the Provisions of the Americans with Disabilities Act.'"

"Dig," says Stanley. "That must have been back in the days when the government didn't just dish out laws but followed them too."

"The plaque," says C. C., "was in English and Braille."

"Well, now, there you are. I could be the McKenzie Field Affirmative Action poster boy. I'd have, like, major rapport with all those black bros up there in the cockpit." Stanley seizes the mike and strikes an air traffic controller pose: "Yo, homie. Get that mofo to three-zero-niner fo I do yo mama."

The radio burps some static, then clears. "This is United 541 confirming turn to three-zero-niner."

Before E. E. can make his way to the mike, two more airliners have acknowledged the change in heading. "This is McKenzie Control. Previous transmission was a test of the Regional Affirmative Action Program. Disregard."

The pilots all come on at once wanting to know if they should resume their previous heading or compensate for the diversion to three-zero-niner.

"Whatever," says E. E., switching off the mike. "Biggest bunch of Mother-May-I's I've ever seen."

"Man, that was masterful."

E. E. shrugs modestly. "You get the hang of it after a while." He finds a coffee cup with nothing in it and pours Stanley a controller-sized serving of Everclear.

Much later, as the gray fades from oyster through dun to drab, ashen, slate, and at last to Dorian, E. E. switches on the field's landing lights and beacon.

Stanley gazes down the runway in awe as the lights pitch and wobble to and fro. "Dude, that's awesome. How you get those babies to perform that to-and-froness? They be like the Vandellas to the runway's Martha."

"The 'to'," says E. E., topping up both their cups, "is a result of the three bottles of Everclear we've polished off. The 'fro' is the rocker platforms I've mounted the lights on. Even pilots who can't tell propwash from mouthwash secretly believe they have the right stuff to be a naval aviator."

"That be," says Stanley. "I recall C. C. Fellows laying it down bout when he be working in L.A. at that Far Eastern boutique, Now and Zen. Some swami come through from Bogustan who claim he be a major navel aviator."

"So I like to give all the pilots who land here a chance to prove they could bring it in on a carrier. Sort of a shit or get out of the cockpit deal."

"I bet them are shittin' bricks right there in that cockpit."

"I believe the idiom is 'they be shittin' bricks,'" says E. E.

"I never could get the hang of that stuff," says Stanley. "Truth be told," he goes on, the Everclear loosening his tongue, "I can't dunk, I can't dance, and my Johnson is almost as small as Buckthorn's."

"We've got more in common than I imagined, son."

Still later, the radio gargles again. E. E. throws up his hands in exasperation. "I thought I pulled the plug on that sucker."

Stanley essays a palms-up gesture, but aborts the essay when he determines that he can no longer reliably distinguish one side of his hand from the other.

"McKenzie Control, this is MegaMax Six-Six-Six. ETA 19:32. Request confirmation of heading and altitude."

E. E. gives Stanley an encouraging knuckle on his noggin. "Okay, son, show me your stuff."

With Stanley on air guitar, E. E. on vocals, and the mike keyed, McKenzie Control breaks into a rendition of "Eight Miles High."

– LVII –

Buckthorn is indeed home, but he is neither watching afternoon television nor dialing a 900 sex number. Rather, he is priming himself for the task to come. Toking away at some of C. C.'s McKenzie Mauve, he turns on and off the single operational burner on the stove, steadying his hand for the plastique detonator. In the mirror, he works out a sincere, resolute, artistic, ingratiating, diminished mental capacity expression for post-kablooie media interviews. He also t'ai chis his shoulders and wrists so he will not be overly discomforted when he's handcuffed behind his back.

What remains is settling on a time. Buckthorn considers February 30, Anzac Day, Alfred Nobel's birthday, and Rosh Kapow before settling on Guy Fawkes Day. He then sets about drafting a manifesto to be distributed to the media. The manifesto will highlight the purity of his intent, the technical wizardry of his craft, the mailing address for ordering maquettes of the stony Johnson, and information on how to contribute to the Free Buckthorn Fund.

He searches for his old college composition text, *The Lap-Dog Handbook*, to refresh his memory on the proper format for manifestos. After rummaging futilely through his library, Buckthorn remembers he used the book some years back to prop up the right rear corner of his toilet when the mounting bolt rusted through and a piece of subflooring gave way. He extracts the handbook and thumbs its mildewed pages. Besides twenty chapters on invention—students being expected, apparently, to actually know nothing—and one on the Aristotelian five-paragraph essay, Buckthorn finds extended chapters on writing memos, committee reports, evaluations, anonymous slander, annual reviews, letters of reprimand, textbook reviews, and self-nomination for awards, but nothing on manifestos.

A timid tapping at his door draws Buckthorn reluctantly from the text. Fluttering there on the stoop is Amanda, clearly wrought and verging, Buckthorn can't help but notice, on overwrought.

"Harley, I must speak with you."

Buckthorn ushers her in, sweeping aside his *Playboy* collection, empty beer cans with their stubble of mold, unopened registered mail, dirty clothes, clean clothes, seven TV remotes, a reproduction of the Mona Wanda from the Laughingstock, Delaware, Museum of Art, and three votes for Al Gore so that Amanda can sit beside him on the couch.

With a little coaxing, Amanda unscrolls the whole tragic story of Reverend Endwell and the Qnxtqkl ceremony, the *coitus* not even getting as far as *interruptus*, and Reverend Endwell's subsequent lack of interest in the entire affair.

"How can the Ford Foundation expect me to develop a community if there's no community to develop? I personally think that whole Qnxtqkl business was a bunch of hocus pocus, hanky panky, mumbo jumbo, or *ipso facto*. I see now that I myself must set an example for the women of McKenzie." Amanda thrusts into Buckthorn's hand the combination to the lock on her chastity belt. "Take me, Harley."

Ever willing to oblige, Buckthorn sweeps Amanda off to his bedroom. Sometime later, as darkness begins to deepen the overcast, Amanda removes Buckthorn's sweaty hand from the lock and for the second time says, "Here, let me," the first time being when Buckthorn gashed his finger while scrabbling away at the coupling mechanism on her bra.

"It's this bandage," says Buckthorn, waggling his bundled finger. "I used to be able to unsnap a brassiere with one hand through three layers of clothing without the hooters in hand suspecting a thing."

With Amanda finally *en déshabillé*, Buckthorn himself disrobes, injuring two more fingers in his haste. Triumphantly, he unfurls the covers. Alas, even in the gathering gloom Amanda can make out on the sheets a mosaic of crumbs, stains, and several small things that move.

"I've always fantasized," says Amanda quickly, "about doing *it* on top of a bedspread."

Buckthorn, who would agree to doing *it* while seated backwards on a dual pogo stick bounding through the drive-in window at Someday My Prints Will Come (motto: "Photo Finishing for Masochists") while singing an aria from *L'Fornicata*, agrees, quickly repositioning the camouflage bedspread he had gotten by mail order from Esprit Décor, a camo home furnishings boutique near Camp Pendleton.

As Buckthorn makes his preliminary amatory move, a rumble of thunder in the near distance announces a tardy summer electrical storm. At once, Buckthorn's Johnson lights up, emitting a spectral glow.

"Holy Hilfiger," exclaims Amanda, drawing back in alarm.

"It's nothing," says Buckthorn. "I'll just pop into the restroom and take care of it." Through trial and error since the Terrell Crisco incident, Buckthorn has learned that by looping his shaver cord around the base of his Johnson and tucking the plug between his cheeks, he can drain off the current, thereby illuminating his asshole, which provides a kind of romantic indirect lighting in the missionary position.

"It's not radioactive or something?" says Amanda, clutching her knees to her breasts.

"Not to worry," says Buckthorn, inching his way past the dresser by feel. A great metallic clattering breaks out, and Amanda fumbles for the switch on the bedside lamp. In the blare of light Buckthorn stands, exposed except for his encumbered Johnson, to which has become attached Buckthorn's keys, pocketknife, silver coins, and Boy Scout Continence medal.

"Oh, my God," says Amanda. "It's like the *Exorcist* or something. Your little thingy—it's, it's not Y2K compliant."

Buckthorn's response is interrupted by an insistent rapping at his front door. One thing at a time, thinks Buckthorn, remembering a cardinal principal he'd read in a book on university management that fluttered free from Stanley's truck one day when Buckthorn went along for the ride: "When the bear shits in the woods, he's not playing pinochle: one thing at a time." He's a little fuzzy, however, on whether answering the door on the way to looping his Johnson with the shaver cord is one thing or two. Whatever, thinks Buckthorn, flinging open the door to reveal Devaney, whose visage recycles his companionable smile into an expression most often seen on first-time viewers of T-Span, the network providing gavel-to-gavel coverage of the Texas legislature.

"Maybe this isn't a good time," says Devaney, backing away slowly.

"No, no," says Buckthorn, wincing as his Johnson whangs onto the doorknob and sticks there. "What's up?"

Casting an appraising glance at the festooned doorknob, Devaney says in wonderment, "I was looking for someone to serve as my best man."

– LVIII –

As Mark Neighbors readies the Jaguar Land Bruiser to fetch Bakersfield—buffing the chrome, platinum, rhodium, ruthenium, and palladium, adjusting the high-definition eighty-inch ConCo TurboTube to ensure optimum satellite reception of the latest dailies of all Disney films in production, saturating the interior with Eau de Mint, a fragrance obtained through back-channel sources from the Federal Bureau of Engraving—Juggernaut calls the State Division of Fish and Game Endangered Species Coordinator.

The coordinator, Agent Knox Orange, tells Juggernaut that DNA testing of the slime trail has proven inconclusive, although tentative matches with Bob Packwood, Martin Shkreli, and Wells Fargo management were ruled out in the end.

"Never mind," says Juggernaut. "We're now talking something much bigger than Albino Banana Slugs."

"Not the Puce-Crested Booby?!" Agent Orange exults.

"Watch your mouth, bub. You angling to be turned over to the Oregon Prohibited Mean Speech Bureau?"

"No offense intended, I'm sure, Ms. Juggernaut. The Puce-Crested B-word is a rare specicritter (formerly specimen) of the family *Bazongas*, more commonly known as the Greater Tit. An unconfirmed sighting attributed to Barry Buncombe placed the creature on the upper McKenzie in the company of a Variegated Narwhal."

"I'm not talking birds here," says Juggernaut. "I'm talking Sasquatch."

"Holy haversack." Agent Orange's vestigial bureaucratic heart thuds against his rib cage. Sasquatch! Centerpiece in the Oregon hagiographic hexagon of endangered species: the Stag-Trousered Logger, the Lesser Linn County Field-Burner, the Free-Ranging

Commercial Fisherman, and the Soft-Shelled Liberal, along with the devilishly elusive Albino Banana Slug. "You have evidence?"

"I don't need evidence; I have Sasquatch."

At once, Agent Orange's voice sinks to a conspiratorial tone. "Have you communicated with him?"

"You can hardly shut him up."

"Did he happen to say whether he favored Ducks or Beavers?" Agent Orange, a graduate of Oregon State University and twenty-seven years in arrears on his student loans, recalls a provision that waives repayment if the debtor can deliver to Reser Stadium a legitimate football prospect.

"It didn't come up, but as far as I can tell he eats pretty much everything."

"I meant his athletic affiliation."

"Now that you mention it, he may have said something about the Katmandu Yetis."

Agent Orange starts to ask something about Sasquatch's time in the forty when Juggernaut cuts him off.

"What you do with the Big S is your business. What I need is certification that Albino Banana Slugs exist in sufficient numbers—and places—that the state green-lights Rancho Rio."

At once, Agent Orange is tossed on the horns of a moral dilemma. "How can I certify something I've never seen that my bosses are going to want to see when they see that I've seen it? I mean, this will be a big photo op."

"When's the last time they were in the field?"

"What?"

"I said, when's the last time any of your bosses found their way out of the Salem Statistical Metropolitan Area?"

"I think my boss's boss's deputy flew to Bromide, Nebraska, three years ago for a conference on carp."

"My point exactly," says Juggernaut. "I can lay my hands on a pod of Albino Plantain Slugs. Unless your guys get up close and personal, they'll be none the wiser."

"None the wiser," says Agent Orange. "They'll go for that. It's the working title of our biennial report to the legislature."

"So here's how it works," says Juggernaut. "Your people show up tomorrow with the documents certifying Rancho Rio slug compliance. I'll deliver the Albino Plantain Slug ringers and Sasquatch."

"Deal," says Agent Orange, visions of sugarplums dancing in his head.

After Juggernaut hangs up, she goes out to see how Mark Neighbors is coming along. All that's visible are the bottom of his Florsheims, protruding from beneath the Land Bruiser. "Should I even ask?" asks Juggernaut.

"Just buffing up the skid plate," says Mark Neighbors, wheezing from the effort and baneful fumes confected by a tincture of Around-the-World and Dr. Pepper, the only compound known to bring titanium to a high shine.

"Can we spell 'over the top?'"

"O-v-e-" gasps Mark Neighbors.

"I mean," says Juggernaut, "attention to detail is one thing; rampant anality is quite another."

"My sources in Bakersfield report that Vlad the Downsizer will be in the corporate party. He doesn't travel with Bakersfield unless they're looking to unload someone. Since we're the only two Mega-Max employees on-site, it's a safe bet who he'll be looking at."

"After tomorrow, who cares?"

"Right. But if we're canned before the deal closes, we walk away with empty pockets." Mark Neighbor's windpipe constricts in a toxic spasm, and he hacks, huffs, heaves, and hawks to clear it. "They worship Vlad on Wall Street. I've seen him fire a whole production shift at Nike when one associate couldn't recite Tiger Woods's third-round score in the 1991 Greater Winnemucca Open and Shut. Could you hand me that toothbrush?"

Juggernaut fetches the implement from the tool tray and lays it in Mark Neighbor's emergent palm like a nurse attending a surgeon in the operating theater. "Have I ever said how much I admire your attention to detail?"

Inside his Florsheims, Mark Neighbors wriggles his toes in delight at the compliment.

"I told Salem we'd deliver Waxwroth's Albino Plantain Slugs plus Sasquatch. I thought I'd round up the slugs and leave the S Man to you. You guys seem to have a certain rapport."

“Piece of cake,” says Mark Neighbors. “I’ve already talked to Carlos. Sasquatch has agreed to infiltrate the ceremony to gather intelligence on MegaMaw, a possible corporate move into antacids.”

“Won’t he be, like, a little obvious?”

“I’ve taken care of that. I picked up a disguise at Easy Ed’s Pawn and Appliance.”

“Just so we’ll all be on the same page, what’s he going to be wearing?”

“An authentic knockoff of a Smokey the Bear suit.”

– LIX –

President York gazes reflectively out his window at the McKenzie, which runs clear and sulky, awaiting the autumnal rains when it can begin its annual nine-month larruping of the retirement homes of Californians who sold their two-bedroom bungalows in Menlo Park as $900,000 tear-downs and have built riverfront Versailles with the proceeds.

Bakersfield has called. President York has been told to yank the funding from Freddy Waxwroth's Slugworks and use the money to recruit student-athlete electronic gamers, taking care not to run afoul of NCAA regulations concerning the total number of recruits under the age of twelve. President York has also been instructed that his choral director will work up a something to perform with the Jakarta Boys' Choir, which will accompany the Indonesian delegation to the Rancho Rio ceremonies.

President York reaches Freddy Waxwroth in his lab and asks to see him at once. After an indifferent interval Waxwroth shambles in, chicly rumpled in the Prada lab coat given him by an anonymous admirer.

"Before you say anything, Dr. York, I wanted to explain about that regrettable episode involving certain Albino Banana Thugs and the Associate Director of Financial Aid and Parking Control."

President York raises a cautionary palm. "Hold on there, Dr. Waxwroth." He buzzes Marsha, asking her to bring in the University Policy and Procedure Statement on Bad News, Delivery of to the President, Person of (for delivery to President, Office of, see Section 139¶28.27[73]609±π4286-6b≥c{lx}1/8). Marsha marches right in with the requisite volume, giving a wide berth to Freddy, the stains and crusting on whose lab coat she believes, rightly, to be slug dung.

Leaving, Marsha ensures that she also remains well upwind of Freddy, while President York reads aloud from the bookmarked passage: "All information, allegations, and rumor (to say nothing of threats and remonstrances) that could be construed by a neutral party as bad news may be presented to the university president or his designee only on the third Tuesday of any month containing more than five but fewer than seven letters of the alphabet. Should the bearer of mediocre tidings have any reason to suspect his or her information may in fact fall unhappily short of mediocrity, said news must be presented to the University Advisory Council on Tidings for a binding finding."

"Now, then, Dr. Waxwroth, you were saying?"

Freddy, catching a whiff of his lab coat, wonders if he might contrive to sit upwind of himself. "I was saying," says Freddy, "here I am."

"So you are," says President York.

An awkward silence ensues, broken periodically by the distant whoosh of flamethrowers as the grounds and building crew lays siege to onrushing blackberry stolons that have made their way through the plumbing to emerge from the commodes in Marguerite Radclyffe Hall, the senior women's residence.

"Perhaps," Freddy suggests, "you had something in mind?"

"I'm sure I did," says President York, wondering if his Springfield clothier, Suit Yourself, carried the Prada Presidential Line.

"Maybe something to ask me, or tell me?" Freddy prompts.

"Tell you, yes, of course. I'm afraid, Waxwroth, that your research funding has been withdrawn." From its stand, President York withdraws the University Ceremonial Mace and lays it conspicuously athwart his desk to forestall harm to his person at the sentence he must now pronounce. "I have no recourse but to return you to the classroom."

"Oh please, please, Brer York, don't throw me in that pedagogical briar patch."

Recognizing at once the allusion to *Henry V, Part III*, President York rises to the literary challenge. "Once more into the breach, dear Waxwroth." Seeing Freddy take apparent heart at his stirring summons, President York presses on. "In fact, twice more into the breach. Frankly, we've had some trouble turning up faculty on a consistent basis for Inorganic Biology. As of next quarter, I'm releasing you from—" here President York consults his roster of university service— "your thirty-seven committee (standing and *ad hoc*), task force, working group, assessment consortium, quality team, and parking scrum assignments and giving you a second class."

"What will become of my lab?"

"It's being reconfigured to accommodate our varsity video-gaming student athletes."

"And what will become of the, uh, entities I have bioengineered?"

"Let's see," says President York, browsing Waxwroth's most recent progress report. "Contractually, the Albino Banana Thugs must be sent to Fox under right of first refusal for a talk show. What becomes of the Albino Plantain Slugs and Electric Bananas is up in the air pending award of our food service contract to one of three bidders: University Gourmet Hash, Professional University Karaokechow Enterprises, or Topnotch University Residential Dining."

Leaving President York's office, Freddy Waxwroth is decidedly of two minds. On the one lobe, he can scarcely refrain from clicking his heels in delight at the prospect of once again teaching students. On the other lobe, it's back to filching heels of bread and unidentified frying objects from the Faculty Club now that his slug bonus is lost. Somatically reflecting his mental quandary, Freddy pauses at the threshold of the outer office and, making certain he remains well beyond Marsha's grasp, leaps from the floor in a vaudevillian turn, clicking one heel and flinging residue from his lab coat across the room.

After an indecent interval, Marsha escorts into President York's chambers Wolfgang Glockenspiel, who has been hunched in the corner of her office reading a magazine of some sort beneath the folds of his raincoat.

"Ah, Glockenspiel," says President York, relishing his Anglo-continental, pan-European tone, which he fancies to be Nabokovesque, perhaps even Proustian.

"*Drang nacht Ostend*!" says Glockenspiel.

"My sentiments exactly," says President York. "Speaking of which, it will be necessary for you to work up a little piece for the Jakarta Boys' Choir, who will be performing tomorrow during the ceremony at Rancho Rio. Something simple, of course, given the time constraints. I was thinking perhaps a piece of Americana, some hearty folk song."

"*Das Volk saugt Eis*!"

"That's the spirit. I knew I could count on you. Here's the schedule," he says, handing Glockenspiel the program that Bakersfield has faxed through and rising to escort him to the door.

"*Arbeit macht frei*!" says Glockenspiel.

"No," says President York, "I don't believe they'll be *machting* a fish fry, but I'm sure there'll be some light refreshments."

When Glockenspiel is gone, President York starts to boogie out the door himself when Marsha reminds him of his 2:30 appointment with Mable Goodchuck to sit for an official portrait.

– LX –

Of the Gulfstream's landing at McKenzie Field, Tice will later write in his memoir, *Shit out of Luck*, that it rivaled in preposterosity only his touch-and-go on the Via Payola in San Mordita, where he snatched off a publicly identified tax-paying Italian just ahead of a mob of his fellow citizens.

On the Gulfstream's final approach to McKenzie, the field's runway lights had begun to wobble erratically and then strobe to the strains of "Eight Miles High." Tice and Wally had a quick but nasty little set-to about whether either or both were having a '60s acid flashback. They settled the matter by jointly grasping the stick, with Wally working the left rudder pedal while Tice handled the right.

On the ground, Mark Neighbors and Juggernaut bundle Bakersfield and the pilots into the Land Bruiser and churn off, giving a wide berth to the tower where E. E. Everclear is showing Stanley how to operate the anti-aircraft gun E. E. had acquired from Easy Ed's Pawn and Appliance after the attack by the ultralight with the Rising Sun insignia.

Settled in at Rancho Rio, Bakersfield lays out the program for tomorrow. Promptly at 8:00 a.m., the IRS Regional Plunderer will auction Buckthorn's parcel to MegaMax. Having confirmed the slimence on property of sufficient Albino Banana Slugs to remove them from the endangered species list, the State of Oregon will certify Rancho Rio as an approved development, eligible to register as a municipal utility district. Following a short musical interlude, Bakersfield will sign over 49 percent of the project to Indonesian interests, who will be motoring in from Twin Titties, Nevada, where they have been observing casino operations. (With big bucks to invest from the International Monetary Fund and given the unsettled political situation back home, Indonesia is looking to diversify investments, especially in countries without an extradition agreement with Jakarta.) After announcing attendant project management changes, Bakersfield will return to corporate headquarters by way of Salem, where formal papers certifying the development must be filed within twenty-four hours of field approval or the project is scuttled onto the Initiative and Petition track, the first stage of which requires seventeen years in the state judicial system before the Oregon Supreme Court rules on the legality of the language in the ballot title. Bakersfield sees no need to complicate the script by including the little post-Salem nip up north to Redmond, where they will announce the acquisition of a controlling interest in their first North American software venture to be renamed, reflective of both parties' relative financial position in the new entity, MegaMicro.

Having given the script to Mark Neighbors and Juggernaut, who will serve as masterpersons of ceremony, Bakersfield repairs to the Buckaroo Room, where it swills a nightcap of Old Apostolic, poured from the jeroboam of brandy knocked back by several Disciples at the Last Brunch and mixed with a jigger of liquefied sildenafil citrate in which has been steeped giant panda spleen, Siberian tiger gonads, and ginseng from a secret remnant patch fortuitously germinated in mastodon dung outside of Far Flung, Alaska. Bakersfield tosses it down, all the while chanting, "We must, we must, we must increase our lust."

– LXI –

From their forest fastness, the Gang of Five makes their way towards the Rancho Rio rendezvous. In his Smokey the Bear outfit, Sasquatch is crabby because the head keeps slipping around, obscuring his vision and causing periodic collisions with immobile impedimenta of the natural world, but Carlos Castaneda insists he must get used to the disguise before he mingles at Rancho Rio, pointing out that the rest of the Gang has redonned their McKenzie Fair costumes without complaint. Tony Ten-Toes Jr. is scrolling through an article on his MegaByte Tummytop (motto: "A Laptop for Baby Boomers") that assesses the impact of an alarmingly Aryan Kennewick Man on the United Nations General Assembly resolution calling on the United States to return to its aboriginal inhabitants all land west of a line running from Un Sound, Maryland, through GS-17, Virginia, to Fester, South Carolina. D. B. Cooper—exhaling little puffs of blue smoke as he sucks on moth balls he has filched from the garment bag the Smokey Bear costume came in, having mistaken them for Tums—whittles phrases into the bark of compliant alder as he trucks along: "If you knew what I was plannin' / Modes of travel you'd examine." Hiro Ishimatsu has flown on ahead, contriving to land on a bare patch of ground atop Buckthorn's bluff scarcely larger than Devaney's bald spot, positioned for a quick extraction or diversionary bombing run if something goes awry.

Down the steps of the rectory of the Church of the Doublewide come Reverend Endwell and the Fell Faller, hand in hand. The reverend has been asked to deliver the invocation at the Rancho Rio ceremony. As good an occasion as any, they have decided, to proclaim their coupledom. Pausing for a mutual grope, they thump lustily into the side of the church, popping a line of rivets.

"Shoddy workmanship," says Reverend Endwell, "even for a Sears secular humanist."

"Not to worry, cupcake," says the Fell Faller, clamping down on the siding with his teeth, crimping it like a stapleless stapler. "In fact, this reminds me of an old falling partner from my early years, Beau Saw, a Mississippi logger who could never remember whether to sharpen the front or back of the chisel bit teeth. And him a college graduate, too."

"I'd like to see his SAT scores," Reverend Endwell says petulantly.

"I don't think Dyslexia Tech requires them," says the Fell Faller. "In those days, I believe they used the hear thunder and/or see lightning baseline for admission."

"A shameful pedagogical passage in our nation's history. I must confess those were the self-same criteria the Free Will Apostolic Church of the Doublewide once employed for ordination."

"Even at that, they were losing prospective students left and right, or right and left, as the case may be. Last I heard, they'd shifted to the Hershey Standard of admission."

"The Hershey Standard?"

"You put one in an armpit applying to get in; if the chocolate melts within half an hour, it's an admit. Anything more than half an hour lands you on the waiting list."

"How come you know so much about this?" Reverend Endwell asks in mild alarm.

"My accountant's been on the waiting list for nineteen years."

Devaney drops by to pick up the soon-to-be-former Widow Wallop. He has agreed to take her to the Rancho Rio ceremony, having extracted a promise not to rend Bakersfield limb from limb for the little spin Beau Zipp took her for.

"I just want to see for myself what these guys look like," says Sheila. "In case they ever turn up in the Pour House."

Sheila is sporting a rock the size of Mount St. Helens (pre-eruption) on her engagement finger. Devaney had budgeted $124.99 for a ring, which Sheila used for an international call to a former business associate of Mr. Wallop's currently in the Federal Witness Protection Program of five countries. She asked him to turn up an eight-carat VVS1 D Sweetheart Cut stone in the next couple of days, reminding him of her copy of the company's books that the International Monetary Fund, the Cali cartel, Carl Woodward, and Semi-Tumescent Copy would like to lay hold of. While she has him on the line, Sheila also arranges the carburetor-capping of Beau Zipp's Camaro. The diamond arrives by courier inside of thirty-six hours.

After waggling her hand around like a signalman waving semaphores, Sheila finally contrives to bang her knuckle on one of the bar's rock-hard sandwiches and proffers the digit for Devaney to kiss and make all well.

Nearly chipping a tooth on the adamantine pledge of his troth, Devaney brings Sheila's hand into trifocal distance and whistles appraisingly. "That's got to be at least a 7.9476294-carat stone. Something that big would have to retail for at least three times $124.99, minimum."

Sheila nuzzles Devaney's earlobe, so like a basset hound's. "You just don't have any idea what a terrific little shopper you're getting."

The sexual debacle at Buckthorn's coming hard, as it were(n't), upon the sexual debacle at the Inn and Out, Amanda has lost hope of prompting, provoking, enticing, inducing, or wheedling community development of any sort on the upper McKenzie. She schemes to slip into media shots of the Rancho Rio ceremony so as to include them in her quarterly report to the Ford Foundation in which she will highlight her role in bringing the Rancho Rio project to fruition, having early on told Sheila she thought Beau Zipp would be a good catch, prompting Sheila's sale of the parcel of land Rancho Rio needed for state certifiable contiguity of turf. Anxious to look her best, Amanda undertakes a two-day desiccant diet in which she powders herself with silicate and cuts back to half pints of Häagen-Dazs.

In Springfield, Rod and Stephanie wheel out of the parking lot at Eyeclueless News in Sam Donaldson, the station's Blitzer-mobile. The chance to film and perhaps interview the reclusive Bakersfield could be a major career breakthrough. Stephanie has honed her reportorial instincts to a razor edge for this one, her Albino Banana Slug investigative reporting having nearly landed her not in Spokane but on the environmental beat, that graveyard of careers. This time, she's leaving nothing to chance. "Did anybody, like, remember film for the camera?"

Orville Crease goes through it one more time. "The suits will be the ones wearing the suits. Okay? They're wearing the suits because they have the money. We don't have the money. But if we play our cards right tomorrow, we'll have their money. Waylon will concentrate on boosting wallets. Wick will arrange to be run over by the Land Bruiser in a nonfatal but tortful fashion. Willa will entice a likely-looking suit into the woods and then rip her bodice and cry for help, bringing Mama and me on the run to identify the perpetrator. Iphigenia will continue to pocket small bills from the register at the Pour House. Any questions?"

Waylon raises his hand. "When we get the money, do we have to wear suits?"

Orville gives him the Arkansas squint. "Any other questions?"

"What's a tort?" asks Wick.

"What's a bodice?" asks Willa.

"Will we have to pay Sheila's bills after I pocket them?" asks Iphigenia.

Buckthorn, too, is headed for Rancho Rio. Having heard of the Rancho Rio gathering, he eschews his projected detonation on Guy Fawkes Day or whenever (Buckthorn having entered the date on his Victoria's Secret calendar, which Stanley has lifted, leaving Buckthorn more clueless than ever) for the grand prospect of sculpturally flashing an audience of MegaMaxers.

Sarah Trip is also making plans to attend, figuring that sooner or later she has to make a clean breast of it. A flyer posted at Devaney's Mercantile had advertised the one-day-only stopover of a mobile breast enhancement company, Noble Knockers (motto: "Flats Fixed"), at Loretta's Curl Up and Dye. While her 36cs were perfectly serviceable, they seemed somehow so average. Sarah had always believed that women should take charge of their own bodies. Biology was not destiny. Less might be more—as was more—but middling certainly wasn't. She had yet to come across a website devoted to ordinary tits.

The nonsurgical procedure ($49.98 for one breast; $129.95 for two ((on the same torso)) involved a vacuum pump sealed around the boobies in question. Drawing four hundred pounds per square inch of suction, the pump lowered atmospheric pressure around the bazooms, which swelled like a balloon rising into the stratosphere. As the milk ducts billowed, lymph and blood rushed into the enlarged chambers through one-way valves. Filled, the ducts remained distended when the suction was removed.

All went exactly as advertised except that the operator—distracted by Loretta's homegrown but cleverly hoisted chi chis—forgot to set the timer. Rushing back to disengage the pump, the operator found Sarah a 55EE. And so she remained, the process irreversible.

Sarah hopes to see Lunelle Johnson-Bender at the Rancho Rio ceremonies to ask if the company that manufactures her industrial-strength girdle offers a line of bras.

As for Loretta, another prospect slipped from her grasp, she must continue to pin her hopes on Bungle, an app for the romantically impaired.

– LXII –

And so it comes to pass that on the appointed day the appointed parties and others without portfolio gather at Rancho Rio. They assemble on banks of the McKenzie, staking out their positions relative to the scrumptious spread on the buffet tables: vegetables catered by Artichoke till You Croak; white wine by Amazing Grapes, red by Beloved Zinfandel, blush by Easy Ed's Pawn and Appliance; beef by Pig Out, a kosher meat market in Springfield; white desserts by Cellulite Express, brown desserts by Insulin Shock, convivial desserts by Sweetie Pies, angry desserts by Crêpes of Wrath, mobile desserts by Rolling Scones, legal desserts by Just Desserts, illegal desserts by Desserted, leftover desserts by ReTorts; natural vitamins by Swallow It Whole; Spam entrée by Corporal Punishment (motto: "Naturally Bulimic"). More than once, the Gang regrets that Hiro isn't here to share recipes.

The various parties eye each other approvingly while casting a skeptical eye at the sundry parties and vice versa. Others cast a skeptical nose as Smokey Bear and a collie with a blunt head, suspiciously pug muzzle, and docked tail circle around sniffing each other's rear end.

Sarah Trip, not yet accustomed to navigating her frontage in public, bumps into Amanda, setting off a burble and trill of greeting.

"There's something, I don't know, different about you," says Amanda. "Don't tell me, you've found the secret to spot reducing. Almost everything looks so much smaller. You *must* tell me how."

Across the way, Mark Neighbors's standard male boob alert rockets beyond the silicon zone into the monumental Zeppelin of Mount Hootmore.

Devaney cautions his oncoming bride to be careful where she aims her ring, having traced a hole lasered in the side of the Land Bruiser to Sheila's diamond.

Juggernaut is escorting Agent Orange and his boss, Commissioner N. Remington Armory, through the Rancho Rio holdings, pointing out periodically the impostor Albino Banana Slugs she has procured from Freddy Waxwroth. Despite avid interest expressed by the university food service bidders, Freddy has turned over to Juggernaut all slugs save one, holding it back at the request of Mable Goodchuck, who requires a model for the body to which she will affix the head of a recently commissioned official portrait.

D. B. Cooper and Wolfgang Glockenspiel are deeply embedded in conversation about lyrics, while Carlos Castaneda scans the crowd in vain for Barry Buncombe, who has gotten stuck in his driveway again.

Reverend Endwell and the Fell Faller stroll hand in hand, provoking nonplussment among all save C. C. Fellows, who figures the reverend has gotten into his crop in the furnace room.

Rod is interviewing Tony Ten-Toes Jr., asking what it was like to ride with the Lone Ranger all those years.

Unsure of his standing with MegaMax, President York tries to appear both actively schmoozing on behalf of corporate interests with those assembled in case Bakersfield is keeping an eye on him while at the same time trying to render himself invisible, not wishing to come to Bakersfield's attention in case he's currently in hot water.

Bakersfield keeps to itself, scrutability being to MegaMax corporate culture what clarity is to the Federal Tax Code. They are cautiously prepared to exchange pleasantries with Indonesia, but Indonesia is having a Bahasa hissy fit trying to get through on their ConCo TurboCell phone to the Aspen Federal Correctional Institution and is not available for idle chitchat.

Stanley and E. E. Everclear are nowhere to be found.

From out of nowhere, a black helicopter appears, its turbines silent as an assassin, its rotors carving air like green beer through a Baptist. Emerging Darthly, a figure makes his Vaderesque way to the podium, escorted by a phalanx of uni-forms. All fall back before the Northwest Regional IRS Vice Plunderer—the Under Plunderer as well as his immediate superiors, the Assistant and Deputy Pillagers, being unavailable as they are currently engaged in seizing Mother Teresa's hovelment on the grounds that doing something stupendously stupid not to mention egregiously illegal is just the sort of thing that keeps your average taxpayer on his toes.

As master of ceremonies, Mark Neighbors asks Reverend Endwell to offer the invocation. The Vice Plunderer steps down off the dais so as to maintain due separation of church and state.

"Dearly beloved, we are gathered here in the sight of God and man to—"

"Hey, twinky," says Sheila, "turn your notes right side up."

"Right," says Reverend Endwell. "Heh, heh. A little liturgical slip-up there." He thumbs frantically through his Bible, at last lighting on the appropriate crib sheet tucked into the Song of Seizures, itself sandwiched between the Acts of the Revenuers and the Book of Lamentations.

"Fellow taxpayers, we gather here today to celebrate the transformation of Brother Buckthorn's property from a debit to a credit. We are reminded on this occasion that one day we must all be held accountable by the Celestial Revenue Service, asking what return of capital gains on our soul. Till then, may the Angel of Audit pass over our door. Amen."

Though the crowd contains not so much as a single Baptist, a mighty chorus of "amens" rises from every throat.

The Vice Plunderer reseizes the podium. Before he proceeds with the auction, he offers a folksy little homily on the IRS as part of the Warm and Fuzzy image buffing campaign, designed for them by Duh & Baldface, a public relations firm that also handles the Bashar al-Assad, Global Warming, Coronavirus, and 115th Congress accounts. The Vice Plunderer reminds the assemblage that without the IRS there would be no money for $20 National Endowment for the Arts grants, $200 standard military set screws, $2,000 lifetime recertification programs for air traffic controllers,

$200,000 congressional junkets, $200,000,000 subsidies to tobacco growers, the $2,000,000,000 invasion of Grenada, and $2,000,000,000,000 to fund Kenneth Starr's investigation.

He continues: "I submit, fellow taxpayers—I see some barely suppressed looks of scorn out there (like you, we too pay less than our fair share every April 15)—I submit that the IRS, cheap target (cheap, that is, if you discount that any public IRS joke triggers an automatic audit of the comedian, who, on average, falling into the 17.417 percent tax bracket, is discovered to have underestimated his tax liability by $2,322.87)—"

"My kind of guy," Devaney whispers to Sheila.

"—for so many hurtful and rarely funny jokes is, in fact, the benchmark institution largely responsible for the greatness of our Republic. Consider: before the IRS was founded, we were little more than a bumptious oaf of a nation, lumbering along like Europe's cartoon sidekick. Today, a scant 104 years after our founding under Commissioner Nelson "Brass" Knuckles, America has put a man on the moon, developed the low-flush toilet, and is the military, cinematic, and fast food envy of the world. A coincidence? I think not."

Wick nudges his father's ribs. "After we get everybody's money, can I have a low-flush toilet?"

The Vice Plunderer continues: "Scoff if you will"—a nudge to a uni-form sends him into the crowd, where he positively IDS Freddy Waxwroth who, truth be told, had been merely sniggering, not scoffing—"but I have just reviewed a study conducted by the Friends of the IRS, currently operating out of the Aspen Federal Correctional Institute, which found that the IRS generated economic activity greater than the combined GNPS of Australia, Brazil, and Nike. Not only do we directly employ 17 million Americans, but our ripple effect affords employment to millions more: accountants, lawyers, comedians, tax shelter annuity salesmen, reform congressional candidates, lobbyists, the penal system, printers and their entire vertically integrated system of loggers, truckers, millwrights, pulp and paper engineers. With the draft abolished and death on the run before our triumphant duo of managed health care and the pharmaceutical industry (the longer you stay alive, the more money they make; this, my friends, is exactly how capitalism works to everyone's benefit), taxes remain our sole national leveler, our singular common ground. The Tax Code unites pauper and plutocrat, cheaters all, in common cause. That we fall short of fiscal rectitude renders us more accepting of the shortcomings of others, promoting civil polity. America, my fellow evaders, was built on derring-do, those undeterable risk-takers out there pushing the envelope. Today, that tradition continues as we provide opportunities for the bold and reckless to claim home office deductions and business losses, run off-the-books cash-only operations, overstate charitable contributions, and neglect withholding on domestic help. Without the challenge of April 15, I declare that America would sink back into the tepid slough of routine lawfulness. Nor is the IRS exempt from doing our share to promote racial conciliation. In fiscal year 2016, for example, we achieved our long-term goal of convicting 184 white taxpayers for every taxpayer of color, contributing importantly to adjusting the racial imbalance in our federal penitentiaries. So when you think of the IRS, just remember our slogan: Your Organization under Reform as Stipulated by Statute: Internal (*Sotto Gaudioso*) Revenue (Affording Sensational) Service."

A hearty huzzah erupts from the throng. The Vice Plunderer nods graciously, then waves the crowd to silence. "We must be about our government's business. We are gathered here in the sight of G word and Mammon to auction to the highest bidder a parcel of property, Township 16S, Range 5E, Section 20, the SW of the NW, colloquially known as Buckthorn's Bluff. Be there any here today who objects to this proceeding, speak now or forever hold your horses."

"I do," says Tony Ten-Toes Jr., waving above his head what appears to be an ancient bar tab with a scriggle of writing on the side opposite the numbers. "It's all here in the original terms of my grandfather's bet with Buckthorn's progenitor, Cecil "Walleye" Buckthorn. If Walleye Buckthorn or his successors ever relinquishes the property, the Qnxtqkl have right of first refusal."

At once, a uni-form and two duplicates are at Tony's side. Lopping off his rear end less than a pound of flesh but more than is strictly necessary, they run a DNA field test, transmitting the results by satellite feed to the IRS central computer bank in GS-17, Virginia. In less than an instant but longer than the time spent writing the script for *Titanic*, the central computer returns a list of every Tony in its data base. Further fiddling produces a roster of every Jr., Mr. Rogers's enemy list, and some explicit .jpg files from Cybersluts. At length, the gene scan hits the jackpot, confirming a positive hit, which the Vice Plunderer reviews on-screen on his IRS-issued wristwatch where the time and date always read April 16, 12:01 a.m.

"I have confirmation here that the taxpayer in question is a lineal descendent of Tony Twelve-Toes—"

"I told you so," shouts Tony triumphantly.

"—who remains on our books as having never remitted the federal blanket tax for the delivery by the Bureau of Indian Affairs of smallpox-impregnated bedding to the Qnxtqkl. The original tax, with penalties and interest, is, even for those of us accustomed to such numbers, no trifling sum. My agents will escort Mr. Ten-Toes Jr. to somewhere we can discuss his personal and tribal tax situation privately."

And so they do, as the Vice Plunderer auctions off Buckthorn's property to MegaMax in less time than it takes to hack Microsoft's operating system but more time than the duration of Rick Perry's presidential campaign. His business concluded, the Vice Plunderer rises with his phalanx in the black helicopter, heading for the Mildew, Oregon, District Office to unruffle the feathers of local agents who are complaining that the Kinder and Gentler Directive, which authorizes seizure of second-born sons but not first, gives them insufficient leverage with the tax-aversive public.

With the contiguous property requirement satisfied, all that remains for full development approval is certification by State Fish and Game that Albino Banana Slugs exist in numbers sufficient to render moot (coincidentally the very law firm, Render and Moot, that got MegaMax off the hook for that unfortunate episode involving the Southern Baptist Convention and MegaMuff, the corporate division that manufactures, fits, and reconditions pubic toupees) the protection of slug habitat.

Commissioner N. Remington Armory, having been assured by Agent Orange that the manifold Albino Plantain Slugs, gamboling amidst fungi, mold, and general rottage on the forest floor, were the genuine article despite the absence of certifying Chiquita stickers, mounts the platform manfully and asks Bakersfield to step forward.

"On behalf of the State of Oregon, I'm pleased to present you with this certificate of development. How rare it is to find a proposal that will take the forest primeval and make of it, if I may say so, a forest prime good." Although he is uncertain what he has just said, Commissioner Armory pauses, according to the stage directions in his script, waiting for the laughter and applause to die down. With nothing forthcoming from the audience save an imperfectly suppressed groan from President York, Commissioner Armory shoots Agent Orange, who has written the speech, a testy glance. Agent Orange shrugs indifferently. When he delivers Sasquatch, his future at the commission is assured. No more mucking about in the field; no more humiliating grade school presentations on Earth Day where all the kids want to know is what he had to do with shooting Bambi's mother. He envisions trips to Scotland to advise on capture of the Loch Ness monster, consultancies in France on the habitat and behavior of gargoyles and griffins, maybe a gig in New York to follow up on the last confirmed sighting of a professional football team in the city.

Commissioner Armory thrusts sheaves of papers into Bakersfield's several hands and concludes: "I must remind you that this warrant is invalid until notarized by the Oregon Secretary of Stuff's Office, said endorsement being affixed no later than sundown the day of provisional award delivery, that day being this day."

At once, Mark Neighbors steps forward with a container made by Rubber Ducky into which the documents are sealed with rubber cement to protect them from conventional drizzle, exotic mists, and stealth downpours. The container is then chained through an open fly to the Johnson of one of the Herbert Walkers brought along for this express courier service.

The papers secure, Mark Neighbors announces a musical interlude with two numbers to be performed by the Jakarta Boys' Choir conducted by Professor Wolfgang Glockenspiel of MegaMax University. The first tune, a haunting folk ballad, translated for the audience by Professor Glockenspiel from Bahasa to German and thence to English, works out to be approximately "The Obligatory Copra Cartel of the Suharto Clan Incites Prosperity to All Who Deserve It." Indonesia breaks into copious tears at the lovely waft of children's voices and the tender sentiments expressed.

Maestro Glockenspiel then introduces the second number, an American folk song, per President York's instructions, this celebrating a mid-Atlantic seaboard state with amended lyrics by D. B. Cooper. The rising buzz of the crowd is at once overridden by thirty dulcet voices raised in heavily inflected but perfectly comprehensible English:

"Nothing could be fina than to be in her vagina in the moorrrrning."

Mark Neighbors leaps from his chair at the back of the platform, rushing towards Glockenspiel. President York hauls out an unopened roll of Tums from his pocket and swallows it whole.

"Nothing could be sweeter than to greet her with my peter in the moorrrning."

As Mark Neighbors nears the podium, Glockenspiel gestures to the choir and twenty-nine boys race randomly about the platform setting off fireworks while the thirtieth fires up the fog machine that Glockenspiel has salvaged from last year's theater department's production of MacBush. In the haze and pyrotechnics, Glockenspiel slips away, later to turn up as choral director for the IRS, arranging a medley of songs to divert taxpayers during audits: "Who's Sorry Now?" "Crying," the sentencing aria from *Madam Helmsley*, and everyone's favorite, "The Taxman."

When order is restored, Indonesia is clearly shaken, and Bakersfield is at some pains to allay their concerns, assuring them that a full investigation will be launched with the innocent punished and the guilty hired on in the corporate black bag division, MegaMum, fronting as the corporate floral division.

Meanwhile, up on the bluff, Buckthorn is sweating over a hot detonator that cannot be induced to detonate, even when Buckthorn applies his secret Boy Scout martial arts move which, administered to the engine block of his Forest Service surplus Chevy, never fails to compel the truck to say uncle and turn over. As Hiro watches, camouflaged in a thicket of Fainting Fern—a non-native species introduced on the McKenzie in the Victorian period and now aggressively replacing a native species, *Lactuca Icebergian*, a colorless, odiferous, uncomely, and violence-prone fern commonly known as Settlers' Bain—Buckthorn fishes around in one of the holes and pulls out an Albino Banana Slug engorged on plastique stabilizer which he finally manages to dislodge from his fingers by applying the Oregon Red Cross Council Slug Sluffer Procedure, taught routinely west of the Cascades along with CPR and the Heimlich maneuver. Then he fishes out of the hole wiring whose insulation seems to have been dissolved by some sluggish secretion, shorting out the electrical charge from the detonator. Even to Buckthorn, whose electrical acumen has served as the inspiration for countless jokes about how many environmental sculptors it takes to fit a three-prong plug into a two-prong outlet, it is apparent that the combination of raw wire and no stabilizer could prove unpredictable.

Back at the podium, Bakersfield is at the microphone to announce management changes at Rancho Rio when a cry erupts from the back of the crowd nearest the river. Upstream, around a sharp bend, a large, quasi-rectangular object heaves into view. Bakersfield pauses as the crowd rushes to the bank, straining to identify the unidentified floating object.

"It's a Great Blue," says Barry Buncombe, who has dislodged from his driveway and joined the throng. "Seen them often in the Arctic fastness."

"It's an Arkansas castle," says Orville Crease.

"It's Imelda Marcos," says Indonesia.

"It's my church," howls Reverend Endwell, as indeed it is.

As it happens, the Sears Siding Man has been lurking for days at the Inn and Out, sharing a room with a vacationing businessman and his family, Oedipus Gypopolis, proprietor of Oedipus Wrecks, a low-end, pre-owned car lot in Buffoon Falls, Ohio (motto: "Birthplace of Presidents"), to save on expenses, waiting for the window of opportunity to repossess the Church of the

Doublewide. All goes smoothly until he takes the historic Belknap zigzag bridge (built in 1894 when the Oregon Ferryman's lobby still had enough clout in Salem to insist that no bridge constructed with public funds could offer a competitive advantage timewise to those who drove across a body of water compared to those who were ferried) at fifteen miles an hour, three times its posted speed. While the Sears man and his truck escape unscathed, the Church of the Doublewide ruptures its hitch at the first zig, sailing through the railing of the subsequent zag and plunging into the mighty stream.

Reverend Endwell's howl of despair is matched by C. C. Fellows, who strips to his hemp skivvies emblazoned with his corporate slogan: "McKenzie Mauve: Official Drug of the Portland Trailblazers." He dog-paddles into the current, hoping somehow to wrest his crop from a watery grave.

While the crowd mills around, aimless as the Jets' offensive line on a pass play, Devaney takes quick stock of the situation. "At 6,300 cubic feet displacement," he tells Sheila, "and assuming breachment of one-third of the windows and one of two doors, given the standard leakage rate of Sears siding with McKenzie running 4,327 cubic feet per second, I'd estimate that the church will go down one-third of the way through Riff Raff Riffle, two-thirds of the way if it enters bow first."

Directly opposite Rancho Rio, Riff Raff Riffle was so named by McKenzie boatmen for its deceptive eight-inch standing wave followed by a suck hole with the hydraulics of a professional blow job, capable of swallowing fraternity rafters, hippie inner tubers, honeymooning canoeists, and entire Boy Scout troops, leaving the McKenzie to the guides and their paying customers.

As the doublewide approaches Riff Raff, C. C. Fellows appears suddenly atop the trailer, wrenching back great sheets of siding to get at his crop in the furnace room. The doublewide heaves and bucks at the top of the Riffle, an especially vigorous heavage leaving C. C. somehow entangled in a seventy-five-foot extension cord that Reverend Endwell has run along the eaves to illuminate his rooftop sign for any nocturnal flyovers: "Heaven/Hell/McKenzie Station," with directional arrows. Halfway through the Riffle, the doublewide begins to nose under, with C. C. lashed atop like Gregory Peck to Moby Special Effects.

Having assayed the situation from Buckthorn's Bluff, Hiro Ishimatsu fires up the ultralight, bursting from the thicket of Fainting Fern and rising into the complex McKenzie air with scarcely a glance from Buckthorn, who is trying to recall how Alec Guinness handled that tricky piece of recalcitrant kablooie in *The Bridge on the River Kwai*.

Two-thirds submerged and approaching the mighty suck hole, the doublewide bears C. C. doomward. Even were he to free himself in time, the cunning currents would bear him down after the trailer. Out of nowhere appears Hiro, engine revved over the red line to match the speed of the current, hovering just above C. C. and flailing with the ceremonial sword he carries in case of capture. After a tricky piece of swordsmanship from which only the most bloodthirsty among the bankside throng fail to avert their eyes, C. C. is free from the extension cord and clinging to the undercarriage of the ultralight as Hiro peels off and slaloms upriver, unable, with the extra weight, to achieve an altitude greater than twenty feet.

At which point several things occur simultaneously, verifying for careful observers Heisenberg's Uncertainty Principle, the Paradox of Schrödinger's Slug, and the Dufus Corollary: "Shit Happens."

In Chigger Knob, Tennessee, Roxie Rae removes her bubblegum-flavored panties from a drier at the Laundromat, Bar, and Detanning Salon (motto: "For That Pasty White Southern Hookworm Look") just as Sarah Trip's 55EEs burst asunder her Lily of Akron, an industrial-strength brassiere marketed to eastern European émigrée over the age of sixty, shredding her blouse and emerging there in their altogetherness, neither sagging nor bowsprinting out in the silicon salute but improbably rising, as if filled with helium, aloft in the same complex McKenzie air that bears up Hiro and C. C., and at nearly the same altitude. The resultant transcontinental erotic charge lifts all Johnsons present in grateful tribute, none more reverential than Mark Neighbors's.

Simultaneously, Waylon Crease seizes the diversionary

moment to lift the wallet of one of the suits. Although it is indeed shiny as sharkskin from thirty years of daily employment, President York's threadbare Harris Tweeds, while academic formal wear, are in fact not a suit but a sport jacket and slacks. The resultant wallet, thinner than the seat of his pants, whisks out of his back pocket in a blue nimbus of static electricity.

Simultaneously, Freddy Waxwroth, shorting out on sensory overload, the avoidance of which drew him to the glacial calm of the lab those many years ago, withdraws from his Watson and Crick lunch pail an Electric Banana and hurls it towards the fraying knot of Bakersfield and Indonesia.

On the bluff, the change in Buckthorn's pocket flies to his Johnson.

In times of crisis, Buckthorn's mind, so often an organ of obliquity—indeed, to put it bluntly, stumpage—processes the world's multiplicity and delivers a digitally direct verdict. "Uh-oh," says Buckthorn's mind, in case anyone is tuned in.

Uncharacteristically, yet fortuitous for future generations of Buckthorns, Buckthorn does not reflexively punch the manual override on his Catastrophic Rapidly Incoming Pulverization Emergency System. Crashing through the Fainting Fern, he bails off the backside of the bluff as the first charge detonates. It is followed by a concussive sequence and Buckthorn, pelted by debris, roars in triumph as his percussive choreography dances on across the bluff face.

Below, all turn as the cliff, shrouded in dust and smoke, continues to erupt, hailing down upon the throng granite, gneiss, gabbro, gahnite, gangue, gley, greisen, and grit along with a deluge of white slime flecks, each of which, upon landing, oozes towards the nearest succulent green. The last explosion launches among the throng several duckable pieces of something man-made. It falls to Devaney to identify their provenance. "Holy harbinger," says Devaney, holding up a Chevy wheel bearing, a worse-for-wear dildo, and an immaculate slice of fruitcake. "These are Harley's."

All of which would have made fine footage for the 7:14 Eyeclueless News at Six, except that Orville Crease has boosted the camera and when Stephanie goes looking for Rod to help locate the perpetrator, she finds him at last in a patch of distinctively three-leafed viny shrub boinking Willa Crease.

By now, of course, Indonesia has pulled the plug on the whole deal and is headed for West Springfield, where they have been invited to advise the city council on how to land a Nike fabrication plant by foregrounding a labor pool of mental patients, county prisoners, and work-study students from local elementary schools who will assemble Air Croesus at 82 cents an hour with half pay for overtime since the company is providing them with more work than contractually guaranteed.

Nor does Bakersfield see any good reason for sticking around. Piling into the Land Bruiser, they look first for Mark Neighbors, who is strolling hand in hand with Sarah Trip along the McKenzie whistling the theme from *Titanic*, "My Heart Will Go Yawn," and explaining how the sinking of the doublewide was a virtual remake of *Titanic II: Down for Keeps* and that though they were from different worlds their love was fated to be. Nor is Juggernaut available to drive, for as the smoke and dust clear from the cliff face all behold what Buckthorn has wrought.

In years to come, though McKenzie citizens will engage in spirited debate over the aesthetic accomplishment jutting from the cliffside, all agree that the sculpture's lifelike fidelity, its embrace of the most exacting tenets of realism—traits, the natives confide, that are engaged only sketchily in Buckthorn's own life—is incontestable, even if you've never laid eyes on the model.

Who is Marta Juggernaut.

For instead of a mighty Johnson, what emerges from the clearing scrim of rock mote and assorted pulverado is Juggernaut herself, or more exactly her torso. At each breast, an infant suckles.

Nip and tuck with the exploded dildo in the worse-for-wear category, Buckthorn scrambles to the edge of the bluff to behold his creation. From above, he cannot make out the resultant form, so he scoots down the mountain to gain a better vantage point. Which, having gained, he stares dumbfounded at his handiwork. Spinning in reverse, Buckthorn's mind, whose comfort zone is neutral and red zone is forward, takes a stab at it. Perhaps his fixation on Juggernaut's bazooms subliminally subverted his intended design. Perhaps the slugfeast and exotic electrical swarm had teleologically altered the explosive sequence. Perhaps MegaMax Minions had ferreted out his purpose and intervened. Most probably, the universe, bored with expanding, had momentarily contracted to inscribe another postmodern chapter in the Carnal Comedy, a chapter in which Buckthorn's name is writ in silly putty.

Weeping in despair at his comeuppance or putdownance, Buckthorn is startled by a firm yet feathery touch on his gritty brow.

"Oh, Harley," says Juggernaut, "Thank heaven you're alive. Tell me where it hurts."

Not unreasonably, Buckthorn tries out the possibilities of hallucination or after-death experience. In either likely event, he sees no harm in going for it. "I believe," says Buckthorn, "that some insult has been delivered to my Johnson. It seems to be wafting uncontrollably." A claim confirmed by the bulge in Buckthorn's pants wagging about like a black lab's tail in proximity to a stick and body of water.

"Well, let's just take the situation in hand and tuck that Johnson someplace snug. We can get a start on the twins."

"Holy humpingworth," is the last thing Buckthorn remembers saying as Juggernaut tugs down his drawers.

With no local driver, Bakersfield takes the wheel, cutting a couple of cookies in compound low as the Land Bruiser plows out of Rancho Rio heading for the McKenzie airstrip, the requisite papers chained to the Herbert Walker's Johnson. With Indonesia out of the picture, a four-banger is out of the question, but the main money from a three-fer—screwing McKenzie residents, Rancho Rio property owners, and the State of Oregon—remains on the table.

Taken by surprise, Wick is caught with his boot laces tied together (something Iphigenia has done to him on every important occasion since his elementary school graduation ceremony, when he was trying to get to the bathroom to shave so as to be presentable) and cannot hurl himself in front of the Land Bruiser per Daddy's instructions. Filling the bill, however, is Bart Bevel, who is so intent on writing up Sasquatch for unauthorized display of a Smokey the Bear suit that he leaps only partially out of the way, landing on his Federal, only to watch Sasquatch stroll away, having eaten not only the citation but Bevel's entire citation book.

As the Land Bruiser roars off, careful observers will later remark on the *faux* collie flattened out on the roof rack.

Wally and Tice have the Gulfstream ready to go as the Land Bruiser skids to a halt at the head of the airstrip. Bakersfield and the Herbert Walker pile out—the Herbert Walker piling very gingerly, to be sure—and clamber aboard, as does a furtive, doglike shape that scuttles unseen into the baggage compartment. In the tower, E. E. Everclear cannot raise the Gulfstream for clearance to taxi, much less take off. Whenever he keys the mike, his electric flosser fires up, so perhaps the fault lies somewhere in the tangle of plugs and cords. But no matter. Rules are rules, and he sends Stanley onto the strip in his Peterbilt to shuttle the pilots to the tower for a personal briefing or, failing that, to block their departure.

In homage to cinematographic if not literary convention, the two vehicles hurtle towards each other from opposite ends of the strip. As the Gulfstream rises, from out of the woods emerges the ultralight, C. C. Fellows dangling beneath. Tice, who is piloting since Wally is nursing a gigantic Viagra headache, threads the Gulfstream through a slot narrower than a sumo wrestler's coronary artery, nipping through just beneath C. C.'s dangle and just above the Peterbilt. Except for the partially retracted landing gear, which the truck shears off.

Five minutes into the flight, another problem emerges as the instrument panel goes postal, dials and gauges spinning wildly while the hydraulic system shuts down save for the independent plumbing circuit, which enables the Gulfstream to tilt and hop like a lowrider whenever they sneak the plane into the Bakersfield Cinco de Mayo parade. Wally goes aft to check out the trouble while Tice wrestles the plane around so he can belly in at McKenzie.

When Wally emerges at length from the baggage compartment, Bakersfield is in no mood for it. Wally, as full of wonder as Speke at having found the source of the Nile, delivers the news: "Some wild creature has et the casing plumb off the wiring and is sucking down hydraulic lines like so much spaghetti."

On their final approach, Wally bets Tice he can't land the

Gulfstream downhill with the wind at his back. Tice takes him up on it and brings the Gulfstream in light as a feather, skidding down the grassy field like a sweet-rolling putt on bent-grass Bermuda.

"Holy Haviland," says Wally. "You never brought it in that smooth *with* landing gear. How come you always do those coyote ugly landings with the wheels down?"

"Those what?"

"Coyote ugly; you know."

"Remind me," says Tice, firing up a cigar as the Gulfstream whispers to a halt.

"Well, there's one-bag ugly, two-bag ugly, and coyote ugly."

"I'm with you so far."

"One-bag ugly, you put a sack over her head before you do her; two-bag, you put a sack over both your heads. Coyote ugly, you come to the next morning and she's sleeping on your arm, you gnaw it off to get away instead of waking her up."

"Been there," says Tice.

Clustered around the Land Bruiser, Bakersfield resolves to drive to Salem, having just enough time to make it before the close of business. Precious minutes are lost, however, as they argue about who gets to ride shotgun, who's wedged in the middle, and who gets the sauna. Ignored, the Herbert Walker wanders off forlornly, the Rubber Ducky container chain beginning to chafe his Johnson. He has begun to wonder whether his MBA from Altered State College of California has really prepared him for the corporate marketplace.

Bakersfield's squabble is brought to a screeching halt (unaccustomed to raising their voice, the corporate octave *in extremis* is the far side of shrill) by a detonation from the opposite side of the Land Bruiser. Rushing to the site, Bakersfield arrives in time to catch a glimpse of Chuck Wepner scooting into a blackberry thicket edging the runway as the Land Bruiser's right front tire wheezes its last breath. The spare, it turns out, has been replaced by the satellite uplink.

But Bakersfield has been in tough spots before. Most recently when they consolidated every HMO in the country under their subsidiary, MegaMed$, overriding opposition from the Democrats, the Republicans, forty-seven state legislatures, the American Medical Association, the Medical Investigative Drug Associated Suppliers, the federal courts, the Girl Scouts, and the *Sports Illustrated* swimsuit issue. Seeing the ultralight idling at the end of the runway while Hiro attempts to pry C. C.'s fingers from the undercarriage, Bakersfield orders Wally to commandeer the device and fly the Herbert Walker to Salem.

Although Hiro does not understand English, he speaks perfectly fluent .45 caliber, as does C. C., who unhands his death grip. Which is replaced at once by the death grip of the Herbert Walker who must turn loose the Rubber Ducky container to fuse all ten digits to the ultralight. The container sways beneath him, the chain tugging prodigiously at his Johnson as the ultralight rises, millimeter by millimeter, from the airstrip.

When rocketing out of the blackberry thicket, as if propelled by a plume of hydraulic fluid—that notorious canine purgative—comes Chuck Wepner, angling towards the ultralight and making up ground. It is a close thing, with Wally squeezing everything out of the plane, hunching back and forth the way he used to get a little extra out of his Flexi-Flier on the sledding hill back in Average, Iowa. He is, in the end, overmatched. At the last moment, Chuck hurls himself skyward, extending his muzzle in an ultimate Frisbee layout and snatching the pendant container.

Which, though stuffed with the entrée of Gulfstream and Land Bruiser, he gobbles greedily, Rubber Ducky being the Häagen-Dazs of rubber, sporting a higher latex content than anything west of Kaputistan's monthly federal paychecks.

In years to come, Chuck Wepner will be feted on the anniversary of his heroic eats. Of the Herbert Walker's unfortunate Johnson, no one speaks.

– LXIII –

Some few weeks later, in a predicted interval between the extraordinary bi-weekly El Niño fronts and the routine tri-weekly northern Pacific fronts known locally as El Hombre, a rash of nuptials breaks out.

First up are Reverend Endwell and the Fell Faller. Having scoured the Postal Code and Oregon Civil Statutes, Devaney discovers that he is empowered as McKenzie Station Postmaster to marry parties of the same sex so long as the ceremony takes place simultaneously on an official Postal Service site and property owned by the State of Oregon. He sends Buckthorn up the highway to saw off a couple of road signs, adding the caution not to take any that would put motorists at risk.

More than once, Buckthorn has been forced to the shoulder when approaching Stanley on a stretch of highway below Bombardier Cliffs as the Peterbilt ambles between lanes while Stanley cranes his neck out of the cab, looking nowhere but up per the sign's admonition: Watch for Falling Rock. Buckthorn also whacks off a sign reading: Caution: Guardrail Damage. As though a driver would otherwise casually careen down the highway like a billiard ball between cushions.

With the three principals standing on the signs behind Devaney's postal counter, he recites the ceremony from the Extended Services Section of the Postal Code, wedged there between guidelines for making book on when a customer's first-class mail will be delivered and instructions on how to perform a bris. The ceremony ends with the time-worn but still deeply moving passage: "Neither rain nor snow nor gloom of night shall stay these Johnsons from swift consummation of their appointed nuptials."

All then repair to the Pour House, where Reverend Endwell will perform a mass marriage before he is defrocked by the Free

Will Apostolics. The Fell Faller, who has always thought the reverend looks especially fetching in his frock, promises a replacement. The bar is bedecked with plastic streamers that Orville Crease—an Ozark sentimentalist when it comes to weddings—has lifted from a Springfield used-car lot. The trip to town has also enabled him to ensure the attendance of Rod, reminding him of the Arkansas Code, applicable to all males over the age of fourteen save politicians:

If you dally a daughter
when you hadn't oughter
you marry her quick
'fore her daddy peels your dick.

Besides Rod and Willa Crease, the couples include Sheila and Devaney, Juggernaut and Buckthorn, and Sarah Trip and Mark Neighbors. Having discovered that Reverend Endwell is performing the service for free and that Sheila is throwing a communal reception while Devaney is springing for a collective honeymoon, having negotiated a group rate from Escalante's Bait Shop and Special Occasions, Freddy Waxwroth proposes on the spot to Mable Goodchuck, who accepts during a span of time longer than the life of a pion but shorter than the life of a muon.

As the wedding march swells from the jukebox, a catchy little tune from Three-Wheel Drive: "I Got Me a Ring (and I Hope I Ain't Got Me No Ringer"), Wick nudges his brother: "I'm glad I ain't refereeing this connubial shebang; how could you tell who was marrying who?"

When all are arrayed before Reverend Endwell, whose eyes twinkle as they reflect the twirling Hamms' display, the ceremony is brought up short by well-bred but heartfelt snuffling from the back of the room. All turn as the snuffles escalate to full-fledged sobs.

"You all are," weeps Amanda, "and I'm not."

Reverend Endwell, moved by proprietary guilt, addresses the room. "Is there no man present who will offer his hand and companion appendages to this woman in marriage?"

Elbows flying as they scramble out of the crowd to be first in line, Chip, the faithful choker setter, Waylon Crease, and Bart Bevel tumble to a stop around Amanda.

Amanda's wails escalate.

"I believe, gentlemen," says Reverend Endwell, snatching the moment as deftly as Chuck Wepner nabbed the airmail pouch from the Herbert Walker, "these are tears of happiness at the plenitude of choice in dazzling array before Ms. Pennypacker. I'm sure you'll understand that she cannot be expected to single out one of these extraordinary proffers without sober or—" wink wink "—unsober reflection."

Amanda nods vigorously and shuts right up.

As Reverend Endwell turns his attention to trying to punch up the appropriate service on the screen of his ConCo TurboPreach, Buckthorn notices someone fiddling around with his nethers. Fearing yet another premarital prank (last night's bachelor party was finally broken up by the Lane County Sheriff's Department with artillery support from the West Springfield National Guard detachment), Buckthorn whirls about, spinning off all fours Chuck Wepner, who has latched onto Buckthorn's wallet pocket.

"Nice doggy," says Buckthorn to the community hero as his trouser pocket rips and Chuck comes away with his billfold.

"Oh, Chuckster, you naughty boy," scolds Juggernaut while Buckthorn tries to recall what became of the citizen who sent Rin Tin Tin to canine heaven when he caught him crapping in his begonias. "You drop that poor man's wallet right now."

With a sheepish belch, Chuck complies, and Juggernaut picks up the billfold, razor thin in the bill compartment but bulging elsewhere.

"We can't have ums biting my betrothed on the tushy. Look, Chuckles, there's nothing here but paper and plastic." Juggernaut begins excavating the wallet, hauling out old lottery tickets, unopened registered mail, box scores from the Brewers' last World Series, a voucher good for one table dance at Titanic Titties, a diploma from the Rhode Island School of Design, a stash of C. C.'s finest, the 1979 West Springfield Junior Geek Bowling League schedule, a signed photograph of Bullwinkle, a church key—oops, a little metal—a corkscrew, a spare key to Buckthorn's second girlfriend's brother's car, a coupon for a complimentary session at O Say Can You Pee, a prostate reduction salon, certification as a substitute pilot for Air Error, Stanley's IOU for $237,000, Hillary Clinton's billing records from the Rose Law Firm, a note from his mommy excusing him from PE and, in the billfold's boondocks, oozing through its disintegrating foil wrapper, a Trojan that Buckthorn has been carrying since eighth grade.

At the sight of the Trojan, Chuck Wepner goes wild, Classic Trojans having a rubber content so prodigious that Goodyear used to hire urchins all over America to scour lovers' lanes for discarded Trojan product, which Goodyear smelted down for their top-end racing tire.

With Chuck Wepner happily noshing behind the bar and Reverend Endwell having scrolled up the wedding service, the ceremony proceeds without incident to its happy end.

"In the name of the Great Schadchan and by virtue of the power vested in me by the State of Oregon, I now pronounce you men and wives." Here Reverend Endwell departs from the script, adlibbing in the interests of inclusiveness in case any Malibu surfers are in attendance. "Whom the Main Dude has twosied, let no weenie poach their wave."

After the requisite smooches, all repair to the bar, where the Fell Faller mans the punch bowl, dishing out Hymeneal Hooch, a special recipe that he turned up in the wedding column of *Chain Saw Monthly*.

As the reception accelerates, Devaney expresses to Sheila his mounting concern at the punch bowl's speedy depletion and replenishment.

"Not to worry, sweetie," says Sheila. "I've cleared it with my silent partners."

"I've been meaning to ask."

"Well, now that we're hitched, I guess you're entitled to know everything besides my age, weight, and hair color." Sheila gives Devaney an affectionate pinch. "The Gang of Five's business manager, Mr. Castaneda, has been putting all their 401(k) money into Pour House preferred stock. They've got 50 percent of the corporation."

Devaney whistles through his nose, a reflexive gesture of grand admiration he hasn't employed since junior high school.

The reception cycles on, the future unfolding not through its customary winks and nudges but with the dazzling clarity of the prospects of Bob Packwood's return to elective office.

Having discovered their common affinity for Tums, Sasquatch and President York have struck up a conversation, which leads to Sasquatch accepting a four-year scholarship at MegaMax University under the federal Species Diversity Program. President York also unveils a new research initiative, headed up by Freddy Waxwroth and financed by an anonymous donor, to synthesize sildenafil citrate from *cannabis boffo mauve*.

Carlos Castaneda hangs up the phone and announces a deal with Polythug Records for his gangmate to front a new rap group, DJ D. B. and the 727s. Carlos himself has just nailed down a book deal with Simon and Shuckster that marketing assures will tap into an inspired blend of ascetic post-millennial yearnings and retro '60s gee-whiz: *The Teachings of Don Barry: A Buncombe Way of Knowledge*. Buncombe himself plans a move to the woods outside of Los Angeles to be more available to media for promotional purposes while remaining an intimate of the bosky hood.

Elsewhere on the publishing front, Sarah Trip gives Amanda John Shine's number at Booty Books. Looking to expand his product line, Shine has proposed a concept book to Sarah that marketing has green-lighted the demographics on: *Air Traffic Control & Virginity for Dummies*. Sarah herself, however, is foregoing the pen to serve as in-house model (tops only) at High, Wide, and Handsome, a San Francisco boutique catering to doper plus sizes, along with its companion luggage shop, Get a Grip, which Mark Neighbors has just bought into at the invitation of an old fraternity brother who had recently hedged his business portfolio by purchase of Esprit Décor. With E. E. Everclear as co-author, Sarah assures Amanda, Shine will jump at the opportunity, not to mention her shorts.

Hiro Ishimatsu ponders the future announced in the fortune inside his roll of Tums: "You become proprietor of Tai Won On—a sake and Spam sushi concept bar." As it happens, at this very moment Hiro's bar-in-waiting, Here's Looking at You, is fixing to go out of business in its current Covert, Kansas, incarnation, this demise a result of inadvertent double booking of receptions for a regional meeting of the Society of American P...ra...oics and a getaway weekend for top IRS 501(c)(4) inquisitors.

Rod cuts on the bar TV to catch the football scores but, having continuing trouble with the big hand/little hand business and unable to go digital since he has no head for numbers, undershoots by fifteen minutes and catches Stephanie with the top of the news.

"This just in. In a development today that sent a financial tsunami—" Stephanie holds a beat after the word to let her audience savor her *savoir* while Stanley says he never did understand how the Japanese could eat raw fish like that— "through the corporate world, Easy Ed's Pawn and Appliance announced the acquisition of MegaMax Corporation on a straight cash-for-stock deal. Reached at Eat It in downtown Springfield where he was lunching with cribbage partners, Easy Ed told Eyeclueless News that MegaMax looked like a good fit with his pawnshop division. He invited all Springfieldians to drop by in the coming weeks as he cycles MegaMax holdings through the shop with the assistance of a key member of the MegaMax corporate team, Vlad the Downsizer. Pressed for details on how he assembled financing for what may well be the largest transaction of its kind since the private sector bought out the public sector during the 104th Congress, Easy Ed indicated that he had recently sold his controlling interest in Up against the Wall, a martial arts framing franchise."

On-screen, with a sly grin and encompassing gesture at his tablemates, Easy Ed adds, "Of course, I owe a great deal to these gentlemen—actually vice versa—whose woeful cribbage games are matched only by their eagerness to bet on them."

"From Eat It in downtown Springfield, this is Stephanie for Eyeclueless News, holding down the fort while Rod honeymoons. If you're listening out there, Rod, when you and your bride get back this restaurant's for you."

A mighty huzzah rolls and flows through the Pour House. Taking advantage of the pandemonium, Buckthorn thinks to slip off unnoticed, having booked a suite at the Inn and Out for a pre-collective honeymoon honeymoon. Alas, the starter on his pickup has reexpired, and he slinks back inside, looking to finesse a chauffeur. He lights upon Stanley, who now owes him $463,000 from post-Quagmire poker games. Stanley is loath to leave the festivities, but reluctantly agrees when Buckthorn offers to cancel the debt and throw in $20 for gas.

In the lot, Stanley fires up the Peterbilt, and Juggernaut snugs in next to him with Buckthorn riding shotgun. The rain, though not immoderate by Old Testament standards, falls in corkscrews and curlicues, a signature move of Oregon meteorology. The passenger window is down, and will not, of course, roll up. Behind the seat, Chuck Wepner snacks on the rubber check Buckthorn has written Stanley for gas. Skirting the Challenger Deep at the last moment, Stanley wheels the Peterbilt out of the lot, tootling his horn in salute.

There goes Buckthorn, his laces loose, his bowels clenched, the rain running into his eyes.

And Juggernaut reaches down, ties two deft bows on his dress boots, slips him a Tums, and draws Buckthorn to her out of the rain in rampant marital embrace.

About the Author

Miles Wilson is an award-winning author of five books including *Fire Season, Harm* (University of Nevada Press), *Woodswork: New and Selected Stories of the American West,* and *Line of Fall,* winner of the John Simmons Short Fiction Award. A graduate of Pomona College and the University of Oregon, he is distinguished professor emeritus at Texas State University, where he was founding director of the MFA program. He divides the year between Texas and his home on the McKenzie River in Oregon.